WATER HAZARD

Also by Don Dahler

A Tight Lie

WATER HAZARD

Don Dahler

MINOTAUR BOOKS

A THOMAS DUNNE BOOK

New York

A THOMAS DUNNE BOOK FOR MINOTAUR BOOKS.
An imprint of St. Martin's Publishing Group.

www.thomasdunnebooks.com
www.minotaurbooks.com

Library of Congress Cataloging-in-Publication Data

Dahler, Don.
  Water hazard / Don Dahler.—1st ed.
     p.   cm.
  "A Thomas Dunne book for Minotaur Books"—T. p. verso.
  ISBN 978-0-312-38353-4
  1. Golfers—Fiction.   2. Golf—Tournaments—Fiction.   3. Bankers—Crimes against—Fiction.   4. Honolulu (Hawaii)—Fiction.   5. Golf stories   I. Title
  PS3604.A343W38   2010
  813'.6—dc22   2009041133

First Edition: March 2010

10 9 8 7 6 5 4 3 2 1

To Katie, Callie, and Jack.
I love you this much and more.

ACKNOWLEDGMENTS

To my publisher, editor, and friend, Peter Wolverton; you have my undying gratitude. For believing in me. For believing in Huck. May the three of us have many adventures together. And to his talented staff of editors and publicists at St. Martin's Press, thank you for being so good at what you do.

To Claudia Cross, my agent at Sterling Lord Literistic, for never giving up, even as the publishing world morphs into—what?—before our very eyes. You have the placid temperament of a saint. Or a really good caddie.

To Lonnie Quinn, Megan Glaros, Joan Thomas, Sharon Newman, and all my other friends who read the early versions of the manuscript and offered both enthusiasm and questions, thank you for making this a better book.

Every city in the world has an underbelly, the murky streets where dark business is conducted and crimes committed. For all its beauty and natural gifts, Honolulu is no exception, and for the most part the places and activities described herein are true and authentic, excluding one: the Relaxation Club is purely a figment of my imagination.

Not that such things don't exist. I just know of none in Hawaii.

I'd thank the people of Oahu for their friendliness and hospitality, but they live in paradise. So they should thank the rest of us for not moving there and ruining the place. If you've never been there, add it to your bucket list.

General Manager Allan Lum of the Waialae Country Club welcomed me warmly and allowed me access to the grounds so as to describe the place as accurately as possible. Head Pro John Harman was more than helpful. His knowledge of golf and the Sony Open added greatly to this project. I'd like to thank them and the members of that marvelous course for allowing me to share this slice of heaven with my readers.

Michelle Yu of the Honolulu Police Department arranged a ride-along with Officer Arnold Sagucio of District One. It was a night I'll never forget; a true education. Officer Sagucio is the kind of cop you want on your corner. He's smart and caring but tough, and like many of the other HPD officers I met during my time on Oahu, completely devoted to making their island a better place. Mahalo.

Thank you to my friends at Somerset Hills Country Club in Bernardsville, New Jersey, for the many hours of joy and frustration that is any golfer's reality. This Tillinghast-designed gem takes advantage of every natural feature of the rolling landscape, and adds a few man-made challenges as well. What I know about golf, I learned there. Head Pro Adam Machala leads a friendly and patient team of real teachers.

Finally, thank you to my wife, Katie, who got me hooked on golf shortly after we first met. True, there are some days I curse the addiction, but the many miles we've walked together over lush, green grass, taking turns wacking little white balls, are an irreplaceable part of our journey together. Truth be told, if it weren't for you, Katie, Huck Doyle wouldn't exist.

WATER HAZARD

CHAPTER ONE

The breeze from the Pacific was for the first time that day barely discernable, the kind that whispers into your hair and nudges the leaves like a nurse idly rocking a cradle. It was warm but not hot, and carried with it the moist, briny memories of my youth, much of which was spent on a surfboard.

And that's what distracted me for that one instant. I shifted my gaze from the tee box on the number seventeen at Waialae Country Club to the ocean a few dozen feet away, when the short little round man who'd just straightened up from placing his ball on a tee let out a small cry and crumpled to the ground.

It took all of us a beat to react, mainly because it's not something you see happen every day on a golf course. And, frankly, the man now lying partially on his side on the Bermuda grass, Sing Ten Wong, was something of a jokester, having kept us in stitches most of the day with his faux Chinese sayings and wacky observations. We weren't a hundred percent sure he wasn't kidding around even then.

The first to reach him was his son, Rick, who was a law-school buddy of mine and, to be honest, the only reason I was in Hawaii at all. It was Rick who'd talked his dad into giving me a sponsor's exemption to play in the Sony Open that next week. Considering it was the beginning of the pro golf season, and considering I'd lost my full status on the PGA Tour again last year by managing to make only a handful of cuts and a single top-twenty finish, it was a very kind gesture by Rick's old man.

We were out this day playing a friendly round to get a feel for the course before we teamed up for the Pro-Am tournament coming up next Wednesday. Rick's dad was to be my partner.

Sing Ten Wong was CEO of the Bank of the Pacific Islands, BOPI for short.

Sing Ten Wong was a very important man.

Sing Ten Wong wasn't looking so good.

Pop! *Pop!* Talk to me!

As Rick held his father's face in his hands, I and the fourth guy in our group, Sam Ching, the bank's VP of public relations, eased him the rest of the way onto his back, taking care to straighten out a leg that was twisted underneath him. I felt for a pulse in his wrist. Nothing. His neck. Nothing. His face was very pale, but it was naturally very pale so that didn't tell me much. One eye was partially open, though, and it had that no-fire-in-the-furnace vacancy that made my stomach seize up. That's when I noticed the caddies and another foursome crowding around us.

Somebody call nine-one-one! And give us some space! Rick, you know CPR?

Yes . . .

You breathe, I'll do the chest.

We worked on him for ten minutes until the EMT guys arrived. They drove the ambulance right up the cart path and parked next to the little footbridge that crossed the drainage canal. They took over the CPR, using one of those squeezer bags with a rubber mask over Wong's face rather than mouth-to-mouth, lifted him onto a gurney and wheeled him back across the bridge. When I stooped to pick up the car keys that had fallen out of Sing Ten's pocket, I noticed a dark circle of blood on the grass, about the size of a half-dollar, and wondered if he'd hit his head on his driver or landed on his golf tee or something on the way down. With everything that was going on the thought came and went like a smoke ring in a stiff breeze.

Don Dahler

Rick, Sam and I followed the ambulance to Queen's Hospital in my tournament courtesy car, still wearing our soft spikes and golf gloves. We had to park the Toyota Camry in an adjacent lot so we didn't see Mr. Wong go into the emergency room, but by the time we ran inside the lady at the desk said he was already in surgery.

Rick blinked hard a few times.

Surgery? Surgery for what? What's wrong with him?

I'm sorry, sir, I don't know. Please have a seat over there and I'm sure the doctor will be out to tell you everything just as soon as they can.

We shuffled over to the vinyl chairs in a fog.

There is without a doubt no more miserable place on earth than an emergency room waiting area, even one as clean and bright and nicely furnished as Queen's. Because no one's there for a good reason. Everyone is either in pain, or scared, or both.

My friend, Rick, was both.

We didn't say a word to each other. We sat, looking at the seascape prints on the wall, or the tree in the corner, or the pattern in the carpet. We certainly didn't meet the eyes of the other miserable wretches in that place. That would have broken the unwritten rule of waiting room conduct.

Twenty minutes after we arrived, twenty agonizing minutes of counting every single tick of the clock, three men came through the double-doors and walked up to us. One wore a suit, the other two surgical scrubs. The suit spoke first.

Mr. Wong? Richard Wong?

Rick nodded.

Mr. Wong, I'm Joseph Wagner, chief information officer for the medical center. Could you please come this way?

We all three stood but Wagner held up his hands.

I'm sorry. Just Mr. Wong.

It's Rick, and I'd like my friends to come with me.

Certainly.

We followed them through the doors and into what appeared to be a doctor's lounge. There was a small kitchen area and couches scattered about, a few low tables with magazines and newspapers. No one else was there. Rick looked confused.

I'd like to see my father.

Wagner ignored the request.

Mr. Wong . . . I'm sorry, *Rick* . . . this is Dr. Luo and Dr. Anderson. Dr. Anderson is chief of surgery.

Hands were extended and shook. Sam and I introduced ourselves. Then Dr. Anderson took a deep breath.

I'm very sorry, Rick. Your father didn't make it. We did everything we could, but I'm afraid he was already gone by the time he got here. In fact, I'm almost certain he died instantly. The autopsy will determine that.

Out of the corner of my eye, I could see Rick physically recoil from the news. I put a hand on his shoulder to steady him. His voice came out strangled.

What do you mean, instantly? Was it a, was it a heart attack, stroke, or what?

The two doctors both raised their eyebrows in surprise at the same instant. They looked at each other. They looked at Wagner. And Wagner spoke.

I . . . we . . . assumed you saw what happened. After all, you were there.

He . . . just . . .

Rick was having trouble finishing the sentence so I cut in.

Mr. Wong just collapsed. That's all we saw. One minute he's teeing up his ball, the next he collapses onto the ground and doesn't move.

You didn't hear anything?

Like what?

All three men looked at each other again. Rick, understandably agitated, repeated my question.

Like what?!

Like . . . a gunshot.

Not one of us could manage more than a blink. Wagner clarified.

Rick, your father was shot.

That's when Rick's knees gave way. I managed to get him under one arm and ease him back onto a couch. Drs. Luo and Anderson pushed me aside and made sure there wasn't a second Wong casualty that day. While they checked him over, I pulled Wagner to the side.

He was shot? Shot where?

I'm told the bullet entered his back.

That doesn't make any sense. We would've heard it. There'd be blood.

Flash on the half-dollar's worth in the grass. Not enough for a gunshot wound. Not nearly enough. I know. I've seen way too many of them.

I don't understand it either . . . Mr. . . . . *Doyle*, you said? But the facts are the facts. Mr. Wong was shot dead. Dr. Luo and Dr. Anderson found an entry wound from a rather large bullet. The police are on their way, as is the medical examiner.

I want to see him.

That was from Rick, who was being helped up by the two doctors.

I want to see Pop. I need to see him.

Anderson looked at Wagner and nodded.

Of course. I'll take you to him.

They left the room. Luo and Wagner followed. Sam felt around his chest for a cell phone that was not, of course, there, considering he was still wearing his company's orange *BOPI* logo golf shirt and no jacket, and cell phones are verboten on club grounds.

I have to make a call. I have to make a hundred calls. What a nightmare. I can't believe this.

He asked for the keys and went out to the car to use my phone.

I sat back down on the couch, trying to replay those moments before Wong collapsed, and I couldn't remember hearing anything that would even remotely sound like a gunshot. It had been perfectly quiet, unusually calm, with just the shushing of water lapping against the beach and the twittering of colorful birds as the soundtrack to that paradise.

The number seventeen was a par three, 189 yards, which ran along Maunalua Bay, with the green lying somewhat in the shadow of the large Kahala resort hotel. One oddity of the Sony Open was that Waialae flipped the out and back for those two weeks only, making the number ten the tournament's number-one hole, and thus the number seventeen was normally the number eight. Get it? Me neither. Anyway, on the second to last hole, Sing Ten Wong had pulled out a fairway metal, teed up his Nike One and was about to take a few practice swings when someone apparently punched a neat little hole in his shirt and ended what up until that very second had been an extraordinary life.

A high-powered rifle and a silencer maybe? On one of those hotel balconies?

I caught myself thinking aloud.

That would explain the lack of gunshot. Except for one thing: Rick's dad was right-handed. His back was to the ocean.

And, while daydreaming about surfing, I'd been looking right at the place where the bullet had to have come from.

And didn't see a goddamn thing.

CHAPTER TWO

I hung around the hospital for another hour until the presence of more and more of Rick's relatives convinced me (a) he was in good hands and (b) I was an outsider. There were almost as many police huddled in the hallways as Wongs, so I wasn't surprised when a rather hefty detective from Honolulu PD approached me as I was leaving and asked if I was Huckleberry Doyle. I said yes but that I prefer Huck. His look said he didn't give a shit what I preferred. He asked me to sit. I did.

I'm Detective Sagulio, Mr. Doyle. How was it you were with Mr. Wong today?

We were playing a round of golf.

He took in my nifty Etonic saddleback golf shoes and color-coordinated Greg Norman pleated microfiber slacks with the little shark logo on the back pocket.

Of course. Is it true you witnessed the murder?

Yes, well, I witnessed Mr. Wong falling down dead, but I didn't see who killed him.

Can you describe exactly what you saw, please?

Sure. I saw Mr. Wong falling down dead. He was getting ready to hit his drive on the number seventeen tee when he made a little sound and collapsed. We tried to resuscitate him—

The detective interrupted.

Who tried to resuscitate him?

His son, Rick . . . Richard Wong . . . and I.

And what was the little sound?

Sort of a surprised sound. Like a . . . *whuh!?* Only higher-pitched.

Did you hear the shot fired?

No.

Did you hear anything prior to him making that sound?

Birds, water, guys talking on the next tee box.

Anything that sounded threatening? Anyone yelling? Anything loud that would be out of place?

Like maybe a rifle bolt being drawn back and a trigger smoothly depressed with four pounds of pressure and fifty-nine grains of gunpowder expanding at a rate of three thousand feet per second which propels a 150-grain bullet three times the speed of sound through cotton and flesh and fat and muscle causing a sixty-seven-year-old heart to switch off like a New York City blackout in the heat of summer?

No. Nothing.

Go back, please, to when you first saw Mr. Wong today.

I had to think for a second.

It was in the parking lot. When he got out of his limo. And I remember thinking, . . . *Rick came from that?*

. . . he looks nothing like his son.

Rick Wong is an inch taller than my six feet, with a thick head of black hair and what they call classically chiseled features. He reminds me of Chow

Don Dahler

Yun-Fat, the guy from *Crouching Tiger, Hidden Dragon,* only younger. And skinnier. You don't have a lot of spare time in law school for dangling alliances with the lassies, but with his face and build Rick never had a problem finding someone gorgeous for a quick hookup.

It didn't hurt that his dad was a millionaire.

So when I saw Sing Ten Wong climb out of the back of his silver $350,000 Bentley Azure convertible, it was immediately obvious Rick's face and build had to have come from his mother's side. Dear Sing Ten stood barely over five-three, with a round belly and head to match. He was wearing the latest in country-club fashion, and man, could he smile. In fact, no matter how many crappy shots that 32-handicapper took that day, the grin never left his face. Until, that is, the very end.

I wasn't sure what the protocol was with someone that important. I mean, I knew Asians had all kind of rules about being deferential to their elders and all, so I didn't know if I should wait to be formally introduced, but when he spotted me in the parking lot he immediately waved me over and escorted me into the clubhouse, cracking jokes all the way like we'd been drinking buddies for decades.

At the door:

> Hey, Huck. Confucius say *Passionate kiss like spider's web. Soon lead to undoing of fly.*

At the lockers:

> What do you call a Chinese woman with one leg? *Irene!*

Climbing into the cart:

> Three Chinese brothers, Hu, Chu and Fu, want to live in the U.S., so they change their names to sound more American. Hu changes his to Huck. Chu changes his to Chuck. And Fu gets sent straight back to China!

And on and on and on, and not quietly either. You couldn't help but like him. And you couldn't help but marvel that someone so successful and powerful could be so, for lack of a better word, goofy. He had all of us cracking up so much we could barely concentrate on the golf. Which, in all honesty, was a problem. I had a tournament coming up, and Waialae is a damn difficult course, probably the second or third hardest on the PGA tour, mainly because of its wasp-waisted fairways as narrow as seventeen yards in places and those towering coconut trees that are to golf balls what fly-swatters are to, uh, flies.

Even though this was supposed to be a casual round, I was hoping to use the time wisely and scope out the course as if this were an extra practice round. It was obvious from the first tee, though, that wasn't going to happen.

Rick started us off and hit a respectable drive into the right second cut, about 240 yards out.

Sam Ching, the bank's PR guy, had a pretty good swing, probably from all the hours he spent schmoozing the local poobahs. His pill landed on the short grass almost exactly halfway down the fairway.

Rick's father then proceeded to flame a hideous slice all of 180 yards into the backyard of one of the single-storey houses that border Waialae. Without missing a beat he teed up a second ball and sent that one just about as far, and just about as ugly, but it nestled into the long grass this side of out-of-bounds. He looked back at me with a grin as he set a third ball on a tee.

You know what they call this, Huck?

Member's mulligan?

No. Chinese baseball! Three strikes, I'm out!

His third drive found the right center of the short grass.

My turn. Playing from the fairways and not the rough is always the goal in golf, but for the upcoming Sony Open it was the golden rule. It's not a particularly long course, but they'd overseeded and let the Bermuda grow so high and thick everywhere else you'd have to use a hoe to chop your ball out of the long stuff. And as for wind, this calm day was the exception. Usually, you have to factor the ocean breeze into every shot here.

My plan for these narrow fairways was to cut corners with big drives when I could, especially on the par fives, but to concentrate more on keeping my sweet little Titleist clean and dry and on the carpet, sacrificing distance for accuracy as much as I could. That's not normally my game. I usually like to bomb them close and hit a short wedge to the flag. But my coach, Paul Warren, had spent a lot of time in the off-season working on my course management thought process. He came up with a mantra I was supposed to keep repeating: 280 on the deck beats 330 in the dreck.

I know. Stupid saying. But he has a point.

The number one is a par five with a slight dogleg right. It's definitely reachable in two but the greedy player flirts with out-of-bounds with the houses on the right and the driving range on the left. I set up aiming at a big apartment tower that loomed in the distance, thinking I'd cut the ball down the left side and let it fade into a good approach angle to the green.

Only, it didn't cut.

It flew straight as an arrow, over those ridiculously tall coconut trees, and splashed into the one and only fairway bunker on the left side. A little over three bills away.

In the dreck.

Sing Ten Wong jumped into the cart and took off before my butt even hit the seat. I almost flipped over backwards.

So, hundred dollars a hole? You give me strokes?

I can't take your money, Mr. Wong. You're sponsoring me.

He laughed and pounded my leg, not bothering to watch where he was going.

Who says you're going to take my money!? I'm in the fairway, you're the one in the sand.

We barely missed hitting a gigantic umbrella-shaped tree.

Point taken. Okay. A hundred a hole and you get one stroke each. On one condition. Well, two conditions.

Two conditions. No problem. What conditions?

No more mulligans.

Okay, sure.

Two, I drive.

He cackled and pulled up to his ball. He chose a fairway metal, looked to be a five from where I sat, and proceeded to top the ball badly. It skittered about a hundred yards and stopped against one of the hummocks that edged the left side, fairly close to where my ball was. I scooted over behind the wheel as Sing Ten let out a chuckle and plopped into the passenger side of the cart.

My swing feels good today! You're in a lot of trouble!

That's really the way he speaks, spoke, I mean; with exclamation marks.

My ball had hit the sand so hard it was half-buried, a real fried egg lie. And I still had a little over two hundred yards to the front of the green. There was no way I could blast it out of there that far, so I'd have to lay-up to a workable distance. I pulled the pitching wedge, reconsidered, and selected a nine iron. I was planning for a hundred-yard shot and figured the buried lie would knock a lot of distance off. Boy was I right.

I swung easy, trying to catch it clean, but instead I hit it a little fat. Sand flew everywhere and blew back into my eyes. When I looked up I could see no ball in flight, and no ball on the fairway. I heard Sing Ten clear his throat loudly and glanced his way. He could barely contain a grin and pointed to my feet.

Look down.

I looked down.

My ball was embedded in the lip of the bunker, a few inches below the edge of turf.

Don Dahler

Shit . . .

Mr. Wong, do you happen to know the difference between baseball and golf?

No, Mr. Doyle, what is the difference between baseball and golf?

In golf you have to play your foul balls.

I forget who said that first. Anyway, this one was plenty foul. My only choice was to hack it out laterally and then hit a long iron to the green, which, lacking any backspin, rolled to the far edge of the table. I three-putted for a double. Sing Ten posted an eight for a net seven with the stroke-a-hole I was giving him. In our silly little contest we were even. But had this been the Open I'd be two over already, on a par five that most of the guys would be shooting at birds on. Not good.

Those nagging little details I left out of my conversation with Detective Sagulio. As a nonpracticing attorney and certified private investigator, I expertly surmised he was mainly interested in Mr. Wong's demeanor and whether he mentioned anything about, oh, people who might want him dead, that sort of thing.

Did you say you're a lawyer, Mr. Doyle?

Yes, I am. Well, that is to say, I have a law degree. From UCLA. I never took the bar exam, though.

And why not?

I found my true calling in life.

Your true calling.

My true calling.

And that is?

To knock little white balls into little white holes all over the world, and get paid for it. Theoretically, that is. No one was throwing the big checks at me lately.

I'm a professional golfer.

I see. You teach golf?

No, I play golf. On the PGA Tour.

Barely. In reality I was bringing a paycheck home once every four or so tournaments I entered, on average. With the PGA Tour's new cut rule, I was all too often among the guys who finished under the line but still didn't get to play the weekend. That paid some money, about nine grand on average. Good enough to cover the rent and expenses, but not good enough to keep my card if I stayed true to these non-winning ways.

My best finish on tour last year was a tie with eight other guys for nineteenth place at the Pebble Beach National Pro-Am. That was a $52,000 payday. But that was my sole high finish of the year. As a result, I ended the season eighteen places out of the magic 125 highest money winners on tour. So I was bumped, yet again, from full Tour card to Conditional status, meaning I don't get to play every PGA event every week. On weeks I can't get a slot on the big tour, I play the Nationwide Tour, which is sort of professional golf's version of the minor leagues.

I do better on the Nationwide than the Tour. Which is not necessarily something to brag about. I was hoping to take it up a notch this season. Me, and about two hundred other guys.

A professional golfer. So you're here to play in the Sony Open?

Yes.

I see.

He consulted his notes, trying to remember if he remembered me.

Sorry, I don't really follow the sport. Huckleberry Doyle, you said?

Huck.

You're a lawyer who now plays professional golf.

Don't forget private investigator.

You're kidding.

Nope.

Nope. I have a license and everything. Courtesy Los Angeles County. Took the test, paid the fee. I needed it to track down a guy who took a lot of money from me and a bunch of other suckers. Got the guy. Not the money. I'm still frosted about that. There's a little over six hundred K of my cash sitting in an offshore account, with an army of bankers and lawyers keeping me from it.

I realize six hundred thousand dollars is pocket change to Tiger and Phil and those guys, but for a grinder like me, that's a lot of money. My entire life savings. And someday, I'll get it back. For now, I'm just scraping along on what we earn for making the cut and the occasional, very occasional, finish in the money. I was steaming over all this, like I do about a dozen times a day, when I realized Five-O was saying something.

. . . mention any concerns? Any stress at work or people who don't like him?

Mr. Wong?

He looked at me like I was a five year old.

Yes . . . Mr. Wong. That's who we're talking about.

Sorry, I got distracted for a second. But, no, he didn't really talk about his work.

Like most of the amateurs golfers we get paired up with, all Sing Ten was interested in was *my* work. And getting tips on how to play better. Which, in Wong's case, would've entailed quitting golf completely and taking up checkers. Yet, I say that, but after three holes we were still even, thanks to two missed birdie putts on my part, and two unlikely bogey saves on his. An inauspicious start to my week. Tied with a 32-handicapper.

We rolled up to the par three number four. Rick and Sam were having a lively debate about who was hotter in her prime, Marilyn Monroe or Britney

Spears, which struck me as totally ludicrous. I bit my tongue. For all of two seconds.

That's totally ludicrous.

Rick looked at me in surprise. I continued.

That's like comparing a 'sixty-five Porsche to a brand new Aston Martin. Or like asking which team was better, the 'ninety-eight Yankees or the 'seventy-six Reds.

Wow. Somebody needs a nap.

Just saying. It's stupid. Can't compare women from different eras. They had different standards of beauty. Besides, when Britney was at her hottest she was still jailbait. Doesn't count.

Who says it doesn't count? Hot is hot. Man, when she was seventeen . . .

Rick's dad piped up.

Confucius say, virginity like bubble. One prick, all gone!

Jeez, Pop. Enough with the Confucius jokes.

Yes, God, please . . .

Sam had moseyed over and took a glance at the scorecard on our cart steering wheel.

Ah . . .

Rick raised his eyebrows, walked over and took a peek, too.

Ah . . .

Which made me look up from cleaning the grooves on my gap wedge.

What *ah* . . . ?! What do you mean *ah* . . . ?!

Nothing.

Nothing. Just checking the yardage.

They retreated to their bags, smirking to each other.

Well, use your own cards. This one's a little ugly.

Those neat little squares you drew on the number one are very artistic.

Shut up, Rick. Your dad's funnier.

You bet I am!

Especially his golf swing.

Hey!

There are little wooden signs at every tee box at Waialae, giving the distances and the Hawaiian name for each hole, along with a translation. The number four is *Apiki*, which means "tricky." And man is it. 203 from the championship tees and fairly wide open to the green, but there are nasty steep bunkers defending the right and left sides and the prevailing winds are usually blowing right into the players' faces. Any spin at all on the ball and that wind would take you way off line.

Rick had the honor, smacked a solid five-metal but still came up short of the green. I chose my number three hybrid and set up for a slight draw, hoping to keep it low. It stayed low, and drew nicely, but found one of the three deep, kidney-shaped sand traps on the left side of the green. Sam and Sing Ten were both short and right.

I scraped by with a par on that hole, and limped around the rest of the course trading birdies for bogeys and having to scramble way too much to save par. I felt out of whack and clunky. My swing, which was humming pretty well before I boarded the flight at LAX for HNL, was lost with the baggage somewhere en route. Despite my best efforts to shut off my brain, I found myself analyzing everything I was doing on every shot, which is a cardinal sin in golf. Work on your swing on the range. Work on your swing in your sleep. Work on your swing while pretending to listen to your girlfriend. Never work on your swing in the middle of a round.

But damn . . . I was in trouble. I had barely a week to get back in the groove, or my Hawaiian vacation would be a short one.

So you and Mr. Wong had a bet?

The Honolulu police officer was winding down his questioning.

A small one. He was about, oh, maybe twenty strokes over par when we got to the seventeenth. I was three over, which means at that point I owed him a hundred bucks.

Uh huh. Do you often wager on your games?

Rounds. They're called rounds, not games. Sometimes. Not usually for big stakes, though.

Most of the guys on tour take the side bet here and there, even though the PGA officially frowns on it. Hell, gotta spice things up now and then. A current favorite among the guys is a no-bogey round. Whoever does that gets a thousand bucks from the other players in his group.

Mr. Doyle, did Mr. Wong ever mention any other kind of betting? Did he talk about other bets he may have made? Any reason to believe he was involved in gambling for larger stakes?

I had to think on that one.

He did, actually. Mentioned something about having money on the Super Bowl. Not sure how much.

And did he seem nervous about the outcome?

Detective . . . ?

Sagulio.

Sagulio. Mr. Wong didn't seem nervous to me about one single thing on earth. He is . . . *was* . . . probably the most carefree millionaire I've ever met.

I see. And in addition to being a lawyer and golfer, Mr. Doyle, are you also a psychologist?

Call me Huck. You forgot private detective. Nope, not a psychologist. Just giving you my impression, drawn from years of dealing with people.

Uh huh. Well, from my years of dealing with people, I can tell you crime is a very straightforward endeavor. Somebody killed Mr. Wong. I assume they had a reason for doing so.

He flipped his leatherbound notepad shut.

Thanks for your time. I'll need your numbers and where you're staying if I think of any more questions.

No problem.

I gave him my cell number and the name of my hotel in Honolulu.

CHAPTER THREE

I managed to avoid the gaggle of media types and cameras clustered at the front of the hotel by taking the arm of an elderly lady who happened to be leaving at the same time and pretending I was a caring relation. She didn't mind in the least and thanked me effusively as I loaded her into a waiting taxi and sent her on her way, clucking about how nice the good folks at Queens Hospital are.

Sam Ching was pacing in circles around the Camry, still on my phone talking, from the sound of it, to other bank officials. He climbed into the passenger seat without missing a beat and we drove back to the club to get his car and change clothes. Along the way he made two other calls and spoke only in Chinese. When we got to Waialae he slapped my phone shut and handed it back.

Thank you. Rick will want you at the funeral. I don't know when that will be yet but someone will let you know.

Of course. Hey, if there's anything I can do . . .

Thank you. I only ask one thing, and this was also expressed by the other BOPI board members on the phone just now. It's crucial you be discreet in relating anything Mr. Wong might have said about his work today, when talking to police or anyone. We are in a highly competitive business and there are things underway, business things, that are highly sensitive. The publicity alone may derail some very important deals that Mr. Wong himself structured. That would not make him happy.

Nor, I imagined, would being dead.

I already talked to a detective, but there wasn't really anything your boss said about his business.

Yes, of course. A detective. What is his name please?

Sagulio.

He jotted that down.

Thank you. And you didn't have anything of substance to tell him?

No, not really.

No or not really?

No. Nothing of substance.

Good, good. So of course you won't mind if someone from the bank also interviews you? Just to make sure there isn't anything you might have discussed that could be proprietary? Sometimes we forget things that don't seem important at the time.

Uh. Well. No, that's, that'll be fine.

Excellent. They'll call on you. Later tonight?

Okay, fine. I'm at the Outrigger. Waikiki Beach.

Very good.

We parted ways. I grabbed my clubs and stuff, thought about trying to go out for another round to work out the kinks, realized that I just witnessed my good friend's father, and my patron, be murdered, and decided that the more sensitive thing to do would be to go back to the hotel.

And hit the bar.

Which I did.

Hard.

After the third Grey Goose I was lubricated enough to play back the last few holes of the day in slow-motion in my brain. I tried to remember everything Sing Ten said about anything, but honestly, his constant patter and puns and silly jokes became white noise to me the more holes we played. I was trying to concentrate on my mechanics, and he was doing everything but.

Kicking back at the beachside bar in bare feet, t-shirt and khaki shorts, with the setting sun warm on my face and my thoughts on Rick and his dad, I was so completely crawled up inside my skull I didn't notice the woman sit down next to me until the bartender asked me, loudly, with a *hey buddy,* and probably not for the first time judging from his tone, what my friend would like to drink. I snapped out of it. Turned to my right. Saw a slim, slight, stunningly beautiful Asian girl in a tailored skirt suit smiling at me politely.

Um. I don't know. Brilliant question, though. Well done. What would you like to drink?

Smooth. Huck Doyle: lady killer. Somehow she managed to keep her clothes on.

The voice was as silky as the jet-black hair.

Manhattan, please.

I gave a nod to the barman, who returned the nod and got to work on the drink. My new friend held out a hand.

Lisa Tan.

Huck Doyle.

I know.

You know?

I'm with the bank. Mr. Ching asked me to meet with you.

Damn.

Of course. And here I thought one of my groupies had caught up with me.

She smiled again, but it was that indulgent smile beautiful women pull out when they're deflecting a flirtatious comment.

The Board wants to make sure there was no information passed between Mr. Wong and you today that might become harmful to the bank's interests.

I already explained to Sam that he didn't really say anything, other than a whole lot of Confucius-says jokes.

Yes. He was known for his sense of humor. And we mean no disrespect to you, but you understand, sometimes things are said that don't seem important except when put into context, so if you don't mind, can we move to someplace more private to go over the events of the day?

More private?

Yes. Where we won't be overheard.

The vodka suggested my hotel room. But then a certain Los Angeles County assistant medical examiner's pretty face peeked around some corner of my brain. Judith Filipiano and I hadn't seen each other for several weeks due to my travel schedule and her job demands. The last few times we did, things had an awkwardness, a lack of synch, like the relationship/friendship/whatever-it-is-ship had suffered a mini stroke in our absence and, though we hummed along our normal Huck-and-Judith-being-together routine on the surface, killer sex and all, something was not quite right.

Whenever we got together it was obvious we both felt something wasn't the same, but we chose to step around the issue rather than talk about it. The long-distance phone calls were becoming shorter; more a list of what we did than an exploration of who we are, perfunctory details not personal discovery. Yet there was still attraction, affection, fun. What's so hard about staying interested in such a great woman? Judith was funny, smart, gorgeous, and God only knows why, but she apparently liked me.

But . . . but . . .

I needed to figure out where things were going with her. So in the meantime, I needed to slap a strong collar and leash on the dog side of my nature. Lisa Tan was watching me as my mind wandered, so I nodded toward the open-air restaurant.

How about that table over there? I hear the grilled Mahi's great.

She arched her back to look past me. When she moved her head I caught a subtle whiff of her perfume. Or shampoo. Or moisturizer. Or maybe it was just the way her skin and hair naturally smelled. I noticed there wasn't a freckle or mole or flaw of any kind on her neck. Her nose was on the smallish side, her lips full, with two tiny laugh lines in the corners of her mouth. Which was moving. Which meant she was saying something. Which meant I should be listening rather than taking inventory.

I'm sorry . . . it's a little loud in here. What did you say?

She laughed.

I said, I think the tables are too close together. Would you mind if we just took a walk?

No! Sure. Great idea.

She reached down, lifted her shoes off her feet, and handed them to the bartender.

Hold these for me, would you please? We'll be back shortly.

Sure. Not a problem.

He took the pointy black Jimmy Choos, appraised them with a raised eyebrow, appraised her with same said eyebrow, and appraised me with a look that said *you're one lucky bastard.*

You wanna leave a pair, too, buddy?

No thanks . . .

I raised up a bare foot and wiggled my toes.

. . . I'll keep these on.

Ms. Lisa Tan from the Bank of the Pacific Islands extended a delicate hand and led me from the comfort of my barstool to the soft, warm sand of Waikiki Beach. We walked close to the water line, past the thinning throngs of tourists who were gathering their towels and umbrellas and beach chairs in the dwindling light and retreating in their sunburned glory to their over-priced hotel rooms.

So how did you recognize me there at the bar?

I Googled you.

Yeah?

The PGA Tour has a website with photos of all the players. Yours doesn't do you justice, by the way.

Thank you . . .

. . . *I think* . . .

. . . I hope the stats don't do me justice, either.

Oh, I'm sure not, although I wouldn't know. I just needed to see what you looked like. I did find some of the news articles interesting, though. You've managed to get involved in some interesting cases.

Yeah . . .

The little girl you found, that was wonderful. And that man who took all those famous people's money.

And some non-famous people's money, too . . .

Yeah . . .

At least she didn't mention Joniel Baker. Which meant my part in all that was still secret.

And that baseball player! I can't believe someone was actually trying to frame him for murder!

Fuck me . . .

There was an article about that?

Yes. One of the New York papers, I think. It said even though the Los Angeles police department took credit for solving the case, sources close to the investigation implied you were the one who actually tracked down the real killers.

Shit.

It said that, did it?

Yes.

Shit.

Did you?

Well. It's complicated. Let's just say I helped out a friend.

Okay. So, that laconic response makes you the silent, humble type, I guess.

The silent, humble, dead type if Pierce Fanagin's mob buddies wanted vendetta on the guy who orchestrated his end. Nothing I could do about that now. I had more important things at hand, like enjoying the company of this tiny, gorgeous, stylish vision in a gray Tahari suit strolling along beside me.

There were a lot of people working that case. I just got some lucky information, that's all.

It sounds like more than that. Maybe you'll tell me more some other time.

Maybe. You have to sign a nondisclosure agreement and post a sizeable bond first, though.

She giggled.

I see. Well, never mind, then. How interesting could it really be?

Darlin' . . . you have no idea . . .

Not very, to be honest. The tabloids always make a big deal out of everything. But, to return to the reason for our little walk here, not that I'd mind your company for any reason, but what is it you want to know about my conversations with Sing Ten? Like I told Sam, he really didn't talk about business much.

Yes, he told me you said that. And I apologize again for taking up your time. But, please, if you don't mind, think back to all the conversations you had with Mr. Wong. Just to make sure. Did any of them involve topics other than golf?

Oh, let's see. Women, sex, girls, sex, cars, movie stars, sex, Chinese stereotypes, sex, Japanese stereotypes, celebrity golfers, Caucasian stereotypes, Black stereotypes, sex.

Not really. As I said, he made some jokes. A lot of jokes, actually. About everything you can imagine. But honestly, I don't recall anything about banking or business. He struck me as wanting to get away from the office, if you will.

Mmm hmm. Did he mention anything that was concerning him? Anything stressful?

No. Like what?

Like, say, any deals he was currently working on?

No.

More specifically, did he mention the merger?

The merger? No. What merger?

She paused before responding, glanced around her to make sure there was no one nearby and stopped walking.

Mr. Doyle . . .

Huck, please.

All right, Huck. I can't tell you much. Suffice it to say, we're nearing completion of a major deal with a very important entity. It will make BOPI by far the largest bank in this part of the world.

Okay.

Although it's far from a sure thing. This hasn't been an easy time for any of us. There's been considerable, even aggressive resistance from certain circles. That's, honestly, why the board is so obsessed with Mr. Wong's last conversations, and why I need to know if he said anything to you. The chairman had just come from a meeting with a very important man who has become key to the merger, right before he joined you for golf. He hadn't had time to tell anyone what the results of that meeting were. We're grasping at straws here, but we were hoping he'd given some kind of indication whether it went well . . . or not. Even in oblique terms. Any clue would be of help. Did he express relief or frustration?

He seemed relaxed, for what it's worth. Sorry I'm not more help. So, forgive me, what exactly do you do for the bank? I mean, what's your title?

The wind off the Pacific had this annoying habit of catching her blouse just so, revealing a nicely tanned, albeit modest cleavage. My dog side whined pitifully. I focused on her face. Most of the time. I shifted my eye line to a couple sitting side by side, watching the ocean paint the shore with big, leisurely brush strokes, which reminded me of the last time I saw Judith.

We'd just taken a run on Malibu Beach and were sitting on the sand, just like that couple, laughing at a group of kids playing tag with the waves, when a miserably small rain cloud dumped on us, and only us, while the afternoon sun beamed through the drops. I remembered what my mom used to call that.

The Devil's beating his wife.

Judith leaned her head back and let the rain mingle with the sweat on her face.

I didn't know he was the marrying kind.

Sure he is. He knows he can cheat.

Ah. And you don't think he feels bad about that?

Cheating? Naw. It's his job to be bad. Just part of his nature.

And his wife? Why would she put up with his beatings and infidelities?

Because she gets to be the Devil's wife, I guess. Go to all the best parties. Penthouse on the Upper East Side. Mani/pedis every other day.

I see. Women are attracted to the bad boys.

Aren't you?

She laughed her best Lauren Bacall, the one that usually has a direct wire to my southland.

Why, Huck? Are you bad?

I didn't much like the way she asked that. With just a shadow of a smirk.

I can be. You know that.

Jesus, that came out like a whine. She leaned over and kissed me on the neck, which felt a little condescending, so I didn't return the favor.

You are the farthest thing from bad, my dear. You are loyal and true as a golden retriever.

Translation: I'm a great boyfriend. Safe. Dependable. Boring. Husband material.

In other words, a frank with no beans.

Ms. Tan was in the process of answering my question.

I am, was, the chairman's chief executive assistant. Which isn't exactly the world's easiest position. Mr. Wong was a very complicated man, involved in a million different things, but he liked to keep much of his business to himself, sometimes not even informing me of his plans.

So why send you to talk to me?

The board asked me to talk to you because they thought you would feel less threatened. We don't want to insult you in any way. We just need to see how far things had gotten and we're looking at every bit of information we can to piece things together.

Doesn't seem like a productive way to conduct the bank's business. All that information in so few hands. Mind if I state the obvious here? Why not just ask the guy he met with?

Lisa turned her head to look at the setting sun, chewing on her lower lip as she contemplated how much she could say. With the golden light and the ocean breeze rippling her hair, she could've been a model on a photo shoot for a fashion magazine. The Asian Adriana Lima. She turned to face me.

The fact of the matter is, and you absolutely must keep this, actually all of this conversation, completely secret, but no one was supposed to know about the meeting. Mr. Wong was hoping for a rapprochement, so at great risk to his reputation and the deal he brokered a personal meeting with a, ah, a very powerful individual.

Whom you won't name.

No. I can't.

Because it was a top-secret meeting.

Yes. Very top-secret. And if it became known that Mr. Wong met with this person, it could be very damaging to the bank and the deal.

I thought she was being a little melodramatic. I mean, we're talking a business deal here with guys in suits and an army of lawyers. How dangerous can it be? Nevertheless I caught myself mid-word as a group of people moved past us, and took a moment to scan the beach. Tourists, tourists, tourists, a cop, a chubby little guy tottling along next to his mom on pink, wobbly legs, more tourists, and a guy in slacks and a white dress shirt with dark shades standing about twenty feet away from us, just looking out to sea. I gave him a second glance, noting he'd kept his expensive-looking shoes on even while standing in the soft sand, before continuing with what I was saying.

This sounds more like a clandestine negotiation between warring nations rather than a bank merger.

Rueful chuckle.

Well, unfortunately there are similarities in this case, that's for certain. So please, if you think of anything he might have said that can at all be related to this issue, please let me know. If anything comes to mind.

Okay. I'll do that.

We started walking again, back toward the hotel. I watched with no little envy as a group of guys with long boards dashed out into the waves to squeeze the last few drops of magic out of the day. She must've noticed my interest.

Do you surf?

Not enough.

Lisa sighed and kicked up some sand with her perfectly pedicured toes.

Never enough, is it? I grew up surfing. On Maui. I try to get out once a week or so but it's hard with my work.

Same here. I hope to take a few days after the tournament and do some rides. Depending on how things go next week.

Which, judging from the way I was playing earlier in the day, would not be good. I pictured myself on the phone, begging the airline again to not charge me the penalty for coming home early on a nonrefundable ticket. But what she said next yanked me out of my funk.

Hey! How about next week? We can do the Pipeline, if you're up for some big water.

Hell yes! Big water! The legendary Banzai Pipeline! Ms. Lisa Tan from BOPI in a bikini! Oops. Wait. Check that . . .

Sounds really great, but I have this tournament. Maybe you heard . . .

Her voice was suddenly higher pitched, more girl-like, full of excitement.

Oh come on, you can't practice all the time! Seriously, call me. Here's my card. Pipeline always has unbelievably good sets. Righteous bombs!

With that, something sizzled in my skull's wiring and I thought a circuit breaker would pop. This five-foot, two-inch stunner in a power suit just uttered the secret code-phrase for the perfect waves. Which pretty much made her the perfect woman. I took a glance at her left hand. No ring. Howls sounded somewhere in the recesses of my skull. Teeth gnawed at leather. Chivalry and virtue looked on in disgust, clucking their tongues like a pair of schoolmarms.

Okay, I thought. Maybe a compromise is in order. Is there any harm in doing a little surfing? Getting to know the locals a little better? I'm told truly beautiful women have a difficult time making friends. People think they're standoffish. Men assume they're taken. Maybe this poor professional woman was actually lonely. Hanging with her would be an act of kindness.

Then, knowing that was all bullshit, and knowing Judith deserved better from me, I gave a little shrug.

> Let's see how the week goes for me. Golf takes a singular focus to play well. I really can't afford a distraction.

> Okay, that's understandable. But, look, if you can't hit the waves yourself, my boyfriend's competing up there on Monday. I'm taking the day off. Come watch at least.

Boyfriend. She has a boyfriend. That's good.

Right?

CHAPTER FOUR

I bid adieu to Ms. Tan after assuring her I'd call her if I remembered anything that might be helpful. She retrieved her shoes at the bar and waved goodbye, leaving a rippling of turned heads in her wake. To a man, they swung their gaze from her shapely backside as it receded from view, to me, curious about the manner of being who warranted such a visitation. I did the cool guy thing and ignored their envious looks.

A bottle of Tsingtao beer in hand, I retreated to my room and rinsed the sand off my skin. When I emerged from the shower, I noticed the red message light on the hotel phone was blinking. The computerized voice told me I had four new messages and no saved messages. Message one, from Kenny, my caddie and friend, wishing me a good week. Kenny wasn't along with me for this tournament, mainly because I couldn't afford to pay his expenses. I'd be picking up a local caddie, the first time Kenny wasn't on my bag since I turned pro. That just shows you the state of my finances. I needed a change of luck, or I might be looking at a change of career.

Message two, from Judith. Just called to say hi. Wished she had some vacay time to join me over there. Hoped I was staying out of trouble and just playing golf for a change.

Of course I was. Merely hearing her voice caused a stirring in the Force. Could it be all the time apart was the cause of the weirdness between us? I really did miss her. All of her. Most especially certain parts of her. No wonder my yaya radar was so keen with the banker-surfer chick. It had been too damn long. . . .

Message three, from my brother, Blue, saying thanks, and that he's really excited to get going, referring to an experimental therapy I'd gotten him enrolled in. Blue's a quadriplegic. A former FBI agent who took a bullet to the spine. I'd read about this radical new therapy that has helped some formerly paralyzed people walk and function again, and I managed to get his name on the list. He starts on Monday.

Message four, with a time-stamp of just a half hour before I came back up to my room, was from Rick Wong. I could hear the hum of conversations in the background. His voice was understandably strained.

Huck. Rick. I need to talk. Can we meet for breakfast tomorrow? I'll come to you. Let me know. Thanks, man.

I called his cell but it immediately clicked over to voice mail. I said of course. How about eight. And said, again, how very, very sorry I was he lost his dad.

I'd planned on ordering room service and settling in with a pay-per-view movie, but thinking about Rick's dad, and hearing the pain in my friend's voice, made me yearn for a little human contact. I slipped on a pair of slacks and a polo shirt and went out to find a good sushi restaurant. Which in Honolulu are about as ubiquitous as palm trees.

There was a table open in a bustling place on Kalakaua Avenue. I ordered an assortment of sashimi and rolls. Plus sake. Ain't sushi without sake. I was popping edamame beans, watching the beautiful people, when I got the funny feeling I was, in turn, being watched. A casual glance around the restaurant didn't reveal anyone staring my way, but when the waitress placed my plate of colorful raw fish flesh in front of me, I caught sight over her shoulder, on the other side of the window, of a guy leaning against a lamppost, looking right at me.

A guy in slacks. And a white dress shirt. And dark shades.

And the sun had set about an hour ago.

Coincidence, right? Waikiki, despite its world-famous name, is really a pretty small area. Walking around, you bump into the same tourists over and over again. I decided to finish my dinner and just relax; Lisa Tan's paranoia had obviously rubbed off on me. And, indeed, when I exited the restaurant, Mr. Shades was no longer leaning against the lamppost looking in my direction.

He was across the street, leaning against the door of an expensive clothing boutique, looking in my direction.

I stood still and stared right back at him, letting him know that I knew that . . . he was looking at me. *Fuck this*, I thought, and started to cross the street to ask him what the hell he wanted.

Hey! *Hey you!*

It was a traffic cop.

Use the crosswalk!

Jaywalking is illegal in Honolulu. As it is most places. Only here, they'll actually give you a ticket for it.

Duly chastised, I moved over to join the crowd waiting patiently at the corner, watching Mr. Shades all the while. He lifted something to his face and said something into it. Just as the light changed and we began shuffling en masse across the street, one of those sleek, powerful, noisy Japanese motorcycles zoomed up in front of Mr. Shades and slid to a stop. He casually walked to it, slung a leg over the seat, and they were off in a high-pitched motorized scream, scattering the herd of tourists and ignoring the red light and the shouts of the traffic cop. I caught what looked to be a smirk on the face of Mr. Shades as he passed about two feet away.

Back in my room, I flipped on a pay-per-view movie but couldn't focus. Tried to read *Golf Digest,* couldn't focus. Changed the TV to an adult channel, couldn't focus. Drank a few microbottles from the minibar. Turned off the tube. Turned off the lights.

Finally fell asleep at about two A.M., I'm guessing, with my dreams visited by the annoying shriek of rice burners and the lifeless eyes of Sing Ten Wong.

Rick was already at a table when I got to the restaurant the next morning. He stood and we gave each other an awkward man-hug. His face was drawn and unshaven, his voice raspy.

Hey.

Hey. How are you doing? How's your mom?

Stupid questions, but what else do you ask in that situation? He just shrugged. His eyes were everywhere; the table, the beach, his hands, anywhere but meeting mine.

Busy. The funeral arrangements are, as you can probably guess, well, they're, ah, complicated with someone like Pop. The wake starts as soon as they finish the autopsy and release the . . . his . . . give him back to us. Probably tomorrow.

So it'll be a traditional Chinese funeral?

Yes. And huge. The wake will go on for five days, then the mourning period for like fifty more. It's really unbelievable to see. You'll have to come.

You know I will.

I'll have someone get you instructions for how things work, so you're comfortable and all. There's a symbolism to every little part.

Okay. Thanks. It's going to be hard for you.

I didn't intend that as a question, but he nodded anyway.

It's like I'm in a dream. No, a nightmare. I can't believe he's gone. And, that way.

I thought back on my own literal nightmares of the preceding hours, and wondered when Rick would stop replaying his father's death over and over again. Probably never.

The waiter brought coffee and juice. I ordered an omelet, Rick said he wasn't hungry. We settled into silence, both of us gazing out at the ocean, sipping coffee. He waited until my breakfast came before he spoke again.

So, Huck, I wanted, I need to ask you a favor. And I realize the timing really, really sucks, with the Open coming up and all. But there's nobody else I can trust.

Okay. You know I'll do whatever you need. Name it.

I imagined there was some duty related to the funeral he wanted me to fulfill, like help track down our college buddies to send funeral announcements to.

But no.

I need you to look into Pop's murder.

The fork full of egg and mushroom stopped halfway between plate and mouth.

What?

This was an assassination, Huck. And I don't think HPD is going to be able to go deep enough to find out who ordered it.

The fork was returned to the plate. I wiped my mouth with a napkin, stalling in order to wrap my brain around what he was saying.

Assassination.

Yes. It was more than just murder. He was in the middle of a gigantic international business deal. There are people on both sides who don't want that to happen. There are billions at stake.

The merger?

. . . Yes. How do you know about that?

Sammy sent someone to quiz me about what your dad said. She mentioned there was a merger but didn't elaborate.

Oh. Yeah. She?

Lisa Tan.

Oh. Wow. She's . . . something.

Yeah.

This merger. It's a really big deal. Very secret.

You said people on both sides didn't want this deal to go through. You mean you actually think people with your bank might be involved in his murder?

See, that's the thing, I don't know. I know it sounds insane, believe me. Someone broke into our house last night, went through the whole place while we were still at the hospital. Someone who knew we'd be gone.

Rick, with all the media coverage of your dad's death, I think a lot of people could've figured out you wouldn't be home.

Maybe. But then what about this: Nothing was taken. Not my mother's jewels, not expensive antiques, not even a flat-screen TV. Nothing.

That is weird. So what were they after?

I know what they were after. I'll tell you later. When I find it.

Okay. That still doesn't explain who would want to kill your father.

I know. But, look, maybe someone from the bank didn't want this deal to go through, maybe it was someone on the other side. I got a sense from Pop there are some pretty scary characters wrapped up in this thing. That's what I want you to find out.

Rick . . . look . . . I understand what this is doing to you. I mean, well, actually, I don't because I can't imagine what it's like to see your own father murdered before your very eyes. But I'm a fish out of water here. Don't you think the local police are better—?

No. Hawaii isn't like the mainland. The rules are different here, because, look, there are such distinct and influential cultures. The balance of power is subtle, nuanced. Cops here are limited in what they can do and who they can go after.

More limited than I am? How do you see that?

Because I'll help you. I'll get you access to documents and people the police can't touch, can't expose. And even if they could, they have no jurisdiction over the ones who are probably responsible.

No jurisdiction? You're talking about people outside the reach of law? Where in the world could someone hide from a murder charge?

He leaned forward on his elbows, his eyes red and exhausted, but his voice, though barely above a whisper, was intense.

China.

CHAPTER FIVE

So, here's pretty much the sum total of what I know about China: Great food. NBA star Yao Ming. Oppressive government. Olympic host nation. Yao Ming. Bully of Tibet. Big-ass wall. Their economy is kicking the crap out of ours. Yao Ming. Guy standing in front of a tank during some protests. Nuclear weapons. Humungous country with a billion or so people. Inventors of gunpowder and pasta. Toys with lead paint. Scares the shit out of the rest of Asia and maybe the world. Communist, whatever that means anymore.

Oh yeah, and Yao Ming.

Rick didn't want to go into details at the restaurant, but I agreed to meet with him later to take a look at what he had that made him so certain his dad had been assassinated. I promised him I'd help him any way I could, and I meant it. Because, frankly, I really didn't think I was going to be much help, so it wasn't going to be much of a drain on my time. I'd take a look at whatever Rick had. I'd bounce a few ideas off him. I'd tell him why this was a job for Five-O or Interpol or the CIA and not some ersatz private detective with a decoder ring and a law degree.

And then I'd focus on the Open and finish in the money to start off the year right.

Confucius say, Man who deceives self lies twice.

We said our goodbyes and I watched Rick move through the restaurant and out into the bright morning sun, his shoulders hunched, his gaze pointed downward, a man with a heavy burden, heavy heart, heavy thoughts.

My breakfast with Rick had cost me a tee time at Waialae for a crack-of-dawn practice round. Most of the Pro-Am contestants would be using the day to get ready for Wednesday's tournament, and tee times were getting harder to come by as more and more Tour pros pulled into town. The nice chubby Hawaiian concierge came through for me, though, scrounging up a slot on Kapalua, a very difficult, very beautiful course up in the mountains.

I signed the check and retrieved my courtesy car from the valet. Fifteen minutes later I was clear of Honolulu traffic and buzzing along the H-2 highway, past sugar, macadamia and pineapple fields. I found a radio station with a guy playing a kickass version of George Harrison's "While My Guitar Gently Weeps" on a, get this, a *ukulele*. Jake something was his name. I made a mental note to track down his CD. The guy is amazing.

I tried to clear my mind of what Rick told me at the restaurant and pass the time by playing a round at Waialae in my mind's eye, shot by shot, but then I remembered my conversation with Lisa last night, and then I remembered Mr. Shades. And that's about when I noticed the three motorcycles trolling along about ten feet off my rear bumper.

They were in no hurry to pass.

I sped up. They sped up. I slowed down. They slowed down.

The guys riding them wore full-face helmets with darkened visors, so I couldn't tell if Mr. Shades was one of them.

But something told me he was.

At the next village, I pulled into a gas station. The rice burners kept going, but all three men turned their heads to eye me as they passed. I went inside the convenience store and bought a beer, walked back to my car and downed it. Just a little morning carbs, that's all. Not to calm my nerves or anything. Although who could blame me? Lisa Tan was paranoid. Rick Wong was paranoid. And I sure as shit was getting there.

They picked me up again as soon as I cleared town, and followed me all the way to the Kapalua turnoff. As I made a right off the highway they stayed straight once again, turning their heads to watch me as they moseyed past. I thought about pulling a quick U-turn and zipping behind them for a tit to their tat, but then I realized my loaner Toyota was no match for those pocket-rockets.

I parked in the club parking lot and paused while retrieving my clubs from the trunk to see if I could hear the high-pitched *yeeeee* of a trio of very powerful motorcycle engines, but only the chirping of birds greeted my ears.

Since it was midmorning on a weekday, there were very few people on the course. Kapalua is rated one of the most difficult courses in the U.S., with virtually no rough. You're either on the fairway or in the jungle. Still, when the starter, not knowing who I was, advised me to take a few extra sleeves of balls, I just laughed.

Yeah, sure thing, sport. Will do.

Huck didn't.

Huck knocked the last Titleist in his bag into never-never land on the four-teenth hole, after playing what was probably the worst round of golf in his young life.

When I slammed the trunk of the Toyota, I noticed it was sitting a little lower on the pavement than it had been.

Maybe because all four tires had been slashed.

The apologetic Kapalua manager had a prepaid taxi idling next to my wounded Toyota before the police even arrived. They looked at the tires, at the shattered driver's side window and the symbol keyed into the paint just below it, and pronounced it a smash-and-grab theft by some local gang-bangers. Five-O took out a notepad.

Anything missing?

No.

You didn't have anything out in the open? Cash? Wallet?

No. Wait. Yes. My iPod.

Is that missing?

I peered into the passenger window.

Nope. It's there.

Well, I guess they didn't like your taste in music.

Har har.

We'll file a report on this. You can get a copy of it on our website. Here's the address.

He handed me a card and told me I could print the police report myself and send it in or the insurance company could access it themselves. I thanked the nice officer, told the club manager for the twentieth time it was okay and don't worry about it, climbed into the taxi, and napped all the way back to Waikiki.

Where I found my hotel room had been ransacked.

CHAPTER SIX

My clothes were strewn about the place. My toiletries were lying on the floor of the bathroom. The inside lining of my suitcase had even been slashed open. And carved into one of the walls was the same symbol that had been keyed into the vandalized courtesy car.

When I opened the closet door I walked into a fist. Or maybe it was a foot. Or a baseball bat. I can't be sure because I didn't really see it. The next thing I remember I was flat on my back, swimming up through pink cotton-candy clouds with sparkly sunbursts all around the edges. I was slow to realize I had a very sore face, and the metallic taste of blood in my mouth.

The EMTs arrived within minutes of my call to the front desk, the Honolulu police a few moments later. This being a tourist town, any crimes involving visitors take first priority. As the medics tended to my busted schnoz, the police asked a few questions, like how much money did I have lying around:

None.

And if there was any jewelry or other valuables missing:

Other than a filling, no.

Two of the cops talked past me as if I wasn't there.

So the way I figure it, we got a break-in going on. They somehow get a copy of the key card, rummage around, looking for the goods.

Yeah. Easy mark. Tourist. They usually carry lots of cash.

Uh huh. This guy surprises the perp or perps and they bust him one.

Gee, ya think? Sherlock Holmes and Watson here obviously thought this was a simple robbery. Until I pulled the ice-pack away from my face long enough to mention the car break-in. Then they got interested.

It's the same symbol, exactly?

Exactly. Gouged into the paint under the driver's side window.

Do you know what it is?

I was hoping you would, seeing as I'm not from around here.

They conferred and came to no conclusion other than it had to be some kind of gang sign, but for which gang was anybody's guess. They asked for a description of the motorcycles.

Japanese. Fast. One was red, I think, and the other yellow. Don't know about the third.

Did you notice a make?

A make? You mean the brand of motorcycle?

Yes.

No.

What were the riders wearing?

Black helmets. Jeans, I think. Black racing leathers on top.

Would you say they were dressed identically?

I resisted the urge to roll my eyes and speak . . . more . . . slowly.

Yes.

Just then I saw a familiar face enter the room, Detective Sagulio, the homicide cop from the hospital. He spotted me and came over.

Doyle.

Detective.

You seem to be in the wrong place at the wrong time these days.

Looks that way.

He sat on the edge of the bed next to me and motioned for the Five-O twins to find something better to do with their time.

How's the nose?

Hurts like hell. How's it look?

Like it hurts like hell. Any reason why someone would be so angry with you that they'd do all this? Vandalize your car and your hotel room? Assault you?

No idea.

Is it your opinion these events and the murder of Mr. Wong have something in common?

Maybe. Could just be a coincidence.

But you don't think so.

You tell me. How many visitors witness a murder, get their car and room tossed and get decked in the space of two days?

None that I've ever known of.

There you go.

He was silent for a moment, taking in the mess around us. I could practically hear the gears turning in his head.

Okay, so someone is either trying to find something you have, find out what you know or maybe scare you off.

Or all three. And I'm pretty sure the guy at the center of it all wears dark sunglasses and is tailing me. But I didn't say that, because I didn't want to tell the detective about Lisa Tan. And I didn't want to tell him about Rick Wong's request. So what I said was,

Makes sense.

So what do you know?

Nothing that you don't.

Sagulio looked at me hard. Thought about saying something. Put on the brakes. Flipped shut his notebook. Stood. Took his foot off the brakes.

You're not telling me everything, Mr. Doyle. Which makes me wonder why.

Hey, I'm the victim here, remember? I'm still trying to figure things out myself. When I do, you'll be the first one I call.

Do I have your word on that?

No.

Of course.

I'll hold you to that.

CHAPTER SEVEN

The cute emergency tech suggested I go to the hospital.

No thanks, I'm fine.

But your nose may be broken.

It *is* broken. I don't need a doctor to tell me that.

She looked dubious but didn't push it. She, and you, may be wondering how I can be so sure. Simple. Because my schnozzola has been broken many times before. In pretty much the same fashion—by violent contact with fist, foot or forehead. Sometimes even by people who claim to love me.

Like my dad.

The first time I was five. Pete, an LAPD cop and one tough sonofabitch, was teaching me how to box. He popped me in the face wearing a sixteen-ounce glove to show me what a punch felt like. I didn't like it. I heard something crack. I saw stars. I was too stunned to cry.

As blood dripped from my nose onto the driveway, Pete went into the kitchen and came back with a piece of paper towel. He tore off a corner, rolled it up tight, and shoved it under my upper lip. The bleeding stopped immediately. So he continued with the boxing lesson. Pete and I had a complicated relationship when I was growing up. Come to think of it, it's still complicated. And he still doesn't think I'm grown up.

When my guests finally packed up their stuff and left, the hotel management kindly insisted I take up residence in one of the penthouse suites with ocean views for all my trouble. I graciously accepted. As housekeeping carefully gathered my clothes and transferred them to my new digs, I took the hotel up on their request that I allow one of their spa's massage therapists to work out the kinks and cramps that bedeviled my poor battered back.

She was tiny, and Asian, and strong, and slightly resembled one Lisa Tan. Which wasn't at all a problem until she finished up on my back and asked me to roll over. Seeing as how I was draped in just a flimsy sheet, and how I'd allowed my mind to wander to lascivious places while she was doing her magic on my legs and gluts, I demurred with a lame excuse about just remembering I was late for an appointment.

Ordinarily, I'm not that bashful. But this wasn't *that* kind of massage place.

I showered off the aromatherapy oil in the spa's shower room and took the elevator up to check out my new accommodations. I wasn't disappointed. The suite was five times the size of my original room. The bathroom alone could've housed a frat party. Now if I could just get Judith to come enjoy it with me. Maybe then I'd quit fantasizing about every attractive double-X chromosome I met. I checked my watch and did a little math. LA is three hours ahead of Honolulu, which meant it was only eight o'clock in the evening there. I dialed the number by heart. No answer. So I dialed her office.

Yes?

Hi Doc. Whatcha wearing?

Oh, nothing much. Little red panties. Matching nail polish. A smile.

Overdressed as usual.

You're right. Are the nails too much?

Judith, the assistant medical examiner for LA county, is one very smart woman, if you don't count her taste in men. After she helped me out with a sticky little problem I'd gotten myself into, we became good friends. With occasional benefits. She wasn't my girlfriend, exactly, but we were developing a very enjoyable, comfortable, unpressured *something*. Or maybe she *was* my girlfriend. Are those things ever expressed? *I now pronounce you boyfriend and girlfriend.* With all the travel of the Tour, I hadn't had a steady girlfriend since college. And she became a stripper. Go figure.

Hey, Doc, can I talk you into zipping over here early? Take the whole week off? I just got a fantastic suite at Waikiki with beach views and a really big minibar.

Aren't you supposed to be concentrating on the tournament? And how can you afford a suite?

Ouch and ouch.

I *am* concentrating on the tournament, thank you very much, and swinging the clubs very well, I might add . . .

Lie.

. . . and the suite's a gimmie from the hotel. I got mugged today.

Truth.

Mugged? In Honolulu? I told you to get rid of that horrific Hawaiian shirt. You must've offended someone.

I should go now. This call's costing me a fortune.

Don't pout, I'm just teasing. Are you okay?

Yes. He broke my nose, that's all. No big deal.

Okay, now I'm not teasing. Are you really okay? And why would someone do that? Are you involved in something you shouldn't be . . . ?

Now, why would you assume that?

Because I'm starting to get to know you.

Well, no, as a matter of fact. I'm not getting involved in anything I shouldn't be. I'm completely focused on the Open. I was just calling to say hi.

Feeling a little lonely?

Nope. I'm fine.

Huck . . .

I should go. Just thought you'd enjoy this place. . . .

Oh . . . I'm sorry, I just can't. An old friend, you know, it's a prior engagement. But I'm still hoping to come out if . . . I mean . . . come out next weekend.

She had started to say *if you make the cut.*

If.

A resounding vote of no-confidence.

Hey, that would really be great. Let's see how things go next week.

Huck, I didn't mean . . .

Hey, come on, Doc! I'm fine! Have a great weekend and we'll talk next week.

Okay. Hey Huck . . .

Yeah?

Watcha wearing?

Red panties. Matching nails. A smile.

Why are relationships so damn hard? When we hung up I took a double vodka tonic out onto the balcony and stretched out in one of the chairs, propping my feet up on the railing, feeling slightly sorry for myself. The relaxed glow from the terrific massage was the only thing keeping me from hauling my ass out to the twenty-four-hour driving range I spotted up the highway for a late workout. That, and the fact that my face was still throbbing. Besides, I reasoned, tomorrow was a workout day at Waialae.

I may have been a tiny bit asleep when I heard the chirping of my cell phone. By the time I found it inside my pants pocket on top of the dresser it had stopped ringing, but the little window showed Rick's name. I called him back immediately.

Hey, Rick. Huck. Sorry I missed your call.

No problem. Just wanted you to know, Pop's wake begins tomorrow.

Oh. Okay. Anything I can do to help?

If you could come by that would really be great. I know you've got to get ready for the Open and all. Can you stop by here, though, in the morning? It's actually on the way to Waialae. Any time after eight. It won't take very long.

Of course.

By the way, one of our senior VPs offered to play for Pop in the Pro-Am. BOPI paid for the spot so they figured they might as well fill it. Guy's named John Ng. The lottery dinner is tomorrow night where you'll find out who else is in your group. You're welcome to go, but you don't have to attend, of course.

I hardly ever do, but thanks anyway. Too many questions about how to fix a slice, you know? Hey, your dad's wake, so what should I know about traditions? I, you know, wouldn't want to show any disrespect.

Don't worry about it. I have some responsibilities as the eldest son but I asked one of my sister's friends to walk you through it when you get here. It's not complicated for non-Chinese honored guests. She'll show you what to do. Nothing much more than bowing at the right place and lighting a joss stick.

Sure. Great. Joss stick?

Incense.

Right. Hey, Rick. You doing okay?

I could hear him take in a long breath.

No, actually, I'm really not. I have to find out who did this. It's eating me up inside. And, well, I hate to ask this, but can you meet me tonight? I want to give you something.

Of course. What time?

In an hour? Is that too soon?

No. Fine. See you then.

Thanks, man.

He gave me the address and we said our goodbyes.

I walked into the bedroom to grab something to wear when I caught sight of my reflection in the mirrored doors of the closet and stepped over for a closer inspection. Things on the facial front had not improved with time. In addition to sporting a still-swollen nose with a fairly useless Band-Aid across the bridge, I now had developed two lovely purplish splotches under the corner of each eye. I was one good-looking hombre.

I pulled on a pair of slacks, and the only dress shirt and tie I'd packed, and grabbed some sunglasses off the dresser on my way out. They were a little painful to wear, and would probably look a little silly once the sun went down, but thus is the price of vanity. I didn't want people to think I'd been in a fight or something. And lost.

I stopped at the hotel flower shop on my way to valet parking and bought a dozen white lilies.

The Open officials had delivered a replacement courtesy car while I was upstairs, and I was happy to see the valet drive up in a big, gold-colored Land Cruiser, with all the bells and whistles. No offense to Camry owners, that hybrid with the four flat tires was a decent little car, but this bruiser was more like my trusty old Ford Bronco that was sitting all lonesome and idle in the LAX long-term parking lot. Except my Bronco wasn't nearly as plush.

I took a moment to plug the address into the built-in GPS before pulling out into traffic on Kalakaua. That took me past the shopping district, towering resort hotels and apartment buildings. A right on Poni Moi Road brought me to a residential area with smallish houses hidden behind seven-foot-high concrete walls and hedges. But when I turned onto Diamond Head Road, I was treated to some of the most exclusive—and, per square foot, most expensive—real estate in the world.

Diamond Head is the iconic pyramid-shaped mountain that dominates the southern tip of Oahu. Around it lies a wonderful state park full of hiking trails and beautiful views. But draped elegantly along the precious strip of land between the state park and the ocean, like a string of gaudy jewels around the neck of a beautiful woman, are the architectural marvels of the island's wealthiest denizens.

The Wong's house . . . *mansion*, to be more exact . . . is a modern glass-and-stucco masterpiece that rises two storeys over the lush landscaping, with a soaring semicircular front window that affords those inside a 180-degree view of the raging Pacific below. As I rolled slowly past I could see delivery vans, workers and florists everywhere, setting things up, making preparations for a week of mourning, ceremony, prayers, and visitations. I found a parking space on the shoulder of the road a quarter-mile away and walked back to the driveway and up to the huge front door, over which hung a large white cloth that billowed in the breeze. An antique brass gong stood to the left of the door.

I spotted Rick just inside and caught his eye. He said something to the young woman next to him and pointed to me. She nodded and waved shyly, then gave him a slight bow and moved away into the next room. Rick came over.

That's Li-Hua, a family friend. She'll meet you here in the morning and help you through things.

Okay, great.

I handed him the flowers. He said thanks and motioned over one of the women to take them.

Gorgeous house, Rick. Really amazing.

Yeah. Pop loved it.

So, for tomorrow, should I get a suit? I don't normally travel with one.

What you have on is fine. Just no red.

No red.

Red is the color of happiness.

Oh.

Some workmen emerged from the house and moved past us, carrying mirrors. Rick answered the question he knew I was thinking.

> Another superstition. Whoever sees the reflection of the coffin in a mirror will soon have a death in their own family. They're taking them out to the garage. That's where we're going, too.

We followed the mirrors around the house to the back, where the open bay doors of the four-car garage revealed his dad's Bentley, a Porsche 911, and a large Lexus sedan. The fourth bay was being used as storage for tables, chairs and, now, unlucky mirrors.

Rick opened the trunk of the Bentley and pulled out a leather bag. He motioned for me to get into the back of the car, and he got in the other side. As he unzipped the bag I took off my sunglasses to get a better look, and he stopped in midzip.

> What the hell happened to you?

> Oh, this? Nothing. Slipped in the bathroom.

> No shit? Damn! You should sue the hotel.

> No. My own damn fault. Floor was wet.

Rick shook his head in wonder.

> Man! Does it hurt much?

Fuck yes.

> No. Not really.

He went back to opening the bag.

> This is Pop's briefcase. I looked everywhere for it before finding it in the trunk this morning. He'd stuck it inside the spare-tire compartment. I should've known it'd be here—he came straight from a meeting to the

golf course. There were a few papers and things in the case that are probably of no help to you, but I think this will be.

He pulled out a very slim laptop computer and held it out to me. I hesitated.

Rick, you sure you know what you're doing? Isn't this company property?

Technically, no. It's my father's, but he did all his business on it.

Well, then I'm certain BOPI will see the information on it as proprietary. You should hand it over to the bank.

He shook his head and placed it on my lap.

I can't do that, not if there's even the slightest chance someone at the bank was involved in Pop's murder. If there's any clue in here that could lead to the killers, I don't want to take the risk that they could get access to it at the bank and wipe out the evidence.

Rick, okay, but look, that's a bit . . .

Paranoid? Ridiculous? Unreasonable?

. . . of a stretch, don't you think? I mean, it's in BOPI's best interest to find out who killed your dad, too.

Maybe not. Not if someone high up ordered it.

Rick . . .

Huck! I need you to do this for me! *Please!* If you don't find anything I'll turn it in and say we simply couldn't find it at first.

But there are others at the bank who know this computer exists?

Yes. And eventually they'll be curious as to where it is. But no one has asked about it yet. Please, Huck. Please. You have to do this for me. For Pop.

I looked down at the laptop. Blew out a long breath. Opened it, and pushed the power button. It barely made a sound as the hard drive spun up.

This is top of the line.

You know it. Pop loves technology. He kicks my ass on Metal Gear Solid. He kept this with him all the time. He'd email the notes and things he wanted in the bank's computer to his assistant, but otherwise he pretty much kept all his stuff in this. I think he was afraid someone could get access to his information if it was on the main server at BOPI. He had this laptop at the meeting he took just before our golf match.

The log-in prompt appeared. In the top slot, the word STWONG was already entered.

He'd set the machine to remember his user name.

That sounds like something Pop would do.

You said your dad was a tech-head. How was he on security? If he didn't trust the bank's computer, do you think he was the kind of guy who was extra careful?

You got me. I don't know. I think his main idea of security for this was to never let it out of his sight. He couldn't remember his own phone number if it wasn't on speed dial. He was always grumbling about all the passwords they make us keep for everything in the world, so I would have to guess it's something simple. Something he wouldn't forget.

Unlike certain computer programs and controlled-access websites, most personal computers give you the option of whether you want a log-in password or not, and if you do there's usually no requirement for how many digits or combination of letters and numbers, nor how often it's changed. I took a chance that Sing Ten would be like most people when it comes to computer security: lazy. I left the password screen blank and simply hit the return key. A warning popped up declaring a password is required, with the numbers 1/10 next to it.

Meaning I had ten chances to get it right.

Next, I tried the world's most popular password: *password*.

The warning repeated. The numbers now read 2/10.

Another shortcut people take to keep from forgetting their password is to make it their user name. I entered *STWONG*.

3/10.

Sing.

4/10.

Wong.

5/10.

What's your mom's name?

Bao.

Nope. I was zero for six. Four to go.

God is another popular one, and I thought back on all the corny jokes Sing Ten told that morning. I tried *Confucius*.

No luck.

Sex.

Uh uh.

Shit! Shit shit shit *shit!*

Rick remained silent.

I leaned back in the luxuriously soft, cream-colored leather seat and stretched out my legs. I noticed the burled-wood armrests and accents, the plush carpet, the sheer perfection of the quarter-million-dollar automobile in which we sat. Smiled. Typed the word Bentley, punched enter.

And the laptop said, Nice try, sucker. One more chance.

He have a favorite pet?

No. He was allergic.

Sports team?

Just golf.

Which player did he like most?

Tiger Woods. Michelle Wie. That kid from China, Wen-Chong Liang.

I thought about it, then entered the name Tiger. Just before I hit the return key, though, I had second thoughts. I didn't know if the computer would lock us out permanently if I got it wrong. Sometimes they simply reset if you power down and reboot, but I couldn't be sure.

If you had to say what was the most important thing to your dad, the thing he thought about all the time, other than you guys, of course, what would it be?

Rick didn't even hesitate. He shrugged.

That's easy. Money.

I tried it. We were in.

The desktop screen had a dozen program icons lined up along the left side, over a picture of Rick's entire family.

Those all your sisters and brothers?

Yeah. And a few brothers-in-law.

I'd been right about Mrs. Wong. She was a full head taller than her late husband, and about six digits more attractive on a scale of one to ten.

If you don't mind me saying, your mom's a stunner.

She was Miss Guangzhou way back when.

I thought, *Couldn't have been too way back*. She looked too young to have had all those kids.

Is she your dad's second wife or something?

No. But Pop married her when she was very young.

How young?

Sixteen.

I looked closer at Bao Wong. The former beauty queen was the only one not smiling in the family portrait. Standing next to her millionaire husband and their large brood, she looked weary, and more than a little sad.

How's she holding up?

Fine, I think, all things considered. I think she's staying as busy as she can with all the preparations. Chinese funerals are really exhausting, especially for the immediate family.

But very important, I'd imagine.

Yes. Very. Which reminds me . . .

Rick opened his door.

. . . I've got to get back to it. Keep the laptop as long as you need it but keep it safe; I'm sure there are ultra-confidential documents and memos in there. The cops should never know about it. People would pay a great deal of money to get that information, and the cops in Hawaii aren't exactly getting rich on their salaries.

Then I have to ask again: Why give it to me? If you don't trust anyone at the bank, then you should look into it yourself. It can wait until after the funeral, can't it?

The look that crossed his face told me he was deliberating how to answer that one. It took him a few seconds to respond. Finally he swung his legs back inside and closed the door again.

It could, maybe. But . . . I just can't. Look at it. I made a promise.

A promise? To whom?

To Pop.

To not look at his computer? I don't understand.

Just, I can't, Huck. Leave it at that.

Rick, buddy, I can't leave it at that. You want me to help find out what happened, and I'll try. But you've got to be straight with me. You're willing to let me look at whatever secret information is contained on this hard drive but you won't tell me why you can't see it too?

It was obvious he was really struggling with it. Then he finally gave a long sigh.

Look, about ten years ago, Pop made me promise to never ever peek into his private life. And I mean to honor that promise.

Why in the world would he make you promise that?

He just did, that's all.

Rick . . .

He opened the Bentley's door again, paused, then spoke without looking me in the eye.

I found out he was cheating on Mother.

Jesus.

With more than one woman.

I . . . man . . . I'm sorry.

So we made a pact.

And the pact was you'd turn a blind eye to his affairs?

Yes.

In return for?

In return for . . . him not leaving her. She couldn't have survived that. She's . . . she's always been taken care of, sort of like a fragile flower or something. Divorce would've killed her. Disgraced her.

Rick placed a hand on the convertible's cloth top and flicked off a stray leaf. He then finally managed to meet my gaze. His eyes were red-rimmed and moist.

Huck, my father was a great man. I mean, a really great man. Name a charity on the islands and more likely than not, his name is attached to it. I mean, parks, Little League ballfields. Theater groups. Homeless shelters. He helped build BOPI into a major financial institution. He is admired and loved by everyone. But even great men can have a weakness, you know? And Pop's was women. He loved women. I can understand that, can't you?

Yes, I had to admit. I could. Any guy could—*understand*, even if not condone.

But would his wife?

After we said our goodbyes and Rick had walked away, I opened the laptop and looked at the family portrait on the screen. Then I realized what was bothering me about it.

Bao Wong looked like a woman who knew.

CHAPTER EIGHT

Okay, I know every family, every marriage, has its moments of extreme crises. They can involve a severe illness, an accident, a financial hardship, or, in many, many cases, a betrayal of trust. We all have our dog sides, I guess. Some are just better trained than others. I've read that a large percentage of marriages don't survive intact after the exposure of an affair, even if the causes for it are often far more complex, and far more jointly shared between husband and wife, than a simple base urge for a sexual tryst.

Divorce lawyers make a nice living by exploiting those complexities for the sole purpose of hacking off a larger share of the family fortune for their client and taking a sizable percentage of that for themselves.

Another reason why I hate law. The first being, it ain't golf.

But even those marriages that do survive are changed forever. Sometimes, I suppose, for the better. Most times, I would guess, the couple limps along with the wounds of war, never quite able to be wholly trusting, nor completely happy, again. Suffering the occasional phantom pain for the innocence that was amputated in the process.

I shut down the laptop and placed it back in the computer bag. This was going to be a problem. My car and hotel room were already tossed by a person or persons looking for something, maybe this thing. So where the hell could I keep it safe?

The question provided the answer: *a safe*.

It wasn't terribly late by the time I made it back to Waikiki, but I decided not to start rummaging around the digital guts of the laptop that night since I had Sing Ten Wong's wake and a full workout the next day. When I told him I had something I wanted to keep secure, the hotel manager tried to talk me into using the in-room safe that was in the enormous closet in my suite, but I insisted that the break-in had me spooked and that this was a very valuable item. He took the computer bag back to the hotel vault and brought me a claim ticket.

Thank you. And exactly who has access to the vault?

Mr. Doyle, only the manager on duty during each shift can open it, and they must use a unique numeric code specific only to them. In other words, mine is different than our dayside manager.

I see. So there's a record of who accesses the vault and when?

Yes sir, exactly. It's kept on file in our computer.

That seemed like pretty good security. Better, anyway, than anything else I could come up with on short notice. I thanked him and made my way back up to my sumptuous penthouse suite, where I poured a cold one, turned on the Golf Channel, and tried to put Rick and his family out of my mind. Which I accomplished for all of about one minute.

Pete, my dad, is an ex-LAPD cop. A disgraced ex-LAPD cop, to be more exact. But when he wasn't stretching the rules or planting evidence in order to solidify his cases against undeniably bad guys in order to get them off the streets by any means necessary, for which he served time in prison, he was exceptionally good at detective work. When he got a case he was like a snapping turtle; you could cut his head off and he still wouldn't let go until he'd figured it out. I learned a lot about how criminals think and work from him, and a lot about how police think and work. He was both, after all, criminal and cop. And what I learned from Pete is, in almost every investigation, the rule of thumb is to look close. At the people nearest the victim. Then slowly, thoroughly, move your investigation outward.

Is a betrayed wife capable of murder? Of course. Prison cells and book pages are filled with scorned women who took Shakespeare's adage to heart, that revenge should have no bounds. But would one wife in particular, Bao Wong, be angered enough, injured enough, humiliated enough, *strong* enough, to take that long step off the moral pier?

For the vast majority of people, it is not an easy thing to kill. Even for men. Even when the killing is sanctioned by society, like in times of war, most human beings cannot willfully end another life. In World War II, studies show only twenty percent of soldiers actually fired their weapons at the enemy. People simply prefer to live and let live, even when the other guy is adhering to only half that philosophy. Pete and his buddies had a name for their fellow officers who couldn't bring themselves to shoot back when shot at. They called them Quakers. Not as in members of the pacifist religion; as in *shaking with fear.*

Pete, in case you hadn't noticed, is not the sensitive type.

So the puzzle pieces that lay before me were these: Sing Ten Wong was shot to death by an unseen assailant. He was in the middle of a huge financial deal with a mysterious partner. He had cheated on his wife, presumably many times, presumably hadn't stopped until the bullet robbed him of his libido along with his life. There were some guys on motorcycles keeping an eye on me and probably trying to get something from me, maybe even the laptop I now had.

My thoughts wandered back and forth among those very muddled bits of information, not making much sense of anything, until they slowed and stopped altogether. It suddenly occurred to me my eyes were closed. And the ice had spilled from my glass when it hit the carpet. And the voice of some guy on the Golf Channel selling a training aid sounded an awful lot like Homer Simpson.

I roused myself long enough to stumble to bed, fully clothed, and fall into that lovely, warm, dark ocean of sleep.

CHAPTER NINE

Mom was calling me to get up already; I was going to miss the bus. Which would've really sucked because I had a big social studies test that day and I hadn't yet read the assigned chapters, surprise surprise, nor written the paper on whether the Electoral College strengthens or weakens our democracy and why. I woke with a start and sat up in the king-size bed with the eight-hundred-count Egyptian cotton duvet wondering where the hell I was.

Looking around the hotel bedroom, realization, as they say, dawned, but the sensation was not unlike what I imagine time-travel would feel like—a whipsaw effect from one era to another. Part of me seemed left behind, in my old bed, with Mom's voice echoing in my ears, and a sense of dread about the coming day.

I hate dreaming about Mom. It only makes me miss her all over again.

The cancer took her from us when I was in fifth grade. Actually, that's not entirely true. It was the .32 caliber bullet from my father's service revolver that took her from us; the cancer was simply the reason why she downed a bottle of Smirnov vodka, sat in the bathtub, put a towel over her head and the barrel in her mouth and waved goodbye to all of us with the slightest pull of her index finger. Not that I blame her. Pancreatic cancer back then had about a zero survivability rate.

I actually think she was trying to be kind to us. I don't think she wanted us to see her go through that hell. She'd called police dispatch and told them to track down Pete, who was off-duty at the time, and tell him to come home right away, I'm sure so he'd find her before we did, and then she just checked out of this world with a click and a bang.

Later that day, Pete sat Blue and me down and told us flat-out what happened and why and that Mom loved us very much and she expected us to be good kids and not fuck-ups. The three of us never talked about Mom again. We were stone-silent at the funeral, even when the minister asked if any of us would like to speak. And the only time I ever heard my dad say anything about her death was in response to a school principal's question about where our mother was.

She's dead. Fuckin' cancer.

The principal, unused to such language in his office and, I would guess, unused to the baleful, challenging look in Pete's eyes, had no more questions.

I climbed out of bed and stepped into a long, steamy shower, hoping to wash those memories from my thoughts.

My dress shirt and slacks were a bit wrinkled from having already been worn, but I'm not sure my clumsy attempts at ironing improved them much. When I opened my door to leave, Sing Ten Wong grinned up at me from the front page of the newspaper placed outside my room. The news coverage of his death had been nonstop, bordering on obsessive, but so far I hadn't been revealed as one of the eyewitnesses. I attribute that to either Hawaii media's relative lack of experience with such high-profile crimes or Hawaii police's unusually tight hold on information. Had Sing Ten been murdered on the mainland I would've been hounded like a rich uncle.

Rick had told me how important a man his father was, but it wasn't until I read article after article about him that I truly understood that was not just a proud son talking. Sing Ten Wong was a pillar of the community in almost every sense of the phrase. There wasn't a charity function or project on the islands that didn't involve him. He sat on the boards of half a dozen corporations. There was even a short-lived write-in campaign to convince him to run for the recently vacated U.S. Senate seat. Mr. Wong managed to put a firm kibosh on those efforts, saying he didn't want to spend that much time in Washington. Can't say that I blame him.

I stooped and picked up the morning's edition of the *Honolulu Advertiser*, probably the most stunningly honest name for a newspaper in the world, and headed down to the restaurant for a light breakfast and a few bracing cups of coffee. As I ate, I took a stroll through one man's life.

The main story was a lengthy obit about Wong and his accomplishments, which were all the more amazing considering Sing Ten came from China as a young boy with nothing more than personality and brains. In a speech he gave decades later, Wong described how much he'd hated the hard, dirty labor of his father's small farm, and decided to hitch a ride on a steamer bound for the islands. The article attempted to plot his unlikely rise from busboy to banker, but I couldn't help notice there were large chunks of time missing in the narrative where the reporter apparently couldn't find out what his subject was doing and where.

There were sidebar stories about people whose lives had been changed by Rick's dad; a young man who couldn't otherwise afford to go to college, a hospital that needed a specialized piece of equipment, a woman whom Sing Ten helped become a U.S. citizen. I was about to fold up the paper and sign the check when I spotted a smallish headline buried inside page four of the paper. The story speculated on who might have wanted Sing Ten Wong dead. That got my attention. For all of ten seconds.

Until I read it.

Three column inches of copy saying, in effect, we have no fucking idea.

Gee, thanks. Two things that article did tell me was, (a) the media wasn't aware of, or wouldn't reveal, Wong's marital problems. And (b) they didn't know about the big merger.

One last sip of coffee and I was driving back toward Diamond Head.

It was barely eight in the morning and I couldn't find a place to park on the street anywhere near the Wong's house. I finally pulled into a spot over a mile away next to a little park overlooking the ocean. The same girl I'd seen talking to Rick the day before was standing next to the front gate, obviously on the lookout for yours truly. Her English was somewhat limited but her accent and voice were cute. I'd put her at about eighteen years old.

Good morning, Mr. Doyle. My name is Li-Hua. Please to come this way.

Sure. *Li-Hua*. Is that Swedish?

I'm . . . ah . . . sorry?

Nothing. A lame attempt at humor.

Oh, yes. Thank you.

Then I remembered why I was there, and stuck the funny stuff back in my pocket.

As we walked up the front path, I noticed a group of four guys squatting on a mat that had been placed on the lawn, inexplicably playing what appeared to be dominoes. Their shouts competed with the wailing that was emanating from inside the house. One man threw a pair of dice as we grew close and the other three cheered. I touched Li-Hua on the arm to get her attention and gestured toward the gamblers.

What are they doing?

Yes. They are, ah, watching, guarding Mr. Wong. It is tradition. They must stay awake to protect the body, so they play Pai Gao or poker or some other game to not sleep.

What are they guarding him from?

I'm sorry?

What are they protecting Mr. Wong from?

Yes. From evil.

From evil, I thought. *They're a little late.*

We passed under the white cloth hanging over the entryway, through the front sitting room crowded with mourners, and into a large, central courtyard.

Sing Ten Wong's coffin rested on two stools in the middle of a temporary floor, which had been erected over a swimming pool. I knew this because the curved chrome handrails were still visible behind some flower arrangements. There was a large group of people gathered around one end of the coffin, and a small table at its foot. I saw Rick sitting on the left side, and his mother, Bao, on the right. Around them were a dozen young men and women dressed in either black or blue. Musicians playing a gong, a trumpet, and some sort of wind instrument accompanied a chanting Buddhist monk, while most of the women and girls wailed and wept loudly. It was, to be honest, a somewhat disturbing clashing of sounds. By contrast, the Irish-Catholic wakes I've attended were relatively silent affairs; a few sniffles, some quiet weeping, maybe, and the low-spoken affectionate anecdotes coupled with the occasional passing around of a hip flask. There was enough going on in the Wong home to, forgive me, wake the dead. And I didn't see anyone sneaking a wee sup of White Bush.

Li-Hua leaned in close in order to be heard above the din.

As an honored guest, you will go to the table there and light incense, then bow toward Master Wong.

Got it. What is the box there, next to the bowl of burning stuff?

The burning is prayer money, for the afterlife, so he is not without. The box is for money money.

Money money? You mean *real* money. Donations?

Yes. Donations. For the family.

I glanced at the mansion surrounding the courtyard. Sing Ten Wong's family wasn't hurting financially.

Tokens of respect?

Yes, exactly so.

I approached the deceased, slipped a couple twenties into the donation box, lit the incense, and bowed toward the open coffin. Sing Ten's face was covered with a yellow cloth, while a blue one was draped over his body. There were some photos, wreaths and mementos arranged on the floor around the top of the coffin, and what looked like half of a hair comb placed inside next to his head. Rick caught my eye and gave a slight nod, mouthing the words *thank you*. I turned to his mother and gave her a slight bow. She dipped her head in return, and I'm not 100 percent sure, but I thought I caught just the slightest hint of a smile fixed on her beautiful face.

Appreciation perhaps? Bemusement?

Or liberation?

Maybe I was overthinking it. Maybe the simple answer was she'd had a few sups of the Irish whiskey herself, just to get through the spectacle.

There were other honored guests waiting behind me to pay their respects. I bowed again and backed away. Li-Hua was waiting at the courtyard entrance and led me into the ornate dining room, where mourners were hanging out, drinking tea and nibbling on finger food.

Very nice, Mr. Doyle. I know Richard is grateful you came. He speaks of you often.

He's a good friend, that's for sure. So how long will this process last?

The wake? I'm not sure. I think a few days. The family is very wealthy, so they can afford a long period of prayer before the funeral.

Uh huh. And Mrs. Wong. Have you known her long?

Yes, since I was little.

Newsflash: You're still little.

I see. So, forgive me for asking, does she seem different to you now?

Different? She is widow now. That is different for her.

Yes, I know she's been married pretty much her entire adult life. That's just it. I saw a family photo where everyone seemed happy except her. And now, here she is, at her husband's wake, and she seemed like she was almost, I don't know, *relieved*.

Li-Hua grew visibly uncomfortable.

I'm sorry. I don't understand your question.

I don't mean any insult to Mrs. Wong. But I guess, does it seem like she's happier now than when her husband was alive? You would know, I figure, since you've known her so long.

She was stone silent. Being the sensitive guy I am, I pushed just a little harder.

I mean, look, Rick himself told me his mother was handling this whole thing amazingly well. And just now, it looked to me like she was very relaxed and content despite, well, despite what all this signifies. Li-Hua, she just lost her husband. He was murdered. Yet there's this sereneness about her.

I'm very sorry. I don't know that word, *sereneness*, but Mrs. Wong is a good wife and is, ah, mourning her husband's death in the traditional Chinese way. Her life has been, not easy. I think marriage is different, our culture than yours. It's too difficult to explain now, and I must get back to my duties. You can find your way out?

For such a young woman, she'd already mastered the art of the dismissal.

Sure, thanks. And thank you for the guidance.

It was truly my pleasure, Mr. Doyle. Goodbye.

Goodbye. Oh, hey, Li-Hua, if it's too difficult to explain now, can we talk some other time? I'm very interested in your culture.

And very interested in Bao Wong. . . .

Yes.

I pulled out one of my cards, asked for her phone number, and jotted it on the back.

I'd like to treat you to dinner later this week if you're available.

She smiled and giggled and turned away.

Which I guess I could take as neither yes nor no. Or maybe a polite Chinese way of saying buzz off. But just by her merely mentioning Mrs. Wong's life had not been easy confirmed what my spidey sense was telling me; that theirs was a troubled marriage, troubled perhaps even beyond the infidelities. So I chose to take Li-Hua's noncommittal response as an unconditional yes. We'd be talking again. Soon.

CHAPTER TEN

It took no more than ten minutes to get to the country club. They were scheduled to play the Dream Cup, a sort of private Pro-Am mainly for Sony executives and celebrities, starting at noon, but I had plenty of time for some practice on the range and then a workout in one of the trainer trailers.

When I made my way past all the sponsor areas and television trucks, I spotted a slot open at the far end of the practice range. A few of the other Tour pros were out getting in a few licks and I said hi to them, but no one was particularly talkative. We're all a bit tense in the days leading up to a tournament; wondering, hoping, praying for one of those weeks when we can put together a stretch of four rounds that'll make a difference in our lives.

For about two seconds I entertained the notion of skipping my routine and just starting to whack balls, then thought better of it. The last thing I needed was a tournament-ending injury. So I methodically went through the whole always-slightly-painful shebang of twisting, pulling and stretching various muscles, tendons and ligaments right there on the range.

I always finish with the hammies, which for the golf swing are like the central springs of a finely tuned watch. Everything flows from the hamstrings; setup, balance and power. The force unleashed at impact between ball and club is born deep in the back of your thighs. When I had that pleasantly warm *hum*, for lack of a better word, cooking in my core muscles, it was time to pick up the sticks and see how the old swing was looking that day.

Not every guy on tour does it the same, but I always start with the short clubs and move up, eventually ending the session by pounding balls with my driver. I've found that chipping a few dozen balls establishes the steady base rhythm and soft hands that I need in order to hit every other club well.

I rolled the brand-new Callaway off the pyramid—Tour players *never* have to practice with old range balls—checked my setup, adjusted my feet in relation to the nearest flagstick down-range, lightened my grip a smidge, hooded the face, took a smooth half-swing back and swept it forward in an even tempo, letting the weight of the wedge find the back of the ball.

It made clean contact.

It rose about twelve feet in the air, then gently plopped down about three yards from the pin and released.

It rolled to a few inches from what would've been the cup had it not been on a practice range.

It felt good.

Okay, nice start. I felt fluid. Felt connected to the club, the ball, the pin, the world around me.

Another ball off the pyramid. Setup, breathe out, take away, drop the club head on the ball, perfect chip. And another. And another. I wasn't hearing anything, seeing anything, but the ball, the pin, the ball, the pin.

The attendant brought more sparkling white Tour ix's with the strange little hexagonal dimples and built another pyramid.

I moved up to my 54-degree wedge and targeted another pin, farther away.

I switched to pitches. Then flops.

As I worked my way from short to long irons, I tried every shot in my arsenal, and every shot was flying true to form. Carve a cut with a seven-iron, no problem.

Draw my five. Done.

Power fade with the three-metal. A thing of beauty.

Everything felt exactly like it should feel. Connected, as I said. Fluid. Meant to be.

Then I pulled out Excalibur. The driver.

You want to be striking every club perfectly, of course, and you certainly want your putter to be a loyal ally against evil greens, but of everything in your bag, it's the driver that can either be Marshall to your FDR, or Brutus to your Caesar. It is a club with betrayal in its DNA and, make no mistake, it will, someday, maybe often, stab you in the back. But it is also the club that can make everything else possible.

So I teed up a ball. Picked an office building in the far distance as a target, imagined a little four-foot high window I would hit through, swept the club back, let my last thought be on keeping the shaft on plane, and let physics and physicality take over.

When you hit a golf ball exactly in the sweet spot on your driver, you don't so much feel the impact in your fingertips or the heel of your palm as you feel it in your soul. It is such a solid percussion that the sensation seems to leapfrog from the club head straight to your brain.

I watched the little pill soar up and up.

And over the back netting of the driving range.

Satisfying as hell. But more than a little dangerous for the folks on the number eight green.

That's when I noticed the guys around me staring. At me. Mike Weir was in the slot next to me, and he leaned over with a smile.

Hey.

Hey.

You might want to back it up a bit.

Yeah. I think you're right.

He nodded in the direction of the chipping green behind us and to the side. I looked and saw another guy was already there, booming drives over our heads and into the net.

Who's that?

Vijay.

Figures.

I picked up my bag and moved over to where Vijay Singh had improvised a practice tee box.

Veeg.

Huck.

Mind if I join you?

Not at all. You staying out of trouble?

Why do you ask?

He waved two fingers in front of his eyes.

Looking a bit rough this morning.

I'd forgotten about the shiners.

Oh that. Yeah. Fell out of bed.

He just raised his eyebrows and went back to smashing golf balls. I fished a pair of Oakleys out of my bag and slipped them gingerly on my still-sore proboscis.

An attendant brought over more balls, and I immediately settled right back into a rhythm, smoking long ball after long ball into the net, some 330 yards away. Vijay, too, seemed to be in the zone, creaming every ball he set on the tee. We began trading shot for shot.

Contrary to the way the public seems to perceive him, the big Fijian is one of the nicest, most well-liked guys on the Tour. We all respect how far he had to come to make it to where he is; Vijay literally couldn't afford golf balls when he was a kid so he developed his swing by hitting small coconuts. Maybe that's why he spends so many hours on the practice range every day, pounding the hard times farther and farther back into history.

He also has a great sense of humor. Vijay stopped smacking those little white coconuts and turned to me with a grin.

Hey. See that radio antennae on the hill, right center?

I peered into the distance. There was a cell phone tower reaching into the sky. It was visible through the net even though it was miles away from the golf course.

Yeah. Got it.

A grand says I can draw one closer to it than you.

Veeg, remember who you're talking to. Better make it a hundred.

Right.

Vijay wastes no time in his setup. He teed up, checked his target and cut loose. It was a gorgeous draw, carving down the far right side of the driving range, then swooping back into the net. From our perspective, it looked like he hit the webbing maybe twenty yards from his target—a pretty impressive feat with a driver.

My turn. I took a wider stance and placed the ball slightly back of center, aiming my feet to the right of my target and standing a bit taller than my normal posture. When I hit a draw I don't change my grip, but I do firm up my right hand a touch and loosen up my left, make a smooth, accelerating swing, and then I let my right hand overtake my left through impact. My little white pill took off down the right, almost skimming the net on that side, before racing back toward the middle of the range and nearly hitting the target dead-center.

Vijay cut loose with a laugh.

Not bad! Okay, there's a crosswind blowing thirty at Birkdale. Gotta keep it low and let it roll.

A stinger.

A stinger.

At the tower or are we playing this imaginary thirty-knot wind?

The tower is the target.

Gotcha.

The honor is yours, Mr. Doyle.

Why thank you, Mr. Singh.

A stinger is sort of like a long punch-shot. You can hit one with almost any club, but it's particularly useful when it's crucial you keep your drives out of the wind and on the fairway.

Once again, I had the ball an inch or so farther back in my stance than usual so as to catch the ball more on a downstroke than the normal up-sweep of a typical drive, and I placed my hands slightly forward. I also choked down on the grip, which helps to keep my arms in a stiff Y through the full takeaway and swing. The left wrist is bowed at impact, closing the face slightly, which gives the ball a low trajectory and a long roll. I have to focus on keeping my lower body very quiet through this swing, or else it can turn into a pretty nasty duck hook. The ball this time didn't make it all the way to the net, but it did get a nice hop on impact and rolled all the way to the base of the webbing, maybe twenty-five yards off-target.

Vijay had obviously been practicing this shot a lot. He put his not more than ten yards away from our imaginary pin, so we were even in our little ad hoc competition.

Our little game had attracted a small crowd of onlookers, one of whom was Nick Faldo, the popular CBS golf analyst and winner of six majors, among a shitload of other championships. He was in town to cover the Sony Open. Faldo is one of the guys I grew up admiring and trying to emulate. He was a bulldog when in the running, as tough a competitor as has ever picked up a golf club. He also had, shall we say, a winning way with the lassies.

Huck Doyle, right? Veeg, nice day. Got up a game of darts have you?

My breath caught in my throat. Nick Faldo knew my name. *Fuck . . . me . . .*

Vijay and Faldo shook hands. I leaned on my driver as casually as possible and did the same.

Hello, Mr. Faldo. Great to meet you.

It's Nick. You fellas are really pounding them out here. Looks like you're putting new holes in the net.

Must be the sea breeze. Gives everything a little more oomph.

Yah, must be. Hey, Huck, so what's the story with your face? You have an accident or something?

No. Allergies.

Allergies.

Yeah.

He and Vijay looked at each other. Vijay shrugged.

Told me he fell out of bed. I think young Mr. Doyle is a bit confused.

So it would seem. Well, I'd take a Benadryl if I were you, young Mr. Doyle. Carry on, mates.

But before we could launch into a tiebreaker round, a man in a suit approached and asked if Mr. Singh could spend a few minutes with one of the sponsors. He said sure with a shrug. I'd hit enough and decided to go work on putts anyway. As we gathered up our bags, Vijay gave me a chuck on the shoulder.

Your swing's looking pretty good, Huck. Might be your week.

I almost tripped. On my chin. Somehow I managed a casual response.

Never know, right? Never know.

He was right. My swing was feeling as good as it ever has, which is what really hit me between the eyes when he mentioned it, because I hadn't even been thinking about that. I'd just been enjoying the day. That, of course, is the hardest thing about golf for amateur and pro alike: to just enjoy it and not think about every damn thing that can, or will, go wrong.

Easy to say, right? When, on that range that day, not a damn thing was going wrong.

I spent another two hours on the putting green, then hit the weight room for some resistance training and core work. It was a little past one by the time I emerged from the clubhouse; showered, shaved and loose as a noodle from the workout. I couldn't wait to get Kenny on the phone and tell him how things were going. I left out the bit about Sing Ten and the condition of my face, but my old friend and caddie fully enjoyed my description of the driving-range competition.

Vijay will make a game out of anything, but nobody works harder.

That's the truth. Hey, Kenny, I gotta say, it just doesn't feel right, you not being out here with me.

No worries. It's giving me some time with K.J. That's always good.

K.J. is Kenny's teenaged son.

Well, take advantage of the time, then, because the way I'm feeling, you and I are going to be doing a lot of traveling this year.

I like the sound of that, Huckleberry.

We signed off. A quick pit stop for a fish sandwich and a six-pack of Tsingtao and I was back at the hotel. The manager on duty retrieved the laptop from the safe. Back in my room, I fired it up again while munching on the delicious Mahi. I typed in the password and studied the icons. It wasn't until I randomly double-clicked what looked like a folder icon with a six-digit number underneath that I realized this was going to be more difficult than I'd expected.

Up popped a log-in screen with the logo *ByteSafe Encryption* at the top. A cursor was blipping patiently below the first of twelve blank spaces. No way would the password guessing game work with that kind of security.

I tried the Word program. It fired up okay but when I tried to open a folder, the encryption program's log-in would reappear. Same with the PowerPoint and Excel programs. In fact, everything deferred to the security log-in except the web browser.

I was stymied.

I tried something different. Rather than going through the proprietary software, I went straight to the computer's hard drive to see if I could at least look at what kind of files were there. No luck. When I tried to expand the list of documents, up popped the log-in request.

Sing Ten Wong had indeed been very, very careful.

Still, if he really did have trouble remembering passwords, a twelve-digit one would be a nightmare. My guess was the security program forced a password change on a regular schedule, too, and it would require a random mix of letters and numbers. So it occurred to me, maybe he had to write it down to remember it.

I turned back to the computer briefcase and rummaged around in the side pockets: Power cord. Plugged that in to keep it charged. Some coins. A gum wrapper. In the bottom of the front pocket, a Medeco deadbolt key, the kind that opens those expensive, difficult-to-pick door locks. I slipped that into my pocket. The computer's owner's manual was in the back compartment, written in English from front to middle, then Chinese from middle to back. Riffed through that. Nothing jotted in the margins.

Nothing else in the case.

Then something made me take another look at the manual. There, in the Chinese section, scattered about every so often on every few pages, was the character that had been carved into the paint of my courtesy car and marked on the wall of my burglarized hotel room.

I picked up the phone and called the front desk.

Yes, Mr. Doyle?

Anyone down there familiar with the Chinese language?

Yes, the head chef at the grill is Chinese. I'll connect you.

The line went dead, then it clicked and a man's voice picked up.

Kitchen.

May I speak to the head chef, please?

That's me. How may I help you?

What's the Chinese character that looks like an L with a line through it?

Hmm. That would probably be *xi*. The number seven.

He pronounced it *chee*.

The number seven? That's it?

I'd have to see what you're looking at to be sure, but yeah, there aren't too many other characters like what you've described. It's probably a seven.

I see. Thanks.

No problem.

I hung up. Thought about it. Called the hotel operator. Asked for the kitchen.

Kitchen.

Hi. It's me again. The number seven guy.

Oh. Yeah?

Does the number seven have any significance other than what comes after six and before eight?

You're asking does it have some other meaning than a numeric one?

Yeah.

Well, it does, actually. It means *death*.

CHAPTER ELEVEN

I thanked him, hung up, emptied my pockets and sifted through the scraps of paper until I found Detective Sagulio's card. I switched to my cell phone. He answered on the third ring.

Sagulio.

Afternoon, Detective. It's Huck Doyle.

Huck Doyle. The golfer.

One and the same.

What can I do for you, Mr. Doyle?

I think I've received a death threat.

Oh?

I told him about the symbol. He was quiet for a moment. When he spoke again his voice was a little less gruff.

Can't believe we missed that one.

Well, not everyone reads Chinese.

Enough do. That shouldn't have fallen through. So, okay, I'll put that in the report. Are you requesting protective custody?

Hell no! I just thought you'd like to know. I've got a golf tournament to play.

That's your choice. You realize we can't assign a patrolman to protect you twenty-four/seven.

I wouldn't want that anyway. Cramp my style. No, I really just thought you should know. In case, you know . . .

In case you turn up like Mr. Wong?

Exactly.

Thank you for your consideration. Good luck. Please try not to be killed. I have enough on my hands already.

Will do.

My next call was to my brother. Only he didn't answer the phone. Lindsey did. My ex-girlfriend. The somewhat wacky, gorgeous little blonde who still visits my clothing-optional dreams.

Hi cutie! How's the tournament going?

Had a good day on the range. Hitting well. Vijay says it might be my week.

Vijay?

Vijay Singh. The pro. Big guy?

Sorry, don't know him. How's Hawaii? You always promised you'd take me there.

She had that slight whine to her voice, counting coup on yet another way I'd let her down.

Get on a plane. I've got an awesome suite overlooking the ocean.

No kidding? Oh, man, I'd love to.

No kidding. Get on a plane. Tonight.

Aww, Huck, you sound lonely. Why don't you fly that new girlfriend of yours out there? The pretty doctor?

She's not a girlfriend. We're friends.

Don't be defensive. I thought you two were dating.

Well, yes. I guess we are. That doesn't mean you and I can't hang out.

I'm not sure how *she'd* feel about that, but I really can't. I'm carrying a full load at school.

Until recently, Lindsey was a stripper. Sorry, *exotic dancer*. Now she's attending nursing school. If she really finishes it and gets a job at a hospital, I pity the poor fools she cares for. Each and every one of them will fall insanely in love with her. Like I did. Over, and over, and over again.

She hadn't stopped listing the reasons why she couldn't zip over to the Islands.

. . . and Blue is going four days a week to his sessions starting this week. He needs help with that. Oh Huck, the more he reads about this the more excited he gets. It was such a great thing you did.

It was nothing. A phone call.

Quite a few phone calls, actually. The folks at the NeuroRecovery Network facility in Lawndale said there were no slots open until next year, but I pulled in a few favors, wrote a big check, and got Blue into the program.

Well, I've never seen him so optimistic. It's very hard work. He was exhausted mentally and physically after today's session. But Huck, he's so happy. So happy. I just love seeing the smile on that beautiful face. And he had this enormous appetite at dinner, which you know he usually doesn't. You've done a great thing, no matter what comes of it.

Okay, okay. So where is he?

Blue?

No, Al fuckin' Capone. I was suddenly in a bad mood for some reason.

Yes, Blue. I need to talk to him.

Okay, let me bring him the phone. I'm down the hall from his room.

I heard some shuffling sounds as the phone brushed against her hip as she walked, the very hip I could picture so easily, sun-browned and glinting salt-water as she sat on a surfboard beside me not so many years ago, and then a door squeaked open and a muffled Lindsey voice said *Huck's on the phone and wants to talk.*

Hey! How's it going out there?

Really well, so far. The swing is really grooved right now. We'll see how it holds up during the Pro-Am tomorrow.

Yeah? You fix that little hook?

All gone. I was doing the same thing as usual. Too flat a take-back.

My chronic problem. Everyone has a hitch in their swing that resurfaces over time. Bad habits that have to be broken and rebroken. Even Tiger. That's why swing coaches get the big bucks.

That's great, Huck. Get a chance to do some surfing yet?

Not yet. I'm thinking maybe today. I had a good workout this morning so a little fun is in order, I think.

Give me a few months and I might be out there with you.

I couldn't tell if Blue was kidding. Only, Blue never kids about his injury. Since being shot during a drive-by a few years ago, the former FBI special agent has been paralyzed from the neck down. I visit him whenever possible, but seeing the athletic guy I grew up idolizing lying in a hospital bed, completely immobile, completely helpless, is one of the hardest things I ever make myself endure.

You feel that good about it?

Hard to believe, but I really do. The way they explain it, it really makes sense. I mean, it's a pretty bizarre process to watch; I'll see if I can email you a video of one of my sessions. They videotape all of them so we can gauge the progress, and it's still an experimental process so they're gathering as much data as they can all the time, but it really is an impressive thing. I'm basically hanging from a harness over a treadmill and a group of guys move my legs in this, I don't know what you'd call it, herky-jerky walking motion. I had my doubts at first, I gotta tell you.

The theory behind the neurorecovery therapy is it helps the spinal cord find new circuits to get signals to and from the brain, past the damaged nerves. Sounds whack but the articles say it's helped a lot of people walk again.

I hesitated to ask. For about a half-second.

Do the doctors think you'll be able, you know . . . ?

He laughed. I couldn't remember the last time I heard that sound.

Got a chance, bro. Got a good chance. My cord wasn't completely severed by the bullet, so they tell me the highway's there. Now we just have to help my body find a new way to get all the information flowing around the damaged parts.

I had to clear my throat before I could talk.

Man, that's, that's just great. Really. Great. Wish I were there to see you doing this.

You will be. The doctors say it's a long process, but we're making headway already, if you can believe it. After just one session, making headway. Hey, you win this thing this week and we'll have two reasons to celebrate!

I'll do my best. Hey, got a question for you.

Sure. What's up?

How can I break a one-twenty-eight bit encryption?

The phone went dead silent.

Blue?

Huck, what are you getting into now?

I told him about Wong's murder. And Rick's request. And the computer. I didn't tell him about Mr. Shades or the break-in or the symbol. Or the broken nose.

He was not pleased.

Can't you ever just pay attention to your golf game? Why *the fuck* do you do this?

Blue almost never uses the word *fuck*. Our dad almost never uses any word *but* fuck.

I didn't do this. This was done. I couldn't say no to Rick, his father's the one who brought me here. It's not taking any time away from my preparation, believe me.

Right. Well, you're a big boy. But it sounds like your game is finally falling into place and I'd hate to see you jeopardize it by getting distracted.

Got no choice. I'm in it now.

You're walking a fine line. The bank could claim that computer's their property and you're conducting electronic trespass.

I realize that. I'm taking the legal view it's Rick's father's personal computer and I'm simply doing the eldest son a favor at his request.

That may not stand up in court.

It won't ever have to. How do I get into the files on that computer?

You can't. Not without a special program that's licensed only to law enforcement and the military. Really powerful stuff, can break pretty much any encryption. But it's illegal to sell to regular folks.

See, the thing is, I knew that. I also knew what he'd say next. After a sufficient pause, that is, during which I knew he was struggling with the ethics of helping me out.

Look, I know a guy who has an older version of it. They're on to an even more effective version so this one's not as restricted. He'll lend me a copy, no questions asked. I'll call him tonight. Lindsey'll FedEx it to you tomorrow. You'll have the disk Wednesday.

I thanked him and gave him the hotel's address. Before we hung up he ended the conversation with the same phrase he does almost every time.

Hey Huck. Be careful, man.

I stepped over to the window and looked out at the ocean. The waves beckoned to me.

Fuck it. Why not?

Her card was in the same pile of pocket junk as the detective's. She had about five different phone numbers listed, but I tried her cell first. When she answered I could hear the sound of wind and waves and voices in the background.

Lisa Tan.

Lisa. Huck. Huck Doyle.

Mr. Doyle! How are you?

Call me Huck, please. I'm fine. Are you on the North Shore?

I am indeed. The sets are fantastic. Luke just took the highest score in his heat.

Hooray for Luke.

Hey, great. So, I have this afternoon free. Mind if I head up your way and do some surfing with you guys?

That's excellent! Please do! Luke can't hang around after the meet, he's got a meeting with one of his sponsors, but I'll still be here. I'll meet you at the snack shack on Sunset. You can't miss it.

Her boyfriend's good enough to have sponsors? Damn. Maybe I should've tried professional surfing instead of golf. . . .

I don't have a board with me.

No problem. I'll have Luke leave his. He won't mind. He's got dozens.

That's a deal. See you there.

I flipped the phone shut and went rummaging for my boardshorts. On the way out I made sure the laptop was locked back up in the hotel vault.

A little over an hour later I spotted the signs for Sunset Beach and pulled into a dirt parking lot across from an elementary school. Finding an empty spot was a bit of a challenge, but a pickup truck pulled out of one on the far end and I zipped over and grabbed it. The lot was full of the odd mix of junkers and hippie-mobiles you see at every surfer hangout, mingled with the rental cars of tourists. A brightly painted blue school bus had been converted to a smoothie shop and was apparently doing brisk business.

She was standing next to a small building that looked as if it were cobbled together from bits of billboard signs and driftwood, her long black hair tied back, her petite yet perfectly proportioned size-zero figure on full display courtesy of a skin-tight blue-and-gray wetsuit. Walking over to her, I couldn't help but chuckle at a small orange warning sign with the dire words, CAUTION, HAZARDOUS SURF, STRONG CURRENTS. DO NOT ENTER WATER WHEN ROUGH. CARELESSNESS COSTS LIVES.

Surfers live for such conditions.

When Lisa saw me her face lit up in a smile.

Hey! You made it!

I did. Like you said, easy to find. You have some good sets yet?

No. The tournament just ended not too long ago. Luke came in second but he had some righteous curls. It's really howling out there.

I looked past her at the crashing surf. She wasn't exaggerating. The waves were easily ten to twenty feet high.

Holy Christ! I can't remember the last time I surfed that big!

Well, it's calmer down the beach a ways. Want to try them first and work our way up?

Hell no! Let's go! Where's my board?

She whooped in agreement and started toward a pair of long boards stuck in the sand. We tucked them under our arms and waded out into the surf. It took us a while to get out to where the other riders were, past the surf line, because we had to dive under each huge wave before resuming our paddling.

Finally, we sat beyond the break, catching our breath. The scene before us, of the big swells rising and rolling away toward the shore, and the perfect, undeveloped sandy stretch of beach, and the tree-covered hills beyond, was one of the most beautiful sights in all the world.

Man. Lisa. This is just unbelievable.

Yes, isn't it? I never get tired of coming here, seeing this.

I'm not sure I would've been disciplined enough to finish college if I lived here. I'd surf all the time.

Like ninety percent of the dudes you see over there. All they do. My parents were pretty smart, though. They sent me stateside for college. UCLA.

No shit? I'm a Bruin, too!

Wow! Small world!

We blathered on about school and football and favorite haunts until we each sensed the perfect wave swelling up beneath us at the same time. With a shout, we both fell forward onto our boards and started paddling like mad, searching for that magic area just in front of where the curl starts to form. She was up on her board first, but I felt mine accelerating just a split-second later and took to my feet, hooking hard right to stay in the power zone. Other surfers who missed the spot pulled up on their boards and let the wave roll past, knowing there would always be another.

It was just Lisa and me, sliding down the face, as it grew, and grew, and grew, our boards slicing through water at an incredible speed as we fought to stay balanced. Out of the corner of my eye, I could see the wave crest and start to roll over on itself, forming that Valhalla of surfing, the perfect pipe. I needed to generate some speed to stay in the curl so I rode up the face to the top of the wave, hung on there for a beat, then, shifting my weight onto my forward foot to keep from falling out the backside, I turned what we call a lip-line floater, leaning forward, flattening my board onto the water, which instantly resulted in me shooting back down the liquid hill as the roar of the wave changed in tone and volume. Within seconds I was in the pocket, engulfed by the blue-green water, with only a small portion of the sky visible through the mist in front of me. Lisa was about ten feet ahead of the pipe, expertly carving the face, dancing the dance between chaos and control. After what seemed like only a few moments, the wave began to come apart. I could see Lisa shift her feet, lean right, execute a perfect cutback and suddenly disappear, up and over the back of the crest.

I crouched and put my weight slightly more forward to increase my speed and shot out of the curl just before it disintegrated, collapsing in on itself behind me with an explosion of water and mist. I snapped a cut right and my board popped into the air as I bailed out.

She was waiting for me back at the lineup, a huge grin on her face. When I paddled up, she gave me a little applause.

Bravo! You really can ride!

What an awesome wave.

Run of the mill out here, my friend. Run of the mill. Welcome to paradise.

No kidding.

We had half a dozen more runs that afternoon. None of the sets was quite as perfect as the first, but still, they were a helluva lot better than almost anywhere else on earth. As the setting sun painted the sky various shades of orange and pink, we hauled our boards up onto the beach with arms so tired we almost couldn't lift them. My legs were shaking, either from the adrenaline or exertion or both. Most of the other surfers and spectators were long gone.

Lisa's car was a Mini Cooper with a Thule board rack on top. The car was so small, the boards extended beyond both the front and rear bumpers, making it look like some sort of freakish insect. I finished strapping everything down while Lisa peeled out of her wetsuit and began toweling off, dressed now in the skimpiest of black bikinis.

She had a perfectly flat stomach. She had a small silver stud in her belly button. She had a tiny tattoo of a tiger peeking over her bikini line.

She had a boyfriend. I had Judith.

I looked away.

She popped me with the towel.

Hey, did you bring a change of clothes? Want to grab a bite on the way back?

Sure. My car's over there.

I motioned toward where I'd parked the Land Cruiser. Which now sat on four flat tires.

With that goddamn Chinese number seven carved into the driver's side door.

CHAPTER TWELVE

What is all that about?

Lisa was driving. We were winding our way back to Waikiki along Kamehameha Highway in her Mini Cooper, the lush farmland of Oahu's interior barely visible in the fading light.

I'm not sure. Same thing happened to another car I had at Kapalua yesterday.

The Toyota rep had assured me over the phone the vandalized Land Cruiser would be replaced by the time I made it back to the hotel, but I detected a note of reluctance in his voice. After all, these were two brand new cars that had been damaged while in my possession. Diminished returns for courtesy extended.

And that symbol, the Chinese number seven, it was on the wall of my hotel room when I got back. I'm told it's the symbol for death, supposedly.

She cut a hard look at me.

Do you think that's what this means? Someone wants you dead?

Not necessarily. If so, they'd probably just do it, not advertise it. Somebody wants something from me.

What on earth could that be?

I instantly regretted saying too much. Lisa didn't know Rick had asked me to investigate his dad's murder. And since she was an employee of the bank there was no way I was going to mention the computer. BOPI would probably consider that bank property and have the authorities seize it immediately, and for good reason.

I'm not sure. Golf is a cutthroat business.

This is serious, Huck. Somebody's threatening you.

Probably just a prank. Maybe some local surfers don't like the out-of-towner stealing their waves. What do you call us?

Haole?

Yeah.

I know most of the Da Hui guys around here. They'd never act like that.

Da Hui?

The Black Shorts. They protect the breaks. You saw a couple of them out there. But they really only get pissed off if you drop on their waves. They get first pick. Even then, the most I've ever heard them doing is roughing guys up a bit or breaking their boards. Nothing like this.

Well, it's probably a practical joke, then. Some of the PGA guys have really strange senses of humor. Don't worry about it. Really.

I could tell she was unconvinced. She started to say something, but the sudden high-pitched roar of two passing motorcycles drowned her out. They shot in front of us and immediately slowed down. Lisa leaned on the horn, which, from that tiny car, sounded about as intimidating as a quacking duck.

Stupid jerks! Now look! They're weaving around so much I can't pass!

I looked back. There was a third bike right on our tail. All three riders' faces were obscured by the dark glass of their helmets, but I was almost certain one would be my good friend Mr. Shades.

The rice-burners in front were zigzagging back and forth, effectively causing Lisa to slow down, guessing, correctly, she wouldn't run them over. I wasn't nearly so compassionate.

Lisa! Speed up! Bump them out of the way if you have to!

What? No! I can't do that! They might get hurt!

That, of course, was entirely the idea. The bikes were so close to the Cooper the front of the surfboards were actually over the riders' heads.

Look, they're trying to make you stop. Which means they probably want to do something bad to us. So rather than give them the chance, *will you please speed the fuck up!*

That got her attention.

But it did no good.

She simply couldn't make herself push down on the accelerator. Some people are just not cut out for harming another human being.

We should stop!

No, Lisa, we should not stop. Now, *please speed up*!

But the speedometer passed fifty miles per hour. Then forty-five. Then forty. The car was so tiny, I couldn't get my foot over the hump to push down on the accelerator. Ahead, the motorcycle kept weaving back and forth. Lisa kept honking the goddamn baby duck horn. The guy behind stayed parked right on our rear bumper. If I didn't think of something, it would be three against one in a very short amount of time. I didn't want to find out how that would turn out.

That was when I saw it. A billboard. With a big pineapple on top.

Hey, pull in there. Up there! On the left!

The Dole Plantation? Why?

They have to have security, right? Sign says it's a museum and store and all. At least people will be there. Right?

Oh, right!

Wrong.

The instant Lisa swerved into the parking lot it was obvious the place was closed. Not a person in sight.

The motorcycles circled around with a squeal of tires, the three guys conferred for half a second, and then they roared into the lot. I reached over and yanked on the hand brake. The little car did a four-wheel skid to a stop.

Get out! Now! And follow me!

We were out and running before the bikers reached the Cooper. Seeing us on foot, all three of them cranked their throttles and shot past the car, gaining on us with terrifying speed. Just as they were on top of us, we reached a small gate and cleared it at full stride like Olympic hurdlers. I caught a face full of branches on the way down.

The bikes all had to power slide to stop.

We found ourselves in a narrow corridor with tall hedges on either side. There wasn't enough room for us to run side-by-side, so I took the lead, running down one way, taking a turn at a corner, running down another way.

We were in a maze.

I'd recalled seeing the words on the billboard. WORLD'S BIGGEST MAZE. To entertain the tourists who come to the Dole Plantation to buy pineapples by the crate. It was constructed of ten-foot-tall bushes grown so closely together there was no way to move in any direction other than on the intricately designed pathways.

Floodlights on the corners of the property bathed the maze in a dim yellow light. I slowed to a stop and held a finger to my lips. Lisa bent over, breathing heavily. I leaned close to her ear.

They'll have a hard time finding us in here. We have to be very quiet and figure our way out before they catch up.

She nodded and straightened, her breathing almost back to normal again. The girl was obviously in terrific shape.

The path was gravel. We had to tiptoe to lessen the sound of our footsteps. As we made our way through the twists and turns, I pulled my phone out of my pocket and started to dial 911, thought better of it, and found Sagulio's number in the call memory. He must've had my cell number coded into his phone, judging by how he answered.

Hello, Mr. Doyle. Nice to know you're still alive.

I spoke just above a whisper.

So far. We're at the Dole Plantation, in the maze, and three guys might be trying to change that. Can you get some help over here quickly?

I'm sorry, I can barely hear you. You say you're at the Dole Plantation? In the maze?

Yes.

And you're being pursued?

Yes.

Stay on the line.

He clicked over. We could hear at least two of the bikers behind us on foot, talking to each other apparently without fear we could hear them. Maybe because they weren't speaking English.

Is that Chinese?

She listened for a beat.

I think it is.

Can't you understand them?

No! My parents are Korean!

Sorry! All Asian languages sound alike to me!

And all you Occidentals sound alike to us. Does the word *asshole* mean anything to you?

You're just cranky because those guys are trying to kill us.

Before she could reply I shushed her, because Sagulio had clicked back on the line.

Doyle?

Yeah.

A car from the Wahiawa PD will be there in ten minutes. Can you hold out?

We'll see. Thanks. Gotta go.

Call me when you can.

Will do.

I slipped the phone back into my pocket and held up my hand for Lisa to stop. We stood still, listening to the crunching and rustling and conversation between our pursuers. They were now to the left, and almost parallel to where we were crouched down.

My internal compass was telling me the entrance to the maze was somewhere to our right. I was pretty sure they'd left one of the men standing guard in the parking lot; that's what I would've done. We began walking again, moving roughly parallel to the direction from which we'd come.

We emerged into an open area, with smaller plants forming some sort of design on the ground, and benches scattered about. Even in the dim light, we were dangerously exposed, so we hustled across to another corridor in the maze.

The voices faded and we began to walk at a more normal pace, twisting and turning our way back in the general direction I thought the gate was. Minutes passed as we wove our way through the tunnels of branches. I strained my ears for the sounds of pursuit, hoping to soon hear the sounds of help.

Suddenly, the crunch of a footstep. And a whisper.

The men had caught up somehow. We had to move quickly, but quietly, back toward the right.

At first, the path we were on was going in the right direction, but then it took a hard turn left. We backed up and started down a different way. Dead end. We turned around and retraced our steps until we found another corner, but by now the men's voices seemed like they were just a few yards away. I held up my hand again and motioned for Lisa to get down. We stretched out prone on the ground. I peered through the lower branches of the hedge and watched two feet pass by on the parallel path. With one correct turn, that corridor would lead directly to the one we were on.

I rose to a crouch, ready to land a quick, hard punch as soon as he came into view.

The crunch of gravel came nearer and nearer. Then came a shout from the other guy, and the footsteps shifted and began moving away.

More shouts. Now we could hear running. And what sounded like someone pushing through the thickly intertwined branches of the hedges. Cursing. Shouting. More crashing through the bushes. One motorcycle started up, then a second, and finally, a third, and they roared away into the distance.

The sound of their powerful engines gradually morphed into another sound:

Sirens.

CHAPTER THIRTEEN

It took us fifteen minutes to work our way out of the maze. There were two police officers from the nearby town waiting by Lisa's car. They were not happy to see us. One of them shone a flashlight on us while the other stepped forward.

You realize you're trespassing? Let me see some ID, please.

He pulled a handkerchief out of his back pocket.

Here, take this. You're bleeding.

He made a motion toward my face. I took it and daubed my cheek. It came away splotched with red. I thought back on getting whacked by the bushes, when we jumped the gate.

Thank you.

I started to hand it back but he shook his head.

Keep it.

Thanks again. So, didn't Detective Sagulio explain why we were in the maze?

Who?

Sagulio. Homicide detective from Honolulu. I called him and he called you.

The cop shrugged indifferently.

Dispatch just said trouble at the Dole Plantation and get over here fast. Why don't you tell me why you're here?

So I recounted the story and showed them the holes in the maze walls and the big comma-shaped tire marks the bikes made on the parking lot when the men took their hasty leave.

Okay. So why do you think they were chasing you?

I don't know. Rob us, I guess. Must've thought we were tourists.

They each made a few notes, took down our names and contact information, and said they'd call in an all-points bulletin on the motorcycles.

After they left, I opened the passenger-side door for Lisa. She didn't hesitate to let me drive. We rode in silence for almost twenty minutes before she spoke.

That wasn't a prank. Those men wanted to hurt us. There's something you're not telling me. What were they after?

After what we just went through, I know I owed her an explanation. But it had to come with a condition.

I'll only tell you if you swear you'll keep it to yourself. Really. No one at the bank can know.

Huck, I can't promise that. My first duty is to my employer.

Then, I'm sorry, no can do.

She slumped down into her seat, arms folded across her chest. I think she was still pissed about the Asian language crack. Not that I blame her.

I glanced over just long enough to catch the angry look she flashed me.

I'm sorry I didn't know you were Korean.

What?! I don't give a crap about that! You put me at risk and you won't tell me why.

I'll tell you why. You just can't tell anyone else, that's all. Because I made the same promise to someone else.

More silence. More stewing in the passenger seat. Then, finally . . .

Okay.

What?

Okay. Okay. I won't tell anyone.

Promise?

Yes, damnit! I promise!

I mean it, Lisa. You cannot breach this trust, no matter what.

I said I promise!

Okay. I guess I owe you that. Rick Wong asked me to look into his father's death, and I think those guys are trying to dissuade me from digging too deeply.

Between the stroboscopic wash of streetlights, I could sense her eyes on me.

The police are investigating. Why would Rick want you too, also?

I think he thinks there are some things they can't, or won't, be able to find out. You said yourself, Sing Ten Wong was a very important, very complicated man. The politics are tricky. Rick is convinced his father was assassinated by someone involved in this big mysterious merger.

Assassinated is a loaded word.

As is *murder*. Near as I can gather, Rick believes there is an element on some side of this deal that either wants to stop it from happening altogether or wants to take more control over the proceedings. Or perhaps the results.

Lisa parsed her words slowly.

But assassinated implies government involvement. Is that what Rick said?

I took a shot in the dark.

Well, you tell me. Isn't China a partner in this merger?

A sharp intake of breath. A long pause.

Huck, you're not supposed to know that. I can't believe Rick would reveal such a thing. He's a vice president, for God's sake.

Rick didn't. Not in so many words. But you just confirmed it for me.

I confirm nothing. The People's Republic of China is not part of the merger.

I had to laugh.

Okay, whatever you say. While we're at it, there was no shooter on the grassy knoll and the check's in the mail. Any other great lies you want to tell me? I mean, come on. BOPI was created by Chinese nationals, is run by Chinese nationals, and you're telling me there's no relationship with the mother country?

That's exactly what I'm telling you. Bank of the Pacific Islands is an American-owned, federally insured financial institution. There are, of course, investors from many other countries, including China, who own shares of BOPI, but the government of China has no part in the bank's business, past, present or, for the sake of this conversation, future.

Jesus Christ. You sound like one of those disclaimers in a drug commercial. Might cause hemorrhoids, hair loss, bad breath or death.

I'm just making sure you're clear about that, that's all.

Then exactly who is involved in the merger?

I can't tell you that.

Gee, thanks. You're a big help.

Besides, it's not germane.

How do *you* know? If Rick's right and somebody wants to reshuffle the deck of cards while the game's still in play, it's perfectly germane. I need to know who's involved in this merger, and Rick can't tell me because he's a sworn officer of the bank.

Well, so am I. It would be a violation of federal law for me to reveal that information prior to the completion of the deal.

You're an executive assistant. That's not an officer of the bank.

You're wrong. I'm privy to all sorts of privileged information, so I had to sign all the same confidentiality documents Rick did. But, getting back to those men, you really think they are connected to the merger in some way?

Can't be sure. But what else could it be about? It's not like I have outstanding gambling debts.

Debts, yes. Gambling debts, no.

Well, perhaps they're working for that mafia guy you exposed back in California. The one who was shot by the police.

Pierce Fanagin? Not likely. Those guys don't work that way. Not nearly so subtle as playing tag with motorbikes.

Not that I was worried about the chances of that happening. Fanagin's crew, what's left of it, that is, had disappeared. Since that shootout on the 101, when two cops pumped bullets into the sports agent I'd found out was the still-murderous son of a New Jersey crime syndicate turned protected federal witness, the Feds had turned up the heat. My guess is the last surviving members of that particular family were quietly living out their retirement somewhere in South America.

Well, Mr. Huckleberry Doyle, I don't know who's after you, or who killed Mr. Wong for that matter. But as a lawyer you should know it's corporate betrayal at least and possibly even illegal for Rick to divulge any proprietary information to you, not to mention having you investigate this murder secretly, and I intend to tell him that.

You're not going to tell him, or anyone, anything. Remember? You promised. And I'm holding you to that.

Her face said either she wasn't at all happy she'd made that promise, or she had absolutely no intention of keeping it. I couldn't tell. She was, for lack of a better word, inscrutable. As we pulled into the entrance to my hotel she sat bolt up in her chair as if the most important aspect of our conversation just occurred to her.

And, hey, by the way, how can you be investigating this anyway? Don't you have a golf tournament to play?

I slipped the transmission into park, undid my seatbelt and opened the door.

Yep. But I'm very good at multitasking.

CHAPTER FOURTEEN

I didn't understand why I was getting all the funny looks in the lobby until I got to my room and checked the mirror. Now, in addition to the two purple marks under my eyes and a swollen nose, I had a nice set of bloody scratches across my forehead and down my right cheek.

GQ would be calling me any day now to be their newest cover boy.

It was then I remembered I hadn't called Sagulio back. He picked up immediately.

You're still alive.

Still alive. Thanks for calling the cops.

Just doing my duty. They catch the guys?

No, they hightailed it when they heard the sirens.

Too bad. So where are you now?

Back at the hotel.

I'll be by in five. Let's take a ride.

Uh, okay. I'll cancel my ballet class.

You do that.

He was leaning against an unmarked sedan parked at the curb when I emerged from the hotel. The detective held out a coffee.

Black okay?

Only way I like it. Thanks.

We got in and he pulled away.

Doyle, it occurred to me today somebody's trying to teach you a lesson and I'm not entirely sure you're paying attention.

Oh?

You're like all the rest of these tourists. You think just because this is such a goddamn beautiful place, nothing bad can happen here.

You mean, like murder and assault and stuff. No, I've been convinced that's all very possible since, oh, let's see, two days ago.

Not just the occasional murder or assault, those can and do happen anywhere. I'm talking about the same social sicknesses that you'll find in LA or New York or Denver. Gangs. Drugs. Rape. All of it. We have it all here. Just the other day, some psycho took his neighbor's toddler, carried him onto the H-1 overpass just over there and tossed the baby off into traffic.

Fuck.

Yeah.

Sagulio let that soak in awhile. We made a left onto Kapiolani Boulevard and drove west, quickly leaving the resort hotels and five-star restaurants behind; replaced by liquor stores and thrift shops, night clubs and convenience stores. What was bustling and bright in the light of day took on a slightly more dingy, more decayed patina at night. The detective didn't speak again until we merged onto South King Street and crossed Bishop.

This is District One. A lot of it's Chinatown. There are eight police districts in Oahu. This is probably the roughest when it comes to crime. Although the Eight can get pretty nasty. That's a big coastal area on the western shore, about 130 square miles, not very friendly toward tourists. Lots of locals there, unemployed and pissed off. Gangs very active. Stay away if I were you.

No problem. I got enough of that action on the North Shore.

So I see.

He slowed to a crawl. Most of the businesses we passed were closed, yet there were still dozens of people clumped on street corners and at the entrances to night clubs. When I commented on that, he gave a derisive snort.

Shoppers of a different kind, out looking to score drugs or sex. Mainly locals. Some savvy, or not-so-savvy, tourists. And lots and lots of homeless people courtesy of the U.S. mainland.

Homeless people from the mainland? How'd they get all the way to Hawaii?

Well, I could never prove it, but I can't count the times one of them told me they were rounded up in some other state and stuck on a plane to here. Don't need a passport to travel to Hawaii, but you might as well be sending them to Siberia since the chances are nil they'll ever show up on your clean streets again. Not like we can mail 'em back home. So we get treated like the dump for the rest of the nation's crap.

We pulled onto Keeaumoko Street and passed a bunch of places advertising massages, and clubs with names like Passion II, Club Saigon, and D'Amore. Sagulio's round face was silhouetted by all the multicolored neon.

We call this Korea-moko. It's a joke on the street name. Lots of the prostitutes here are from Korea. The massage business is just a front, of course. At the very least guys get the standard rub and tug, a massage with a happy-ending hand job. But for a little more cash, anything is available.

Are all the hookers Korean?

No. We got 'em from all over. China. Thailand. Vietnam. Hell, Wisconsin. Girls looking for a way to make money and get a tan. You name it. Tourists see the advertisements on the Internet for these places or in those little flyers you see being handed out all over town, come out here and get into trouble.

How so?

Well, not just the risk of catching AIDS or some other STD, but there's also a lot of robbery going on that simply never gets reported to us. The tourists are too embarrassed to admit what they were doing out here. The pimps and hookers know that. Makes 'em easy marks. They get jacked and limp back to their hotel, a little poorer, a little wiser, hopefully. Although, I don't know—like Forrest Gump said, stupid is as stupid does.

That took my thoughts back to when I was in high school, and the golf team made a trip to Tokyo to play an exhibition match with the Japanese amateur champions. After a series of close matches between my teammates and some of the best young players in Asia, the contest came down to my thirty-foot putt for birdie on the eighteenth. From the size of the gallery at the Tokyo Golf Club, you would've thought it was the final round of The Masters. They held their collective breath as I rolled my ball to the center of the ridge that dissected the green, and it turned sharply left and trickled downhill into the bottom of the cup. The huge crowd erupted in appreciative applause, and I remember wondering if American fans would've reacted the same way had a foreign team come to our shores and beaten our best. I sure hope they would. Good play should be celebrated, no matter who wins.

But that night, we slipped away from our coaches and found Tokyo's red-light district. Lindsey and I were in an *on* phase of our on-again, off-again romance, so I reluctantly begged off a trip upstairs.

The guys had some great stories for the long flight home about the exotic young girls and what they were willing and, to all appearances, happy to do. My impressions of the night were slightly different. I saw older, tough-looking guys, loitering at the entrances, closely watching the comings and goings with lethal eyes. I saw girls on break, smoking cigarettes in alleyways, talking, gossiping, complaining, with faces that suddenly looked twenty years older than their bodies, and expressions that did not convey a love of their work, nor a love of their clients.

That's what I was seeing here, on the streets of Honolulu. Lots of faces of people who weren't exactly enjoying what they do for a living.

Sagulio drove slowly, pointing out a Chinese temple used as a popular drug-buy spot, because the dealers can toss the goods into the river if the cops show up. Heroin was making a comeback here, in the form of something they called *cheese*. A cheap mixture of heroin and Tylenol cold medicine, sold for two bucks a hit. But so addictive, the junkies needed multiple hits a night just to stay sane.

Each kind of drug had its particular spot where it could be found, like aisles in a grocery store.

Maunakea Street for crystal meth.

North Kukui for cocaine.

You could score some good local *ma'a*, crack, over on Merchant Street, which during the day was Honolulu's financial district, and at night was popular with trannies and street walkers. Sagulio explained you could always tell the difference between the two, if only because the transvestites avoided the streetlights, which revealed the shadow of a closely shaved beard, or the dead giveaway of an Adam's apple.

I noticed a Grand Am with a green National sticker on the bumper parked in front of a bank, guy sitting inside talking animatedly on his cell phone, and pointed it out to Sagulio.

Tourist looking to score?

He peered over.

Nope. That's a pimp. In fact, I know the guy.

In a rental?

Yeah. They all use rental cars, because they know by law we can't confiscate 'em. Private vehicle being used in the commission of a crime is going to the impound lot, but not rentals. They're also big on using taxis. Lot of the cabbies are on the take from the dealers and pimps. They'll offer to take you to whatever you need, then get a nice little cut on the backend. The pimps will also send taxis to bail out their girls, so there's no connection made that we can use against them in court.

Got every angle covered.

You know it. Sometimes I wonder if the laws are written to protect the innocent, or protect the guilty. See that group over there, under the streetlamp? Two girls and four guys?

I see them.

Ten bucks says they just made a buy. Probably a few rocks of *ma'a*. Now, if we walked up to them and ask to see what they have, all they gotta do is close their hands into a fist, and we gotta get a warrant to see what's in there.

What? You're kidding.

Nope. Courts here say a closed hand comprises an enclosed container. We're required to have a magistrate give us a court order to make them open their damn hand.

That's rough. How do you ever get a bust, then?

Vice finds the ones who don't know that rule. Mainly tourists.

He pulled away from the curb and we continued our tour of the dark side of paradise. Business was brisk in Honolulu's underbelly, and there were signs of serious money on almost every street, mainly in the form of four-wheeled currency. A Mercedes here, idling next to a streetlight as its occupant negotiated a quickie. A Lambo there, cruising the cocaine district, eliciting friendly waves from the neighborhood suppliers. When we reached a rundown place with a sign announcing POOLI'S ARCADE over its entrance, the detective pulled over behind a bright red Maserati and slipped the transmission into park.

Let me show you something.

We got out and walked up to the bouncer, a burly Samoan with tattoos covering almost every visible inch of his body, including his bald head. Sagulio and he were obviously familiar, even friendly.

'Tsup, Oleo?

Not much. Quiet night. Who's the *haole*?

He motioned to me.

Not on the job, if that's what you're worried about.

Okay, cool. You the one beat the shit out of him, then?

They had a good laugh at my expense.

No. He's got some rough friends. So what're you doing here tonight? You still work the Bangkok Club, don't you?

Lennie's sick. Just filling in.

Lennie your brother.

Yeah.

Sagulio tilted his head.

Gotta take a look.

Help yourself.

He waved us inside.

To my surprise, Pooli's Arcade really was an arcade. There was a row of pinball machines down the right side and two video shoot-em-up consoles, the kind with the plastic pistols connected by a metal cord, down the left. Large chunks of the linoleum floor were missing, revealing patches of black adhesive-coated plywood. Where it remained, the floor was yellow and stained by ages-old gum, or God knows what else. The fluorescent lights hummed like angry bees, coating everything in the place in a sickly green wash.

At the back of the room were a half-dozen electronic poker machines. That's where the only customers in view were congregated. A very bored-looking older man sat in an elevated booth behind what looked to be a bullet-proof glass, watching us with bloodshot eyes.

Sagulio looked up at him and nodded his head toward the door at the back of the room. An electric lock buzzed and clicked. Sagulio opened the door.

We stepped through into a narrow hallway with what looked like ten fitting-room doors down either side. A mélange of sounds greeted our ears;

moaning, low conversation, heavy breathing, laughter. My tour guide didn't bother to lower his voice.

These are porn booths. Not illegal in Hawaii for their intended use, that of the viewing of adult films. But they also happen to be popular with druggies and hookers. In fact, I'd bet that there's some criminal activity being conducted in at least half of these rooms right now.

The hallway had gotten much quieter, with only the recorded sounds of sex coming from the various rooms. Sagulio had obviously gotten the clientele's attention. We turned and exited the hallway, back through the arcade area, and back to the street. The bouncer named Oleo and the detective exchanged cordial goodbyes.

Back in the car:

Okay, so if you know they're in those rooms committing crimes, why don't your buddies in Vice bust them?

Another lovely court ruling. Because, Mr. Doyle, there's a presumption of privacy in those booths. To just enter, we need more than probable cause, we need a warrant. Don't you just love lawyers? Oh yeah, I forgot, you are one.

There was more than a little disgust in his tone. I redirected the subject.

Your friend Oleo out front there, he sees the cops coming, something tells me he has a way of warning those folks inside.

A doorbell to be exact, on the wall behind him. But Oleo doesn't usually work Pooli's. His addict brother does. Lennie's probably not really sick, probably strung out somewhere. Oleo works two blocks over at a strip club.

Those are some fierce tattoos he's sporting.

Prison art. You can tell by the color. In good light the black has a greenish tint to it. Black's the only color ink available inside but it's in limited supply. Guys'll make their own ink by burning rubber and mixing it with urine.

Jesus. You'd have to really want a tattoo to put that stuff inside your skin.

Prison life is boring.

So why didn't he warn them you were coming in?

He knows I'm Homicide. No worries about me, unless somebody offed somebody in there. By the way, don't take offense he called you a *haole*. It's not really an insult. It's more a description, like *foreigner* or *white guy*.

Which can be an insult in some quarters.

That's true. But not in this case. *Ha* means to blow on the feet of the king, out of respect. *Ole* means, literally, none. So a *haole* is somebody who refuses to show respect for the king. Hawaii stopped being a monarchy about a hundred years ago, when a coup orchestrated by American businessmen, thank you very much, forced Queen Liliuokalani to abdicate the throne.

So, then, if there's no monarchy, who's the king of Hawaii now?

Sagulio's cop eyes scanned the streets, the alleys, the rearview mirror, in one uninterrupted, unending loop of concentration. He took in a deep breath and blew it out slowly.

Same as everywhere else. Money.

CHAPTER FIFTEEN

It was ten minutes past midnight when the homicide detective pulled to the curb in front of my hotel. I thanked him for the coffee, and the ride.

But there's one question you haven't answered. Why?

Why what?

Why show me all that?

Because you don't get it. You don't understand that nasty shit happens here, like anywhere else, and it's looking more and more like nasty shit is getting ready to happen to you. I know what you've done in the past. I did some checking. You helped some folks. Big hero. And now you think you're bulletproof. You got away with messing with some rough guys and now nobody can touch you.

I pointed to my sore, bruised, scratched face.

Evidence to the contrary.

That didn't scare you enough. The apple don't fall very far from the tree. I know who your dad is, and by the way, while I don't condone what he did, I can certainly understand why he did it. A lot of us, we watched the trial on TV. And we know what he was trying to do. Believe me, there are plenty of times I'd like to stack the deck in favor of the prosecution, but I just can't cross that line.

Pete doesn't care about that line. He only cares, or cared I guess now, about the line between people who hurt other people, and people who need protecting.

Well, that's not how things work. Not there. Not here. Look, we're digging away on this case. It's a tough one. No witnesses saw the shooter, including you. No obvious suspects . . .

Except maybe his wife. I wondered if Sagulio knew about their troubled marriage. And of course, knowing your husband is cheating is one thing; killing him for it is another. But even if Bao Wong wanted her husband dead, that still doesn't explain how she did it. The detective was still talking.

. . . we do know Sing Ten Wong was involved in a huge business deal. Huge. Talking billions. With at least one very powerful international partner. And . . .

China.

That stopped him midsentence. He started to say something, paused, started again.

Yeah, China. But maybe not only China. Point being, I also know you're sticking your nose in this thing for whatever reason, maybe out of loyalty to the guy who invited you out here . . .

Loyalty to his son, actually. Rick. He's an old friend.

I thought as much. Well, if he was really a friend, he'd put you on a plane out of here.

He thinks his father was murdered because of this merger. He thinks somebody involved is trying to throw it off-track by killing Mr. Wong.

I think that's highly likely, too, I gotta tell you. But regardless, what I know is where there's money, there's crime. And where there's big money, there's big crime. And little guys like you don't fare too well if you're poking around the wrong places and end up meeting the wrong people.

I thought of Mr. Shades. *Already met them.*

I don't expect you to protect me, Detective Sagulio. But I sincerely appreciate your concern. And the social studies lesson. One last question, though: If it's so futile, if the laws are so restrictive and the bad guys so numerous you have no hope of cleaning things up around here, then why try? Why put your neck on the line to help people, most of whom you don't even know?

He snorted. Looked to the moonlit sky. Brought his weary eyes back to meet mine.

Because who the hell else will?

I gave him a slow nod.

Exactly.

Beat. Two. Three. Four . . .

Okay, I hear you. But the difference between us is I'm a cop—

And I'm just some guy. But it's been my experience that people are sometimes more open to talking to just some guy than they are a cop.

He shrugged and let it go at that. We shook hands goodbye.

I had two big dudes from hotel security accompany me to my room and give it a thorough search before I collapsed into the bed, a flurry of ugly, streetlamp-lit images dancing me to sleep.

CHAPTER SIXTEEN

Tuesday morning came about four hours too soon. My tee time for a practice round at Waialae was scheduled for 8:10. I almost overslept, having forgotten to request a wake-up call the night before. If it wasn't for the chirp my cell phone makes when there's a message waiting I would've stayed in dreamland for the better part of the day. When I pushed up from the bed I noticed a few dots of dried blood on my pillow, reminding me of the adventures of the previous day.

I skipped the shower, jumped into some golf clothes and called down to valet parking for my car.

I'm sorry, Mr. Doyle. You never returned it last night. Your car isn't here.

Which meant the good folks at Toyota hadn't yet sent over a replacement vehicle. Can't say that I blame them. Maybe they're hoping I'd take up bicycling instead. I thanked him, hit the disconnect and dialed the concierge.

Hi. I need a taxi to Waialae, please.

Certainly. There's a line of them parked out front.

Great, thanks.

The day was as gorgeous as advertised. Low eighties, a few zaftig clouds waddling across the azure sky. While in the taxi, I flipped open my phone to check messages.

Lisa Tan, needing to meet again. Sounding official but friendly. Has some information.

Judith, just checking in.

Waialae, saying they had a good caddie lined up for the week and he'd meet me there this morning.

My financial manager, Louie. The check I wrote to the spinal cord therapy place had more than wiped out my money-market account. I was overdrawn. What did I want him to do?

Um, let's see, sell a share of Berkshire Hathaway. It's running at, what, $130K per share right about now? That ought to cover it. Except I don't own Berkshire Hathaway. I don't own any stocks. Anymore. Not since a certain slick con artist had taken me, and a lot of other people, for a very expensive ride a few years ago.

I called him back.

Hi Louie.

What exactly were you thinking, writing that big a check without telling me?

Sorry. It was something I wanted to take care of quickly before I left town.

Well, I convinced Wells Fargo not to bounce the check, but we'll have to make good on it in thirty days. Meantime, they're making eighteen and a half percent on the overdraft loan. Now, how do you propose we cover it?

I'm selling the Aston Martin.

The phone went silent.

The gorgeous sapphire blue DB-9 Volante had been given to me by a very wealthy friend I was able to prove was being framed for murder. It's worth about $180,000. It has under two thousand miles on the odometer, only a few hundred of which I had the joy of contributing. It also happens to be my dream car.

I'm sorry, Louie. I meant to tell you but as usual, things got hectic at the last minute, trying to get to the airport and all. I'd hoped there was enough left in that account to cover the check, but now I remember I had to dip into it to pay rent last month.

And the month before . . .

Yeah, right. I know, I know. We've had a rough stretch lately. But anyway, my plan was to sell the car to pay for Blue's spinal cord therapy. I don't know how long it's going to take, or even if it's going to work for him, but I wanted to make sure I had enough to cover it for the long term.

He was silent again. Louie's tone was markedly different when he finally spoke up.

I see. That's . . . well . . . that's an amazingly generous . . .

It's a car, Louie. It's just a car. So, you have the title still, yes?

Yes. It's here.

Well, if you don't mind, why don't you start checking with your wealthier clients to see if anyone's in the market for a gently used sports car? Maybe put it up on eBay too and see if anyone bites.

You're absolutely certain you want to do this?

Absolutely certain, Louie. Talk to you later. . . .

Okay. Well. Okay. Goodbye.

Lisa didn't answer her phone, so I left a message saying I was returning her call and to please remember her promise.

Judith didn't answer her phone, so I left a message saying I was returning her call and to please remember her red panties and smile when she came out to the Islands. I didn't add, *if* I make the cut. My swing coach always hammers the idea of positive thoughts into my head, so I was determined to give it a shot. I mean, what could it hurt?

God knows I couldn't play any shittier than I had the past few years.

I spotted my golf bag next to the curb, with the man I assumed was my caddie standing next to it. He was a short guy, middle-aged, African American, with close-cropped white/gray hair and skin the color of toast. He stuck out his hand with a grin when I got out of the cab.

Bobby Carter! Really great to meet you!

Hi, Bobby. You with me this week?

That I am, that I am. It's an honor, Mr. Doyle. I was actually in the gallery when you won the U.S. Amateur. I remember thinking, this kid's destined for greatness.

Actually, what I was really destined for was a desultory year on Tour, a quick exit from the PGA, a torturous detour into law school, and a long, long struggle to return to professional golf, and stay in professional golf. Pretty much anything but greatness.

Well, we have yet to see, don't we? And call me Huck.

Naw, you're wrong. The greatness is there, brother. I seen it. You just haven't tapped into your potential yet. It'll happen. Hey, maybe this week!

Maybe . . .

But I was thinking, this guy's had too much caffeine this morning. Still, okay, I was a little flattered.

He glanced at his watch.

It's about that time! Wanna get into your spikes and I'll meet you on one?

That's a deal.

The other players were already at the tee box when I got there. Other than Adam Scott, none of the rest of us was a household name, so I was a little surprised to see there were camera crews dutifully taping every group as they teed off. Probably getting in their own practice round before the big televised event starts, I surmised.

The problem with sleeping in so late was I didn't have a chance to warm up at all. As I took my place on the tee box and set up for my drive, I kept telling myself at least *please God* don't do anything embarrassing.

And I didn't. My first drive was actually a nice, long draw that landed squarely in the fairway and gave a good roll. Bobby winked at me as he put Excalibur back into the bag.

And away we go!

I already liked him. But still, I would've given anything to have had Kenny on my bag. This guy didn't know my game and had no idea how to club me. Here I was, going into battle against the forces of evil course designers, greens keepers, and nature, with an untested Robin to my Batman. It was going to be a struggle to keep my confidence up.

Now, to be clear, a practice round is really just that: for practice. It's a way of familiarizing oneself with the course, of figuring out your best approach angles, of taking notes about preferential landing zones and places to avoid and how the greens break. As a result, they're typically slower rounds than usual for everyone on the course (the only people on the course this day were the professionals entered in the Open), and you don't typically worry about, or in some cases even keep, score.

But that said, as the round went along I found myself making some pretty damn nice shots. It was one of those very rare days when the ball was doing exactly what I wanted it to.

Bobby had been a caddie there, on and off, for twenty years. He knew everything about the golf course. Even so, I could see him make notes in his notebook after every shot, marking down what club I selected and why. He knew the various distances by heart; the yardage from the edge of this sand trap to the center of that green; what he didn't know was how I liked to approach different situations. I appreciated the fact he was obviously trying to learn that fast.

A perfect example of how dialed-in my irons were happened on the fourth hole, the relatively short par three with the nickname *Apiki*, or Tricky. I'd found the sand there on Saturday but managed to save par.

I tested the wind; blowing five knots straight into our faces. Bobby checked his notebook.

Two hundred three to center. Pin's on the back shelf, so plus five. There are two ridges running diagonally on either side of the center swale. The back one is slightly steeper. So you want to get it all the way to the back or it'll either roll back down to the front or stay stuck in the ditch.

Okay. Gotcha.

He'd just described a two-hundred-eight-yard shot requiring at least two hundred three of that distance be carried through the air, rather than running it up the front of the green and trying to chase it through the swale.

Three days earlier, I'd played a hybrid. This day I pulled the five-iron. Set up for a straight shot, no draw, no fade, because I didn't want the wind to take the ball too much in either direction. Checked my line. Checked my grip. Pictured the whole thing in my mind. Took an easy breath and let it out.

And hit a solid shot that took off like a jet from an aircraft carrier, rose until it almost reached the green, then became a dying swan and plopped gently onto the green. We couldn't see from our perspective how close it came to the cup, but the grounds crew working next to the green cut loose with some yells and applause.

The other guys in the foursome all found the green, too. When we got up to the pin, my happy little Titleist sat not two inches from the hole. One of the grounds crew came up to us, all excited.

It lipped out, man! We couldn't believe it! You almost had an ace!

Bobby caught my eye as he handed me the putter. I shrugged as I tapped it in.

Wish I'd saved that one for Thursday.

Plenty more where that came from, my brother.

I carded not one bogey that round. Nothing but birdies and pars, and *almost* as many birdies as pars. The day reminded me of playing at the collegiate level, where the enjoyment of the game outweighed the pressure of having to win about a thousand to one. I was having so much fun just hitting a golf ball, while also focusing on the mental challenge of plotting an assault on this venerable, and tough, golf course, I'd completely forgotten what happened there three days earlier.

Until, that is, we stood on the seventeenth tee.

When Sing Ten Wong took a bullet to the heart at that exact location, I'd been gazing out at the ocean, day-dreaming about surfing what usually, that day excepted, were perfect waves. Looking out on a glassy sea, I don't remember seeing anything, except maybe a few gulls meandering through the sky.

This day, there was more wind, and waves, and I noticed a large cruise ship in the distance, and some sailboats meandering closer to shore.

I scanned to the left. A grayish naval vessel appeared to be at anchor or moving imperceptibly slowly about half-a-mile out. I don't know anything about navy ships. This one was smaller than a battleship but larger than a tugboat. It had big white numbers painted near the front: *52.*

I scanned to the right. Four guys were taking turns carving the surf, such as it was. The swells were only about three feet high.

Looking at the scene of the murder again only puzzled me more. My memory had not played a trick on me; there was absolutely no way somebody could have taken a shot at Rick's father without being seen. There was simply no place for the gunman, or gunwoman, to hide.

And yet, someone did.

I finished the round with back-to-back pars, but the memory of Sing Ten's death draped a cloud over an otherwise blue-sky day.

CHAPTER SEVENTEEN

When Special Agent Vida Blue Doyle went down with a bullet in his neck during a drive-by shooting at a softball game in East LA, I came running over from the other side of the field. We were playing in a Bloods versus Crips, Red against Blue game my brother had organized to bring gang members together in a more constructive pursuit than drugs and death. To this day, we have no idea who did the shooting. Maybe there was another color, some obscure gang, that felt left out of the fun that day, I don't know. I just know when I looked down at his dirt- and blood-covered face, I couldn't imagine him dying. It was inconceivable that such a little thing as a bullet could end his life, because he was Blue. He was invincible.

But the damage that little piece of metal did to him, to all of us, was enormous.

Almost as much damage as a similar little piece of metal did to Mom. And to all of us.

So forgive me if I have no love for bullets, nor for the various mechanisms from which they're fired. Growing up the son of a cop, I learned more than my share about how firearms are used. Being the brother of an FBI agent, I learned more than my share about how they work. And being a lawyer, I learned more than my share about what they leave in their wake. In addition to broken lives and broken families, bullets leave behind very specific clues as to where they came from, and who may have wanted to send them on their merry way.

Which reminded me, I needed to make a call to my new friend, the homicide detective. When we finished the practice round, I found my phone in the locker and left a message for Sagulio to please call.

Bobby declined a quick beer in the clubhouse, explaining the visiting caddies were allowed there but the local caddies were not. So we parted ways in the parking lot.

I wandered over to the Toyota tent, sheepishly poked my head in and asked if they'd managed to scrounge up yet another courtesy car, and the buxom sponsor's rep cheerfully informed me yes, they had. She escorted me to the parking lot, where sat a tiny little car about the size of my shoe. Well, okay, to be completely fair, it was about the size of the box my shoe came in. The rep was ecstatic.

Isn't it the cutest little thing? It's a *Yaris*. It gets really fabulous gas mileage. You probably won't have to fill it once all week.

Hey, great. Great. Where do I wind it up?

She giggled. I wondered if she was even old enough to drink.

I think we also have one in red if you'd like that.

No, thank you. This one's perfect.

This one was blue. Almost sapphire blue. Which reminded me of my Aston Martin. Which soon enough wouldn't be mine any longer. Which depressed me to no end.

Any chance I can have the Land Cruiser back when they replace the tires?

Oh, I don't know! Let me check, though. I'll ask. So you prefer that?

Let's see; embarrassingly small somewhat feminine subcompact versus manly mountain-crushing machismo machine. Tough choice.

Yes, if that's at all possible.

I thanked her as sincerely as I could and folded myself into the driver's seat, wishing all the while I had just one credit card that wasn't maxed out so I could rent a proper damn vehicle.

I was planning on spending part of the afternoon with a visit to the hotel gym followed by a run on the beach, and then some study time in my room, working out a battle plan for the week ahead, hole by hole. But when I got back to the Outrigger, the concierge informed me a package was waiting for me at the front desk.

It was from Lindsey. The disk. She'd sent it counter-to-counter with Continental and arranged to have a courier bring it over to the hotel. I requested the laptop be retrieved from the safe and headed back up to my room. Stopped. Backtracked. Asked the desk if they could spare a few security men for a quick once-over of my room.

Certainly, sir.

They gave it a good twice-over. No Mr. Shades. No sign of a break-in. I thanked the two guys and shut the door. Propped a chair under the handle, just in case. Threw the secondary sliding lock.

And powered up the computer.

There was a handwritten note inside the DVD case. It was Lindsey's handwriting, but Blue's instructions:

> *Boot up the computer with this disk already in the machine. It's automatic. It will search the route directory and prompt you for the files you want to gain access to. DO NOT let this get into anyone else's hands.*
>
> *Play well! We're rooting for you! Team Doyle.*

Blue had almost certainly said *root* directory, but Lindsey heard it as *route.* I turned off the laptop, slipped the disk in the slot and turned it back on.

My brother had no reason to know this, but I was actually very familiar with what this software could do. My second year of law school, a radical professor of law and government spent three weeks raging against the government's use of such things to undermine our civil liberties. He ultimately lost his teaching post when he was convicted of setting up a wireless nanny cam. In the nanny's bathroom.

128-bit encryption is several orders of magnitude more difficult to crack than the old 40-bit, given the enormous increase in variable choices, the formula being two multiplied by two, 128 times over. That's a number so huge it would take longer than the age of the universe for a conventional computer to happen upon the correct combination of letters, numbers and symbols. Every encryption is based on a key; a code for the program itself to unscramble the mess in order for it to be used by the intended persons. This particular program was designed to figure out what that code is.

Password breaking, what I was attempting, is only slightly different. Instead of looking for the encryption code, the software tests billions of combinations of words and letters and symbols in order to happen upon the correct sequence that comprises the password.

This U.S. government–developed decryption program is, in effect, a digital sledgehammer.

In most cases, computer security is still based on human psychology. Among the seventy-six characters, letters, numbers and symbols used for passwords, the thirty-two most common are, in order of their most frequent occurrence: ea1oirn0st2lud!m3hcyg94kSbpM758B. Security experts rest uneasily in the knowledge that probably 20 percent of all passwords are made up of *only* a combination of those thirty-two symbols. So the decryption program starts from that basis and works its way outward, testing millions of random passwords a second. The process is called *bruteforcing*. The hyperfast processors in today's computers allow the crunching of combinations to happen considerably faster than even a few years ago. In addition, the program simultaneously scans all files on the computer's hard drive, looking for the most commonly used words, names and numbers, and giving them priority in the testing.

There's also a host of other nifty little algorithms written into this particular deciphering software, which was developed by the Pentagon's Defense Advanced Research Projects Agency, or DARPA, using good old U.S. taxpayer greenbacks, in order to keep an eye on what good old U.S. taxpayers are doing, among other folk. But I don't know what those additional methods are. Because they're highly top-secret. In fact, I was breaking a few laws by even using this program. Blue had broken a bunch more by getting it to me. And, apropos, when the laptop finished spooling up, a stern FBI warning appeared in big red letters, threatening prosecution to the fullest extent of the law should any unauthorized persons attempt to use this proprietary software.

I affected my best Monty Python:

Your mother was a hamster, and your father smelt of elderberries.

The computer had no witty retort.

The FBI warning disappeared, to be replaced by a rather austere welcome screen. DARPA obviously wasted no money on pretty graphics or animation. It said simply, *Begin scan?* Next to that were two buttons: *Yes. No.*

I clicked *Yes.* The computer whirred. The screen said *Working* . . .

Less than a minute later, up popped a short list of programs that required passwords. Top of the list: *ByteSafe Encryption.* I moved the cursor over to the little box next to that line and clicked it. A checkmark appeared in the box. I then clicked on the button at the bottom of the screen that said *Begin decryption.* Once again, a plain screen with the single word, *Working* . . . on it. I stared at the laptop, transfixed by the black magic I imagined going on inside it.

My cell phone buzzed.

I jumped. Answered it.

Yes?

Doyle? It's Sagulio. Everything okay?

Oh, yeah. Everything's fine.

You sound stressed. You sure everything's okay?

Some spy I'd make.

Yes, yes. I just walked in from the gym. A little winded.

Ah, okay. So, you called.

I called? Right! Right. I called. Any chance I can take a look at the autopsy report when it comes out?

Absolutely not.

Oh, come on.

No.

We're on the same team here.

Can't do it. Not until the case is closed and the family okays it.

Then I suppose the ballistics report on the bullet is out of the question, too?

Out of the question. Anything else I can do to help?

No, that's plenty. Thanks so much.

Anytime. Glad to be of service.

He hung up. I checked my watch, dialed her number. There was conversation in the background when she picked up. She spoke in a low voice.

Hi there!

Hi. Out on the town?

Kind of. Cocktail party for an old friend. I've told you about him, Henry? He just sold a movie script and we're sort of celebrating. Steven Soderbergh is already attached to direct. Isn't that exciting? They're thinking Clooney will play the main character.

Judith's ex-boyfriend, Henry, I'd only recently learned, is a successful screenwriter. Drove an antique Porsche 356. To make matters worse, he's a USC Film School grad. Broke up with Judith to date starlets. And somehow he and the rookie Assistant M.E. for Los Angeles County had managed to stay good friends. Downright chummy, in fact.

Yeah, hey Doc, got a favor to ask.

Want me to talk dirty?

Maybe later. I need an autopsy and ballistics report on a murder that happened to a friend's father out here last Saturday.

It's not uncommon for medical examiners to share information about cases, looking for similarities, connections, exciting new ways people are offing each other.

The banker?

Obviously the news had made it to the mainland.

Yeah. He's the guy who gave me the sponsor's exception. I kind of owe the family.

Huck, what you owe *yourself* is a chance to focus on the Open!

Sheesh . . .

I am. Don't worry. I'm playing well. I just need some help with this.

I knew you were wrapped up in something. . . .

Doc . . .

Okay, okay. No lectures. I'll put in the request tomorrow. I really shouldn't, you know.

I know. I'm very grateful.

Yes, well, I'll figure out a way you can pay me back.

You do that.

It might involve some slight humiliation on your part. Nothing terrible. Balloons. Body paint. Some baby diapers maybe.

As long as they're not Depends.

You actually think they make *baby* diapers your size?

Oh . . . they're for me?

She rewarded me with that delightfully husky laugh I'd grown to . . . like. Yeah, *like*. Let's not get carried away. We said goodbye. She went back to her Hollywood party. I went back to staring at the laptop's screen.

Working . . .

It dawned on me, given all the various combinations the security program could suggest as passwords, this could take a while.

A very long while.

I didn't want to be anchored to the hotel room as the laptop crunched through its combinations, but neither did I want to stop it. The battery life of the computer was, at best, six hours. Actually, maybe not even half that given how much the dual processors and hard drive were working. So I couldn't simply return it to the hotel safe and let it keep grinding along. Nor did I want to risk letting any hotel employees get their hands on the DARPA disk.

It was a nasty quandary: I couldn't bring the laptop with me anywhere. I couldn't leave it here.

Or could I?

I went to the bedroom and found the room safe in the closet. Read the instructions, opened the safe, and coded in a random four-digit number that would become the safe's combination.

Back into the living room. Picked up the laptop. Returned to the safe and checked that it would fit inside. It would. Barely.

I was again faced with the issue of battery life. A coffee maker sat on the dresser next to the closet, plugged into an electric wall socket. The power cord that led from the computer's AC adaptor to the wall would reach, but it was too thick to allow closure of the safe's door. The thin little cord that ran from the charger to the computer itself seemed like it would work, but I didn't dare try it for fear the safe's door would sever it.

I looked around the room and my eyes fell on my iPod charger. It had a cord about as thin as the laptop's. I laid it in the corner of the safe's opening, near the lower hinge. It took a bit of a push, but the safe closed shut with a muffled *thunk*.

I entered the safe's combination and opened the door. The power cord was bent but not cut by the edge of the door. I was in business. I exchanged the iPod cord with the laptop's, put the computer inside the safe and gently pushed the door closed.

CHAPTER EIGHTEEN

The Outrigger has a nice, albeit smallish, gym. No one was in it that afternoon so I could move from machine to machine without having to wait. After forty minutes of resistance work and another twenty of stretches, I headed out the door and down to the beach for a leisurely jog.

Running on a beach is always slightly dangerous for me. Not because of the soft sand.

Because of all the visual distractions.

Bikinis to the left of me, gnarly waves to the right. What's a guy to do?

But I had to be disciplined. There'd be plenty of time for more surfing . . . and bikinis . . . after the tournament was over. Besides, with the way my face was looking lately, I'm pretty sure none of the babes would be the slightest bit interested.

When I got back to the room and showered off, I checked the laptop in the safe.

Working . . .

It occurred to me there was a good chance I might never know what was on Wong's laptop. Even with that high-tech software, passwords can take days or weeks to bruteforce. And even if I did crack it, there's no guarantee I'd find anything that would finger his killer. I returned the computer to the safe and called Bobby Carter, the Waialae caddie.

Hey, it's Huck.

Hello, Mr. Doyle. I was just tellin' my wife about you.

Oh yeah?

Told her you got something special this week. Told her to watch out for us. We got the juju.

The juju?

The magic. I can always feel it. We got the juju.

I sure hope you're right, Bobby.

Man, did I ever.

Say, Bobby, so something I always do with Kenny, my usual caddie, is sit down before the tournament starts and go over a plan for how to attack each hole. If you're free sometime this evening, do you think you could come by for an hour or so and we can compare notes?

Normally, Kenny and I would plop ourselves in front of a TV and use one of my many Xbox golf simulation games to get a feel for playing the particular course. But I hadn't packed my game console this time. And anyway, I couldn't recall if Waialae was a featured course on Tiger Woods or Links. Paper and pen would have to do this time.

You know, my brother, I would really love that. I'll bring my course notebook along.

Bobby showed up twenty minutes later with some damn good pizza and a few Cokes. Between munches and sips, we worked through our strategy for the days to come, all the while sure in the knowledge that for all our good intentions, the weather, and the golf course itself, would conspire to knock us off our game plan. We wrapped it up at nine. Bobby and I said our goodbyes. We'd link up again in the morning for the Pro-Am.

One more peek at the laptop: *Working* . . .

The HBO movie of the night was *Ocean's Thirteen*. The last thing I remember before nodding off was Brad Pitt's car blowing up in the parking lot.

CHAPTER NINETEEN

The next morning I was up and out the door by 5:30 A.M. I wanted some time to warm up before playing in the popular charity event. The first groups teed off at 6:50; ours was scheduled for 7:07. They were starting players on the first and tenth tees to get through everyone faster. Each year, celebrities like Will Smith, Adam Sandler and Marc Anthony show up at Waialae to entertain the crowds with their quips and slices. It's good fun all around. The pros get to rub elbows with movie and television stars, and the stars get a walking lesson from the pros. Everyone's happy as long as no one brings up politics.

Professional golfers tend to be very conservative.

Celebrities tend to be very liberal.

I've seen more than one shouting match erupt at one of these events, especially during election years.

At the range I was relieved to see my swing was still in the groove. I finished the warm-up with a few dozen putts, which were also rolling nicely. A good sign, but the fact is any golfer, professional or amateur, will tell you what happens on the practice range means nothing.

I made my way to where all the players were gathering and spotted Sam Ching, the VP from the bank. He extended a hand.

Huck.

Hi Sam. How're you doing?

Okay, I guess. Rick said you made it to the wake.

Yeah, you?

Yeah. Still can't believe it. He's really gone.

I know. It takes a while, believe me. When it's that sudden.

Well, Mr. Wong was really looking forward to today. It's a shame. Huck Doyle, this is John Ng, our senior vice president of mergers and acquisitions. He's taking Mr. Wong's place today.

We shook hands. John Ng looked exactly like a bank senior VP should; a little balding, a little paunchy and a little dour. In fact, he seemed downright unhappy to be there.

John, is it? Do you get to play much golf?

He glanced around nervously.

Not really, no. Not much. But I was the only one with the bank available today.

Ah. Well. I'll do my best to make it a fun day for you.

Not very likely. . . .

Two other men stepped forward. The first I instantly recognized as the lead actor in a popular, if slightly sophomoric, television sitcom. He was round and loud and very likeable. He wore his TaylorMade lid backwards. His hand completely engulfed mine.

Dave Planter. How ya doin'?

Great, thanks! Nice to meet you. Enjoy your show.

You learn to lie at these outings. I actually hadn't watched a sitcom since *Friends* went off the air.

Yeah, bullshit. It's crap, but it pays for all my expensive sins!

Dave gestured to the man next to him.

Hey, this is my new friend Buddy Mano. He's evidently a very popular disc jockey on the radio here in the islands.

Buddy Mano was a muscular guy about my age, maybe a bit younger. He rolled his eyes at Sam even as he took my hand.

Dude. We're not called disc jockeys anymore. It's *radio personality*. Or DJ.

Then to me:

Nice to meet you, man. Looking forward to watching you play.

Likewise. You get to play much?

Yeah, I do. I work the morning zoo so I'm free by nine. It's sweet. Out the door and on the cart by ten.

With this weather you must play year round.

He gave a tilt of his head.

Year round. It rocks. It really rocks. My only problem is deciding each morning whether to hit the waves or hit the links.

Surfer?

Yah.

Me too.

No shit?

Yes shit.

Awesome. Hey, give me your digits after the round and I'll hook you up with the four-one-one on where to go.

Sounds good. I had some good sets up at Sunset a few days ago. Unbelievable waves.

Monday?

Yeah.

I was there. Had a little competition going.

I know. I hit the surf right after it was over.

You must've just missed me. Well, you're pretty good then if you can surf the Pipeline. So I may just have to join you next time.

The marshal stepped onto the tee box and recited the rules of the match; best ball, stroke play, 100 percent handicap, keep up the pace and please replace your divots. In the distance an air horn sounded, signaling the start of play.

For the tournament week, Waialae's number-one hole is a par five that's almost perfectly straight, with just the slightest bend right. A strategically placed bunker lurks on the left edge for those big hitters who try to take too much of a bite out of the fairway, and a row of houses and very tall coconut trees are stacked down the right. At 517 yards it's definitely reachable in two, but Bobby had warned me a big greenside trap out front tends to be a magnet for aggressive players.

John Ng was the highest handicap in our foursome, so he had the honors. He was nervous as hell, his hand literally shaking as he set his ball on the tee, but he somehow managed to make solid contact and knock his drive a respectable distance down the right side of the fairway.

Dave and Buddy both found the right rough, with the comedic actor twanging his pill off a tree trunk first.

Buddy's swing looked like he was a player, even though I could see he was a little quick with his hands. Dave's swing was that of a sitcom actor; all elbows and wrists.

I stepped to the tee, and replayed my drive on this hole in my mind from the last round I'd played here, the day Sing Ten Wong was shot dead. I'd sent a bomb out toward center and it folded over into the bunker. I managed par, but it's the par fives where we go bird hunting, so a par is never a good score on a five.

As I planted my tee and weighed my options for this drive, I felt another twinge of regret that Kenny wasn't here, since he was really great at working out the angles. And, well, I missed my friend. The relationship between caddie and player is a complex one, sort of a combination of frat brother, comrade-in-arms and wife. Without the sex, of course. But the fact is, I was broke and Kenny knew it. I assured him we'd pair up again once the Tour came stateside. And I had to admit, Bobby had a wealth of local course knowledge that would come in very handy.

My strategy with this round was not necessarily to try and win the Pro-Am, but to treat it like yet another practice round. I wanted to have fun, but make it a useful outing, too. Which meant continuing to plot out my plan of attack for the Open by trying different things.

My set up this time was down the right side, aiming at a large office tower that rose in the distance. I cut loose a smooth rocket that soared over the right-side trees, took a lazy turn left and found the middle of the fairway, about 320 yards out. Our modest gallery let out a communal *oooooo!* Except for Dave. Who had something a little more colorful to say:

Holy mother fucking shit! You smacked the hell outta that thing!

I'm not sure those exact words had ever been uttered on the verdant grounds of Waialae, and certainly not at that amplitude. But the folks around us exploded in laughter.

That set the tone for the entire round.

The fairway was relatively flat, but there were rolling hillocks in the rough on either side that were causing my playing partners a lot of trouble. As for my little Pro V1, it was waiting patiently for me about a hundred sixty yards from the front edge of the green. Bobby read off the exact yardage to the center. He pointed out the flag placement was toward the back left.

Water behind the green, and it slopes back to front, so you'll want to keep it below the hole.

Gotcha. Do you think they're sticking today?

They're fast. Not sure how well they'll hold, I gotta be honest. But the grain this time of day is going to be toward you.

The grain he referred to is how the grass is lying on the green, in this case, pointing away from the pin and toward the front of the green. Most people don't realize a golf course is an animate being, a living thing, which moves and grows and changes even in the span of a round of golf. Most kinds of grass change positions during the day relative to where the sun is in the sky, and a green you're putting on in the morning will have slightly different characteristics in the afternoon determined by the blades of grass seeking their best exposure to the sunlight. Some pros downplay the amount of influence a green's grain has on how a putt will roll or break, but for me, any additional information helps.

The shot was 160 with a good roll. That's between a nine and eight iron for me. The eight would guarantee I'd make the distance, but with a creek flowing behind the green, I'd risk overcooking it and reaching the water hazard. I could make it with the nine, all carry, but a shot like that would almost assuredly have a lot of spin, negating some of that distance and leaving me with a lengthy putt.

So here's what you do when you're between clubs and you really don't want to be short: You choke up.

I moved my grip about half an inch lower on the eight iron's shaft and concentrated on executing a smooth takeaway and follow-through. It was a solid hit, with a huge divot flying through the air after the ball. That's a good sign. It meant I stayed down through the shot and met the ball cleanly with a still-descending blow. It streaked through the air straight as a dart, right at the pin, hit the middle of the green, popped in the air then released and rolled an additional ten feet. Another chorus of *ooooooos* from the gallery. Another comment of appreciation from Dave.

Fuckin' fantastic fuckin' shot! Goddamn! You should really think about turning pro!

I'll do that, thanks. As soon as my ears stop bleeding.

He grinned.

Oh, I'm sorry! Am I being inappropriate? A little coarse on the course?

Not at all, not at all. But that nice matron over there just fainted.

Dave peered over at my imaginary doyenne.

Oh her. Yeah. She's okay. We did a little too much toot together last night. She's a real tiger in the sack.

Okay, that's nice.

No really. What she can do with some Crisco and a vacuum cleaner . . .

I get the picture.

. . . rocked my world, I'm telling you.

Thank you for that mental image.

Just sayin'. Old don't mean cold.

Okay, right. Thanks.

It took the other guys three more shots each to make it onto the plate. When we walked up to the green, my beautiful little pill was eight, maybe eight and a half feet from the cup. When it came time for me to putt, Bobby helped with the read.

I see it pretty much straight in. Maybe a smidge inside right. It's still slightly uphill, so roll it firm.

I took my time. Walked around to look at the line from the cup to the ball. Walked to the side to see if there were any surprises from that angle. And had to agree with Bobby's assessment. I lined up the arrow on the ball to point at the inside right edge of the cup. Picked up my lucky NYC subway token. Checked my feet alignment. Loosened my grip. Took a few practice swings to get the feel of the distance. Shuffled closer to the ball. Gave the cup one last look, and swept the Odyssey two-ball putter back and forward in an easy pendulum.

As if on railroad tracks, the ball rolled up to and into the center of the cup.

The gallery erupted. Bobby winked.

Easy game, isn't it, brother?

Starting a round of golf with an eagle is a great confidence booster. But starting a round of *tournament* golf with an eagle is dangerous. For this reason: It gets you thinking maybe this is the day. Maybe this is the week. Maybe this is the year. So for a lot of us, as soon as we make that eagle putt, we focus hard on anything else but that double circle around the number on our scorecard. It's way too early, we tell ourselves, to let any of those thoughts start to creep in. We all have our little tricks. For me, it's picturing a certain former centerfold and B-level actress's bulbaceous attributes.

When I made the mistake of telling my friend Judith that little secret, she went all apoplectic about how sexist that was and that anyway, those are so grossly fake and oversized and unsexy. I tried to explain that was entirely the point, that I didn't really find them that attractive, but rather they were an exaggerated mental distraction from the stress of whatever shot I was facing. It was no use. The damage had been done. That particular evening ended early. I guess Pamela Anderson's breasts are lucky for golf, unlucky for getting lucky.

What is it with women?

My group moved on to the next hole, the 426-yard par four. A lake with some picturesque fountains defended the left, and bunkers threatened the landing zone on the right, squeezing the fairway's waist between them at that point, like a corset on a pudgy bride. The danger here for players is if they shy too far away from the water they will invariably find the sand.

Even though the prevailing winds were blowing directly into our faces, I knew better than to take out the big dog. Instead, I lined a solid hybrid 230 down the right side, leaving a clear shot at the green with a middle iron for my second.

Dave was up next. He dared to hit a driver and put his ball about ten feet away from mine, in the long grass but not in terribly bad shape either.

Buddy, the lowest handicap of the three, took out his three-wood. It looked from my angle like he was setting up to hit a fade, but he hooked it out over the lake and his ball dove in with a soft plop. The folks around us groaned.

Dave ambled over and gave him a big hug, faking sobs and sniffles.

Surfer dude! I . . . you . . . it . . . we . . . you're fucked.

The gallery loved it. People watching the group behind us on the number-one green noticed all the laughter and began to trickle over, curious about why this foursome was having so much fun. Our crowd was now about twice the size we started with.

The somewhat humorless banker, John Ng, was next. He'd posted a snow-man, an eight, on the last hole and looked about as happy to be there as, oh let's see, a snowman in Hawaii. John pulled out his driver. Put it back in the bag. Pulled out his three-wood. Put it back in his bag. Put a hand on his driver. Moved it over to his rescue club. Finally Dave walked over and made a big show of drawing Ng's five-iron out like a sword from its scabbard.

M'lord! Me thinks thou shouldest hit the Holy Five Iron. Would that a slice by any other name be as ugly?

The audience giggled. The bank exec blushed. I decided to step in.

That's actually not a bad idea, John. Play conservatively early until you get a feel for your swing. It's a relatively short hole. You can still reach the green in three and post a good score. But if you drive it into the hazard, like surfer boy here did, then things become a lot messier.

He nodded, managed a grim smile, took the club from the comedian, and hit a perfectly fine drive 150 yards down the middle of the fairway. He gave a shrug.

Better safe than sorry, I guess.

That's the golden rule in golf.

Thank you.

No sweat.

I could tell he wanted to say something else, but he cut his eyes to all the folks around us and evidently thought better of it. As we started off down the fairway I moved in closer.

Anything on your mind, John?

He glanced around.

Yes, ah, yes, actually. I know Rick asked you to look into Mr. Wong's murder, and I wanted to let you know I'm at your service. If there's anything at all you need.

Rick told him? Why?

Uh, well, that's very kind of you, thank you. I do have quite a few questions.

There are, of course, certain limitations to what I can tell you, but I can perhaps help you in other ways. Certainly I can let you know if you're off in the wrong direction.

Which begged the question, how would he know that? But I didn't ask.

So, but, why would there be limitations to what you can tell me if I'm trying to find out who killed your bank's executive director?

Because I'm legally proscribed from disclosing certain information. Federal banking laws limit what inside information I can divulge and as you know, there are delicate negotiations underway. But believe me, I will help you any other way I can.

We stood at his ball. He again selected the five and hit another pretty good shot, clearing the edge of the lake and dropping his pill a little over a hundred yards from the center of the green. As we started walking again, we continued our quiet conversation.

Well then, for starters, I need to know who Mr. Wong's enemies are. Uh, *were*. He gave millions to charity. He was funny. He was successful. Who would possibly want him killed?

Ng shook his head.

I do not know, Mr. Doyle. I do not know. He was a very respected man.

We waited while Dave hunted around for his ball. He finally found it at the base of a tree, and had to chip out laterally to find the fairway. He was still away, and knocked his third shot to the left of a green-side bunker. Buddy made like he was going to mimic the whole hugging and sobbing shtick until Dave threatened to brain him with his sand wedge.

From his drop, Buddy had about 230 to the pin, with a stiff wind blowing right to left. He grew serious for a moment and had a little discussion with his caddie before choosing to hit a three-wood. He caught it a little thin, but that ended up being a good miss because his ball stayed low in the wind, hit the fairway in front of the green and chased on to the putting surface.

He jumped around and hollered like he'd just won The Masters.

My distance was a touch under his, probably closer to 190 from the pin placement, which this day, Bobby had just informed me, was a yard below dead center. I thought about playing a British Open–style approach, hitting a punch-shot and letting the ball roll onto the green like Buddy's. But with the wind blowing as steadily as it was off the ocean, I realized I could take advantage of that.

190 yards is a six-iron for me, which gets the ball pretty high in the air but has considerably less spin than a more-lofted club.

I aimed out over the far edge of the sand trap that guarded the right side of the green, and concentrated on keeping my lower body still while letting my wrists rotate naturally through impact. The result was a ball flight that started down the right of the fairway, then, riding the Pacific wind, it looped gently left, plopping onto the right center of the green. It bounced maybe a foot and came to rest no more than four feet from the flagstick.

Come to daddy, big guy!

That was Dave, arms outstretched for his hug. I complied. A few minutes later, I sank my birdie putt. Two holes played and I was already three under par.

I sidled up to John Ng again and spoke in low tones.

> But, you're in charge of mergers and acquisitions, yes? So you must know who Sing Ten was dealing with on this big thing you have going on?

> Mr. Wong insisted on handling some of the more delicate negotiations alone. Frankly, the board did not approve, but as CEO, Mr. Wong's instructions had to be respected.

> Did he often handle the bank's affairs that way? Alone?

> Never. It was highly unusual.

Ng glanced around at the gallery.

> Perhaps we should continue this discussion later. This is very confidential information.

> Okay, yeah. Sure.

I could understand his nervousness. Thanks largely to Dave's antics, the crowd of people following us continued to grow. As we made our way to the third tee I could've sworn I caught sight of a familiar face out of the corner of my eye, but when I swung around to get a better look, I saw nothing but a sea of ball caps and smiles. And then, farther up the cart path, there he was. The only person walking away from us rather than with us.

A guy in a white shirt. And dark wraparound sunglasses.

Mr. Shades.

Just before he disappeared into the throng he glanced back at me. I think I saw him smile.

CHAPTER TWENTY

At some point, I was going to have a conversation with that guy.

There was little doubt Mr. Shades was connected to Sing Ten Wong's death somehow, and I looked forward to asking him exactly how in as polite a fashion as I could muster. I couldn't prove he was the guy who decked me in my hotel room. I couldn't prove he was among the guys chasing us through the maze.

But my gut told me he was.

This, of course, was not the time to ask him about those incidents. So I did my best to push him out of my mind and think about the task at hand, namely, keeping the wheels on the cart and this good round going. It wasn't easy. He was just one more question in a sea of questions, with not a drop of answers in sight.

At the turn, I was seven under par. I gave one back on the number ten when I went fairway bunker to greenside bunker, but recovered it when I birdied the fourteenth.

Hey Huck!

The British accent was familiar. I turned and spotted Nick Faldo with a camera crew standing near the line of television production trucks. I waved.

Nick!

How's it going today?

Good. Having a good round.

I'd say so. You're seven bloody under.

Yeah. The greens are running true.

What else could I say?

He laughed.

That must be it. And, how are those allergies?

The what?

He made a motion toward his face.

Oh, yeah. My allergies. Better, thanks.

If you say so, mate.

Faldo stayed put, but the camera crew joined us at the next tee box and followed us through the rest of the round.

My twenty-foot birdie putt lipped-out on the fifteenth, and our now-sizable gallery groaned in unison. Dave slung his arm around my shoulder.

Now you're really fucked. They're rooting for you.

For us. Don't forget. For us. This is best ball. We're a team. I win, we win.

Holy shit, that's right! Don't screw up again, you bastard!

Waialae's number sixteen is one of the prettiest in all of golf, a carbon-copy of the number-six hole at the National on Long Island. Most days the winds off the mighty Pacific are at your back, so this par four is a great driving hole. The fairway takes an almost ninety-degree left turn, but if you keep your drive to the right you have a clear shot at an open, relatively flat green, which is very bird-friendly.

The tee box was situated so far back the only thing between it and some guy's tiny backyard was a cast-iron fence. A row of really tall coconut trees marched down the right in close order, a threat to anyone foolish enough to attempt too big a draw.

I felt relaxed and content as I teed up my Titleist, but the adrenaline must've been coursing through my veins, because I absolutely smashed the ball through the dogleg and into the fairway bunker at the far end.

Our audience groaned again.

Dave uncharacteristically kept his mouth shut.

Bobby leaned in close as he slid the driver back in the bag.

They think you're in trouble. You're not. The sand is firm in there.

Buddy's drive ended up in fairly good position, just to the right in the first cut. Dave was not quite so lucky, bouncing his behind an umbrella-shaped tree at the fulcrum of the dogleg with absolutely no shot at the green. John Ng wisely hit another five-iron into the middle of the fairway, following on with a seven-iron to safely make the turn. He had settled into playing bogey golf, which, with a high handicap like his, is how you win tournaments. Take note, amateurs: Play within your abilities, play smart, play the scorecard, and you'll almost always be in contention. If you can't really commit to hitting driver or a long iron with confidence, put it back in the bag and hit what you feel good about. You can still score well. It's when you keep putting drives in the woods or the water and have to take drops and penalty strokes that you really start cranking up the big numbers. The more frustrated you get with this game, the worse you'll play.

Dave took a crazy chance and tried to hit a low shot out from under the kiavi tree, which reached out and grabbed his ball and knocked it to the ground not ten feet away. He still didn't have a clear shot, but this time he took his medicine and chipped back out to the short grass. His fourth shot found the front edge of the green.

Buddy's second landed in a steep-sided bunker right of the green, and from our perspective it looked like it plugged into the wall pretty good. Before Dave could utter a word, the DJ had his iron raised over his head ready to strike. Dave shut up. The gallery howled with pleasure.

As we made our way down the fairway, we passed a huge pink stucco-and-glass house on the left where a few very attractive bikini-clad young women were stretched out by the pool, casually following the match through designer sunglasses while chatting and sipping from large tumblers of colorful cocktails. Two black Porsches sat in the circular driveway next to a sleek red Maserati Quattroporte which looked vaguely familiar. Three men who looked to be in their sixties, also in bathing suits, were clustered against the fence, beers in hand, watching the golf match with considerably more interest. I caught Bobby's attention and nodded toward them.

That's the life.

He glanced over.

You have no idea, brother. He's a member here. Part owner in a hotel in Waikiki, among other things.

Which one?

Old guy on the right. That's his wife in the middle of the babes.

The girl in the middle looked like she was still getting carded at nightclubs. She had blonde hair down to her butt and world-class knockers.

The one barely out of high school?

Yep.

Damn. He likes 'em young, huh?

Yes. Real young. Rumor has it . . .

Bobby slammed on the brakes, shut his mouth hard, put his head down and started walking. I caught up with him.

Rumor has it what?

Nothing. Nothing.

C'mon! There's no better story than one that begins, *rumor has it!*

Nothing. I really shouldn't talk about a member, Mr. Doyle. I could lose my job.

I glanced back at the house, trying to figure out what was piquing my interest all of a sudden. Then I remembered where I'd seen that red Maser before.

> Well, shit, Bobby. I wouldn't want that to happen. But you know you can trust me.

I let it drop. For the moment.

We came to a stop beside the bunker in which my little white pill sat, barely nestled into the sand. Once again, I had to push some unpleasant thoughts out of my mind and concentrate on the job at hand. Bobby was right; it was as good a lie as if I'd landed it on the Bermuda. He read off the distances from his notebook.

> Ninety-two to the front. One-oh-five to the pin, which is cut back left. Green's pretty flat, with a little tilt toward the water but not much.

He tossed some grass.

> Wind is at a slight cross, from a little behind you going left to right. I put it at ten knots steady. You have two steep-sided traps there on the left to contend with and two more on the right.

A steady wind is something you can factor into your shot; it's the gusty winds that can really mess you up. So with the pin placement toward the back left, and the wind pushing the ball toward the right, the safe play would be to go left center green. I put my hand on my sand wedge, pulled it, thunked it back into the bag, looked down at my ball in the sand and ran through my options in my head again. As I said, the safe play was left center green. But at this distance and with this lie, I could be pretty damn accurate. The trick is controlling the spin, but I figured if I could lay one up near the cup, let it bounce past and then spin back, I could very well end up with another short birdie putt.

I decided to go pin hunting. I pulled my gap wedge from the bag. Bobby approved . . .

> Good club.

. . . and hefted the bag onto his shoulder, backing a few yards away.

I checked my line, shuffled my feet a bit to get a firmer footing, and checked my line again. The ball was slightly below my feet, meaning the bunker was a little higher where I stood than where the ball lay, so I flexed my knees ever so slightly more than usual to make sure I caught the ball clean and not thin. Then I took a nice, fluid backswing and a nice, fluid follow-through, after having made sweet contact with the ball somewhere in between the two. The ProV1 rose out of the bunker with barely a mist of sand in its wake, drifting up toward the expensive houses along the left side before swan-diving onto the green. It took a mighty hop past the pin, but before it could catch and spin back as I'd hoped, it settled into the long grass at the back of the green, all but disappearing from view.

I handed the wedge back to Bobby without comment. He took it. Without comment.

The other guys wrestled their way onto the green, none of them looking at anything better than a double-bogey for that hole. When we got up to my ball and I saw how far down it was in the grass I was pretty sure I'd be lucky to make par.

Until, that is, I managed to pop it out of the rough with a wide-open sixty-degree wedge and the damn thing gave one bounce on the fringe and then ran all the way to the bottom of the cup as if nothing on earth was going to stop it from going in. Bobby and I looked at each other with identical loopy grins.

Nice bird!

Yeah. Jesus.

Hey, brother, don't you wish today was round one of the Open?

That made me stop. And think.

And wish today was round one of the Open.

I've gotta figure out a way to keep this going, Bobby.

He pounded me on the back.

Just keep doing what you're doing. Man, you are playing some golf.

We stood to the side, watching the other guys putt. Dave finally tapped his ball into the cup and we all started toward the seventeenth tee.

And once again, I stood at the exact place where Sing Ten Wong was shot dead two days ago.

CHAPTER TWENTY-ONE

The half-dollar splotch of blood was no longer visible on the grass. I still didn't know why there wasn't more. Fascinating detail of the day: the average body holds ten pints of blood. That blood is under pressure, like water in a garden hose with someone's thumb plugging the end. Even if the bullet stopped the heart immediately, it stands to reason a few of those pints would've sprayed the ground around him. I was hoping the autopsy would explain why they didn't.

A gull cawed. I looked up. Out on this ocean this day, there were more sailboats and surfers enjoying the breeze than the day he died.

I tried to lose the image of Sing Ten crumpled on the ground, but I couldn't. His ghost was all around us. Then, as I gripped my six-iron for the 189-yard shot, I got an intense itching sensation in the middle of my back. I imagined the reticle of some high-powered scope was centered there. With a mysterious finger silently easing back on a trigger.

I backed away and nonchalantly looked around. Took a big breath. Set up again. Got the cold sweats. Backed away again. Bobby stepped forward.

Anything wrong? Too much club?

No. This is the club. Just . . . nothing.

Forcing myself into position, I hastily set up and swung, just to get it over with . . .

. . . and pulled it badly. My ball thwacked the fronds of a coconut tree and dropped hard into the sand of a steep bunker on the front left side of the par three's green.

Fuck. Me.

The crowd buzzed.

Dave and Buddy both found the plate on their first. John's came up short but in pretty good shape on the false-front of the green.

The willies were less once I got away from the tee box and up to the trap, but the news there was not good. My ball was plugged deeply into the sand, meaning there was no way I could control the spin coming out. All I could manage was to splash it out onto the putting surface about twenty feet from the pin, then two-putt for bogey. My playing partners, however, managed par, every one of them. So in best ball scoring our team remained eight under going into the last hole.

Dave, Buddy and John all had good drives on the eighteenth. John even dared to hit the driver and put one down the center a respectable distance. I was still feeling a bit shaky, so rather than try to bomb one over the traps down the left side and go for the green in two, which was our battle plan, I decided to play conservatively. Bobby raised his eyebrows when I reached for the three-wood but said nothing. My ball ended up about in the same position as the other guys. We all four finished with par.

The gallery cheered as the last putt fell. We'd run away with the Pro-Am, winning by three strokes. As we made our way off the eighteenth green, I was basking in the glow of back pats and autograph requests, until one guy's voice rose above the chatter.

Hey Huck! Whatcha been doin? Hitting drives with your face?

Everyone chuckled and I turned to the guy with a smile.

It's working, isn't it?

Then I noticed the television cameras next to him. A few hours later, that exchange was a highlight on *SportsCenter,* with my battered mug blown up full-frame and the anchor quipping about golf being a full-contact sport.

At least they mentioned I'd won the Pro-Am.

I hadn't won anything in a very long time.

The awards dinner was scheduled for eight, so I had a few hours to kill. I thanked Bobby for his great work and made sure he was coming to the dinner before we parted ways. Buddy and Dave were heading to the bar, which was exceedingly tempting, but I wanted to peek in on the laptop and see how the decryption program was coming along. I told the guys I'd catch up with them at the dinner.

John Ng stopped me in the parking lot as I was getting into my midget car. It's funny, on the golf course he seemed like a fish out of water, nervous and unsure of himself. But the man who approached me, already showered and dressed in an immaculate black pinstriped suit, had the aura of authority.

Mr. Doyle, a quick word please, now that we have some privacy?

Sure, John. And call me Huck.

Very sorry, I keep forgetting. I must ask, do you have any idea yet who may have killed Mr. Wong? Have you made any headway whatsoever?

I'll be straight. Not a clue. All I have so far is this big merger everyone's so hush-hush about, and that's about it.

I wasn't about to mention my suspicions about Bao Wong until I'd gone a little further down that road. In fact, I wasn't going to give Ng much of anything. I was still surprised Rick would've told him, after emphasizing the need to keep the bank in the dark about our little investigation.

Yes, the merger. Well, there's some question now as to whether that is going to happen now. Mr. Wong was instrumental in shepherding it forward, and with him gone, the deal is much less a certainty.

But it was before? A certainty.

Don Dahler

He nodded.

It was. There were still some difficulties to work out, but the board was, shall we say, guardedly in favor.

So who, then, would most benefit from the merger's failure? Who was so against it?

The bank executive shook his head.

I wish I could answer that. Usually, partnerships like this are strictly financial transactions. Numbers. Very large numbers, to be true, but numbers nonetheless. All the parties involved in this deal stood to benefit, although some more than others.

Can you confirm China is one of the parties involved?

His face didn't change one iota.

As I told you earlier, there are certain things I simply cannot divulge to anyone.

Okay. Then let me ask you again, who would want to see Sing Ten Wong killed?

No one at the bank, that's certain. He was a very respected and admired chief officer.

Gee, thanks, that's a big help.

But everyone has enemies, John. Especially those in positions of power.

That is perhaps true. But if Mr. Wong did have enemies, they are not employees of Bank of the Pacific Islands nor any of the parties involved in this merger.

I see. And you're sure of that.

Inasmuch as I'm in a position to know, yes. I cannot imagine who would want Mr. Wong dead.

I got the distinct impression Mr. Ng was not as interested in helping my investigation as he was in making sure that investigation didn't splash back on the bank.

Thanks, John. Will I see you at the awards dinner?

I'm afraid not. I have a prior engagement.

Right.

I extended a hand.

Best of luck to you.

And to you, too, Mr. Doyle. Here's my card. Please keep me informed of whatever you discover. Richard is well intended, but he's young still, and in light of this incident he may not be thinking as clearly as he should. The board is not entirely pleased about an investigation separate from the one the authorities are conducting, but I've managed to convince them we should give you some time.

Well, that was nice of you. Considering Rick was the one who asked me to do this, not the board.

He leaned forward.

Please make no mistake. My duty is to protect the bank, its stockholders and the people who trust us to care for their money. There are billions of dollars at stake here. Not to mention the reputation of a respected financial institution. You must be careful how you characterize the actions of the bank and any of its employees. You should be very certain of anything you say, of any suspicions you have, because you will be held responsible for whatever comments you make to anyone.

I knew this wasn't John Ng talking. He was just repeating the words of BOPI's Board of Directors. But it still pissed me off. I hate it when people try to intimidate me, especially in subtle ways.

And here I thought we'd gotten so warm and fuzzy on the golf course.

I'm serious, Mr. Doyle. Be very careful. Richard Wong has put the bank at risk by employing you in this capacity; therefore his position and career at BOPI is, shall we say, under scrutiny. There will be a vigorous internal investigation to see if any of the bank's proprietary information has been compromised. And furthermore, I've been instructed to tell you the board insists you inform them, through me, of what you find, every step of the way.

I mean, if you're going to try to intimidate someone, don't be subtle. Pull out the bazooka, for God's sake.

Every step, John? Really? Does that include bowel movements?

Mr. Doyle . . .

Just kidding. Fine. I'll inform you every step of the way.

Like hell . . .

Ng gave a slight nod of his head and walked toward a limousine idling at the club's entrance. I got into my car, pulled out my phone and called Rick.

Hello?

Hi, Rick. It's Huck.

Hey! I heard you guys won! Great going!

Yeah. It was a good day. How're you doing?

Oh, okay I guess. Getting really tired of all the ceremony, you know? Sometimes it sucks to be the eldest son. You got anything yet?

Not really. But I wanted to ask, what made you decide to tell the bank about my investigation?

What? I didn't! They know?

Yes. John Ng was just quizzing me about it.

Shit. I really didn't want them to know. How'd they find out? He said I told him?

Yes.

Well, I didn't. I haven't told anyone.

Think back. Are you certain? No one? Not even casually?

He was silent for a few minutes.

No, no one around here. I mentioned it to Carter Driscol over the phone yesterday. He called to give his condolences.

Carter was a UCLA chum of ours.

So you said it over the phone, then.

Yes. He asked if I'd seen you lately. Wait. Shit. You think . . . ?

Call me on this cell phone from now on. And watch what you say over your home phone.

Okay, will do. Holy cripes. Hey, any luck with the—

—*Careful,* Rick. Not yet. Still working on that. It'll take some time.

Right. Yeah. Sorry. Okay. Well, see you later.

Later. Oh, and hey, I need to talk to your mother. Whenever you think the time is right. I'll be gentle, I promise.

Ten seconds of silence.

Man, wow, I don't know about that. Why do you need to talk to her?

You want me to do a thorough job. I have to ask her some questions about your dad.

Right. Well. Maybe in a day or two, okay?

Okay. Bye.

Yeah, bye.

While it's common practice and completely legal for corporations to monitor employee phone calls and emails, even on personal accounts, from their company phones and computers, it's still, thank the baby Lord Jesus, illegal for them to do so in the employee's private residence. Only law enforcement agencies can do that, and they have to get a warrant. I think. Unless the Patriot Act has been amended and nobody told us.

BOPI had obviously been keeping an illicit eye, and ear, on the Wongs.

The question was, for how long?

CHAPTER TWENTY-TWO

I spent thirty minutes on the phone with my friend and caddie whom I'd left back in L.A., Kenny, sharing every detail of the round I could think of with the guy who should've been there with me, who deserved to be there with me. He was, of course, nothing but cool about it. Par for the course for Kenny.

Hey, it's a great sign, Huckleberry. I couldn't see anything wrong with any part of your game. I think it's come together.

Feels like it, Kenny.

We got plenty of tournaments ahead of us. I'm glad for you.

For us, man.

Right. Have a good round tomorrow.

I said goodbye and flipped the phone shut as I walked into the bedroom, opened the safe and took out the laptop. Its screen announced the decryption was successful.

The password was a mashup of what appeared to be a series of random numbers and the nonsensical word *PearlR*. But that rang a bell in my head, and I looked around for where I left the newspaper article about Sing Ten Wong. Sure enough, the series of six numbers was his birthdate. Wong was born in the city Guangzhou, where his still-young wife was once a beauty queen. The river that flowed alongside that particular city was the Pearl. Thus *PearlR*. The decryption program's artificial intelligence had obviously zeroed in on data from the deceased CEO's life to find the right combination of things he would not have trouble remembering.

I poured a tall Absolut on the rocks and sat down at the table with the laptop before me, unsure of why I was so hesitant to proceed. The icy vodka slid down my throat like a Rocky Mountain avalanche, crashing into my empty stomach and leaving me momentarily lightheaded.

My finger hovered over the enter key. It would take but one key stroke to activate the password and open everything on the computer's hard drive. Of course, there might be absolutely nothing in those binary guts that would point in the direction of Sing Ten's killer. But I had nothing else to go on. Still, it felt like a violation of his privacy to break into his personal files like this and go snooping around the digital dark. I've sat in on autopsies before and wondered the same thing; would the deceased have preferred to let his/her murder go unsolved rather than be subjected to such raw, unblinking, unsympathetic exposure?

Sing Ten's dead, I told myself. *And Rick is desperate for answers.*

I hit the enter button. The screen blinked, went black, then rebooted.

The computer had the usual programs on it, from word processing to an Internet browser to solitaire. I noticed a popular accounting program and one for presentations. He also had a few icons for various games, and I remembered Rick saying his dad really liked Metal Gear Solid, a fairly violent action game made for the PlayStation console.

I never really got into the first-person shooter games. I guess when you've seen what real bullets do to the people you love up close, the fun in make-believe killing is harder to find.

A number of the folder icons on the screen had various years as their titles, 2007, 2008, 2009, etc. I clicked open the one from last year and found myself looking at a collection of the Wong family's financial records. The taxes were professionally prepared and very complex. I'd need more time than I had right then to take a closer look at them. I did notice there were two real estate properties listed; the family house on Diamond Head, and a building in downtown Honolulu.

I closed out of that folder and went to the PowerPoint program. In the projects list I found graphic presentations for a host of ventures the bank was involved in, from real estate to commodities investments. All the presentations were very slickly produced. I scanned through them all, dating back three years. None dealt with a major bank merger.

There were no files in the word processing program. Not a single one. Which I took to mean any letters or documents Sing Ten Wong wanted to draw up, he dictated or roughed out in email form and had his staff compose.

So I then waded into Wong's Microsoft Outlook folder and started looking at his emails. There were over a hundred from the day he died alone, half of which were time-dated after his murder. I didn't take this as suspicious; most of the bank's employees wouldn't have heard the news for hours. I quickly culled through the corporate announcements and company spam that all large institutions clutter up their employees' inboxes with, and started taking note of who was requesting meetings and opinions and on what subjects. I noticed Lisa Tan was cc'd on pretty much every email.

To keep things straight, I created a temporary folder and copied those emails over into that for later review. I then checked his Outlook Calendar. There were only two items listed for that past Saturday: Golf at 8am. And Meet GW at 6:30. Clicking over to the email system's Global Address Book I scrolled down to the Ws and looked through all the BOPI employees whose initials were G.W. There were fourteen such persons, none of whose names immediately jumped out at me. Nonetheless, I copied and pasted the list of G.W.s into the notepad and transferred that to my keepers folder.

I then clicked back to Wong's inbox and spun through the messages from the preceding days, looking for emails from anyone with the same initials. No luck. But then, something unusual caught my eye: A single message from one person in particular whose name showed up in the "from" box as Chinese characters. When I opened that message, the entire text was comprised of Chinese script, too. I copied it over to my keepers folder.

All emails, in fact all documents, files and folders on every computer, are embedded with microdata. It's invisible unless you know where to look. It contains information about when the particular document or message was created. When it was modified or sent. And when it was responded to. Near as I could tell, Wong never printed the Chinese message. Never forwarded it. And, interestingly, Lisa Tan was not cc'd. But the microdata showed he did respond to the sender.

I clicked over to the sent-messages folder. It was empty. Completely empty. I checked the settings on his auto-archiving function, which allows a user to schedule regular maintenance and clean-up of their email folders, and sure enough, Wong had the computer set to delete his sent messages every night at midnight. The auto-archive function on messages in his inbox was set to be deleted once a week. The deleted-messages folder was empty, too. The computer was scheduled to empty the wastebasket, in Microsoft terminology, every morning at 12:01 A.M. So Wong had set it up so that all the sent messages would be duly wiped out as soon as they were transferred to the trash folder.

But what I hoped Rick's dad didn't know, what most people don't know, is that just cleaning out the computer's wastebasket doesn't actually erase items from the hard drive. The data remains until the drive fills up and the information is overwritten with new material, or the user runs a disc-defragmentation program or disc-wipe software specifically designed to clean off the hard drive. One quick check of the computer's maintenance schedule confirmed that Wong had not.

I breathed a sigh of relief. There were email messages hidden somewhere on Wong's hard drive. The trick would be finding them. A quick glance at my watch told me it was time to get cleaned up. I slipped the computer back into the safe and locked it.

The autopsy of Sing Ten Wong's digital life would have to continue after the Pro-Am awards dinner.

CHAPTER TWENTY-THREE

Buddy Mano was already at the table when I arrived, a tall, leggy blonde attached to his hip. Bobby Carter was chatting at another table nearby, and Dave Planter was on the makeshift stage. He was the night's master of ceremonies. John Ng was, as expected, a no-show. A waiter came by and I ordered a Macallan, neat. He needed clarification.

Would you prefer the eighteen- or thirty-year-old?

We can discuss my choice of women after I've finished ordering my Scotch.

He didn't crack a smile.

Very funny, sir.

Yeah, I can tell. So you don't have the fifty-five?

We do, sir, but it's not being offered tonight.

But the thirty-year-old is?

Yes.

A bottle of Macallan thirty-year-old single malt goes for almost $900. The fifty-five-year-old will set you back a tasty twelve grand.

Well, I guess I'll have to settle for that.

Very good.

Dave started things off by telling a few jokes, then introduced the president of Sony USA, who made a little speech about how much of an honor it is to sponsor the Open but how the Pro-Am is always the high point of the week for everyone. He then announced the winners, my group, and Buddy and I walked up to the stage amidst some pleasant applause and cheering.

Dave made a big deal out of grabbing the plaque out of the presenter's hands and running off the stage with it. In an obviously prearranged gag, two burly cops brought him back out to huge laughs. He then had a few comments about having to play with such a hack pro as myself, who could only manage to shoot a measly sixty-five, and how they had to save my ass on the eighteenth.

Buddy's turn. He was funny, too. Until he called for a dimming of the lights and a video was played of the *SportsCenter* bit that aired earlier that evening about the ever-deteriorating condition of my face. The audience howled. I winced. When the lights came back up, I was expected to speak. I pulled an old standard out of my hat and waited for the applause to dwindle.

Thank you. So, a group of college buddies meet for golf every Tuesday morning. But one week, one of the group is home with a cold, so the starter completes the foursome with a gorgeous young woman. She confides in them she's just a beginner and has only played a few times, but as the round continues, it becomes obvious she has a great deal of natural talent.

Finally, they're on the eighteenth green, and the woman is looking at a tricky three-foot sidehill putt for birdie.

I've never made a birdie in my life, she tells her partners. Whoever can help me with the right read on this putt, I'll take home and give them a night they'll never forget.

I had this putt last week, one guy offers. It's five inches above and putt it firm.

His buddy disagrees. No, no, he says, it's two and a half cups high and hit it softly. It'll curl right in.

The beautiful woman turns to the last golfer. And you? What do you advise?

The guy leans over and picks up her ball.

That's a gimmie, he says.

Best I could do on short notice.

I offered a few more words of thanks to my playing partners and made a graceful exit from the podium.

After the food and dessert came and went, Bobby and I sat drinking some mighty fine cognac as we watched Buddy dance with the life-sized Barbie doll. Her snug dress offered a generous décolleté, giving full view to her twin assets. Which then reminded me of the bikini-clad, surgically enhanced young women at the glass house. Which then reminded me of what Bobby started to say earlier.

Hey. The guy we saw on sixteen today. The one with the Victoria's Secret wife.

Mr. Anders.

Anders. That's his name? He drive a red Maserati QP?

Yep.

So what were you going to say about him?

Mr. Doyle . . .

C'mon, Bobby. It's just us now. No one'll know. You have my word.

I could tell his resolve was wavering. The booze was helping.

Bobby, what did you mean?

Well, you know, there are rumors about him. Pretty nasty rumors.

Like?

Like . . . he likes girls.

Obviously. His wife looks eighteen.

No, *girls*. Young girls.

Younger than his wife.

He nodded and took another swallow of his drink.

Word is he goes for what they call *untainted meat*.

Untainted. You mean virgins?

Another nod.

Underaged virgins?

Nod. Swig of his drink. Long sigh.

Hard to believe, ain't it?

Bad people all over, right? But how did you hear this?

You know how guys talk on a golf course. Like us caddies aren't even there. They think they're being cagey but you can connect the dots, especially when you've already heard things. You'd be surprised what guys talk about around us. Who they're screwing, pardon me, both in bed and in business. What kind of tax loopholes they're trying out. You name it.

Bobby, did *you* actually hear him talking about this?

Naw, naw, naw. Some of the other loopers was carrying for him and some others. They kept using the word *cherry,* only they didn't mean the fruit.

They? You mean there are more than just Anders doing this?

That's the talk. Some sort of club that brings the girls in from all over. But who knows? Might just be, whatcha call it, *apothecary.*

Apocryphal.

What you said.

I sure as hell hope so.

Me too, Mr. Doyle. Me too.

Bobby stood, stretched, drained his glass of Hennessey and patted me on the shoulder.

But to happier thoughts. Don't we have a golf tournament to play tomorrow?

That we do. Going to bed?

Yes I am, after what will probably be an unsuccessful attempt to rouse the wife for a little action. See you in the A.M.

See you there, Bobby. Have a good night.

The crowd was thinning. Buddy and Boobs said their so-longs too, and kind of ice-skated out the door the way drunk couples do when they don't want to take their hands off each other but can't quite get their legs moving together in synchronicity.

Alone at the table now, I started to stand when I felt my cell phone vibrate. The little caller ID window said it was Blue.

Hey! You're up late.

All I do is sleep. My brain works best at night. Can you talk?

Sure. What's up?

I did some checking on Bank of the Pacific Islands and found out a few things I thought you might be interested in. But first, what the hell happened to your face? I caught you on ESPN tonight.

Let's see: Tripped in the bathroom? Ran into a closet door? Allergies?

Naw. Not with Blue.

Some guys are putting the squeeze on me. Trying to scare me off, I think.

Scare you off what?

Wong's murder, I guess. That's the only thing I can figure. Maybe they don't want me to look too closely.

Which means you must be getting close to something. You've run into them more than once?

Yeah. We've had a few encounters. They might know about the computer, too. I'm sure they'd love to get their hands on it.

Looks like they play rough.

Well, they've had the upper hand so far.

I haven't had my turn at them yet, I didn't say.

Do you know who they are?

Asian. Young. They ride motorcycles. I think one of them has been tailing me pretty close. I saw him at the Pro-Am today, as a matter of fact.

Oh, hey, man, I'm sorry! I should've congratulated you on that first thing. Great round! Sixty-five. Very nice.

Yeah, thanks. Thanks. It felt really good to win something. Now if I can just carry that over to the real thing.

You will. I saw some of your play during the *SportsCenter* piece. Your swing looks smooth.

Feels smooth.

So these guys, you sure you can handle them?

I think so. It's not like they've taken a shot at me or anything.

Yet. . . .

Could they be the ones who killed Wong?

Maybe, but I don't think so. It doesn't feel like that. And besides, whoever shot Wong had to either be invisible or underwater. I was looking right at the point of origin, and there was nobody in sight.

Blue chewed on that one for a second. An attractive waitress, on the skinny side but with long legs and really pretty eyes, came by, pointed at her tray of empties and mouthed the words, *Need another?* I answered with a shake of the head and a silent *Thank you.*

> Go over those few moments again for me. You were right next to Wong and didn't hear the gunshot?

> Didn't hear it.

I repeated everything I could remember from the time our foursome walked up to the tee box to when Wong fell over dead. Blue was quiet again. Then I heard him blow out a long breath.

> Well, I'm stumped about that one.

One of many things my brother is truly great at is bouncing around ideas about things. He always has a clear-eyed take. I told him about the naval vessel I saw earlier in the day.

> So that made me think about navy frogmen. Like what a SEAL could do. You know, a diver comes up from underwater, takes the shot with a sound-suppressed rifle, and disappears. But what gun would work after being submerged in seawater?

> Well, let's see, the Soviets developed a fully functional underwater assault rifle back in the seventies called, if I remember correctly, the APS. I used to know what that stands for . . .

Blue had obviously paid attention at the academy. He continued,

> Regular bullets are inaccurate and don't go very far when fired underwater, so the APS fired specially designed steel bolts. The weapon's barrel wasn't rifled; instead the hydrodynamic effects kept the bullet going in a straight line. But that made them very inaccurate when fired above water. They became more or less like a shotgun firing a slug. The bullet's trajectory through air becomes unpredictable, like a knuckleball. Wong took a shot in the heart; that would necessitate a high degree of accuracy. Do you know what the caliber was of the bullet that killed Wong?

No. Not yet. Big is all I know, from what the attending surgeon said. I hope to have that info soon.

Note to self: Call Judith tomorrow.

Well, the APS used a special size, five-point-six-six millimeter, I think. And again, the bullet can't be mistaken for any other kind. It's a steel bolt. But frankly, you know, you wouldn't need a special underwater weapon to do what you're describing.

Really?

No. For example, the SEALS carry modified Colt M4A1s they call the Integrated Carbine. Five-point-five-six-millimeter rounds. Very rugged. Very accurate at short and long range. One of the best all-around assault weapons in the world today. You can submerge this rifle in seawater for relatively short periods of time and it'll still come out firing. As long as you strip, clean and oil it quickly after use, it shouldn't have any adverse damage, either.

Except to whoever's on the other end of the action.

Yeah, exactly. But it would definitely take a military-trained shooter to pull that off. Swim up. Take one shot, dead-center mass. That's skill. You honestly think that's what happened?

I don't know. But I can't come up with any other likely scenarios yet, other than a woman-scorned sort of thing; Wong had been cheating on his wife for a long time. And she didn't strike me as all that torn up about him being gone now. But that doesn't solve the puzzle of how the hell he was shot.

Maybe she hired an ex-military type to do the job?

Maybe. That's one theory I'm checking on. She does have the money. But, the other puzzle piece has to be China. It fits into this merger somehow, maybe trying to take a big bite out of the bank on the sly. Everybody gets really hinky when I ask about their participation in this deal. I would guess there are all sorts of laws against foreign-government ownership of U.S. banks. Maybe they're working up something off-the-books and Wong got in the way.

Interesting theory . . .

Yeah?

. . . but you're wrong.

CHAPTER TWENTY-FOUR

The busboys were starting to clear all the tables, including mine, so I wandered over to where the spare chairs were lined against the wall and sat in one, my phone still pressed to my ear as Blue filled me in on the world of international finance.

He explained there are actually no laws forbidding foreign-government ownership of U.S. financial institutions. In fact, it's becoming more and more common. Blue said there is a federal committee that oversees all foreign investment, but it's widely seen as passive, and the complexity of some sovereign wealth funds—SWFs in banking terminology, which is what foreign governments establish to undertake state-financed investments—makes it impossible for the committee to really know what's going on.

China, in fact, has invested tens of billions of dollars in U.S. financial institutions in recent years through its China Investment Corporation. They've bought large parcels of numerous banks and mortgage companies, and after the collapse of most of the premier Wall Street investment firms, the CIC snapped up millions of shares in firms like Blackstone and Morgan Stanley. What my brother was telling me made no sense.

But, aren't there limits to how much of an American financial institution CIC can buy?

None. And they've been on a shopping spree for years now. Although my guy at the Bureau says no one can really be sure what they own and how much because their investment patterns are so unconventional and obscure.

But isn't the Securities and Exchange Commission able to track the purchases of large segments of banks and investment houses?

Huck, you know how many trades happen each day just on the New York Stock Exchange alone? Millions. The Chinese are very busy with this and the CIC works under numerous brokerage houses and accounts. It's not exactly a transparent system. Especially with hedge funds and REITs that are required to do only a limited amount of reportage. There's been a push by some in Congress to change that in recent years, primarily for national security reasons.

It wasn't hard for me to understand why they'd be concerned. Imagine what influence a foreign government could have over policy decisions if they owned enough of the world's largest economy to crash the system at their will. With billions of dollars of America's capital and debt in their pocket, China could, for instance, invade Taiwan and threaten to send the U.S. into a crippling recession if we tried to intervene.

Holy shit. The weapon of the future isn't nuclear. It's financial.

And not the future. Now. China and Russia are just two of many countries with substantial investments here who are not exactly interested in our best interests.

So what are we talking here? What kind of money are they spreading around?

We know CIC has at least two hundred billion to play with. But the CIA thinks it's closer to a trillion dollars the government of China has secretly funneled into its sovereign wealth funds. They see this as not only a way of growing their own economy through foreign investment, but gaining unprecedented political influence in the West.

Jesus Christ! I sat absorbing that for a moment.

Huck, you still there?

Yeah. Just trying to wrap my brain around this. So, this merger thing, you think China is using their investment corporation funds to get a chunk of BOPI?

Well, that's the thing. They don't have to. China already owns thirty-four percent of the bank.

If I hadn't already been sitting down, I would've had to sit down. Blue was still talking, although my mind had blanked off for a split second. I caught up with him midsentence.

—of the Pacific Islands was actually started eighty years ago by Chinese immigrants who objected to high interest rates imposed on them by Japanese and mainland-based banks. But it wasn't until about five years ago that China evidently took an interest in BOPI and started quietly buying up shares through numerous brokers. All very legal.

So this big merger . . . ?

It's not with the People's Republic of China. The preliminary SEC filings list a Hong Kong–based investment group, Zhonghua Holdings Limited, as second party, but so far I haven't been able to come up with a whole lot about who they are or why BOPI would even want a partnership with them, since their assets seem considerably smaller than BOPI's.

Does the filing list the corporate officers?

Yeah, hold on.

I could hear some rustling and clicking and pictured Blue propped up in bed, using a stick in his mouth to flip through files on his laptop.

Let's see. Here it is. Wei Wu, president and CEO. Zhuang Li Yang, CFO. They're the only two listed. I'll do some digging on them tomorrow.

I found a scrap of paper in my pocket and waved down the skinny/pretty waitress to borrow her pen. I had Blue spell out the names.

That's great. Thanks a lot.

No problem. It's good to have something to work on between sessions.

I handed back the pen. Another mouthed *thank you* to her. She returned the smile and added a wink. I enjoyed watching her walk away. She glanced back, caught me looking, gave me another smile, this one with a hint of a question mark attached, causing my dog side to raise his head and perk up his ears.

Blue and I chatted a bit about how well his therapy sessions were going, turned the discussion back around to golf and wrapped things up. After we hung up I started to call Judith for a little phone flirting but realized how late it was back in LA. Then I caught sight of the waitress's slim-but-pleasant backside again, waved her over, chatted her up, found out when she was off duty that night. Considered asking for her number, then yanked on the leash and quit being a jerk.

Which wasn't easy.

CHAPTER TWENTY-FIVE

I came out of college ready to dominate the PGA Tour. I fully expected to win every tournament I entered or, failing that, place a heatedly contested second. That confidence was, frankly, based on winning a lot at the high school and collegiate level, being voted top amateur golfer in the nation two years running by *Golf World* magazine, and taking the U.S. Amateur title by five strokes my senior year. I had an agent. I had offers for endorsement deals. I had a glorious, rosy future.

Then, like a spurned Mrs. Faldo to Nick's beloved Porsche, the game of golf took a six-iron in hand and beat that confidence right out of me.

The Amateur champion wins the right to play in the U.S. Open, The Masters, and the British Open. I stank up all three of those. Somehow I managed to get my Tour card by squeaking through Q-School, and then proceeded to play horrifically badly in every tournament after that. In fact, I stank up pretty much every round of golf I played my first year as a pro until I pulled my old Bronco over by the side of the highway, coming back from some po-dunk charity event in Scottsdale, which I also stank up even though there wasn't a scratch golfer in the field, and heaved my bag of clubs into a ravine. I'd quickly gotten to the point of not expecting to win. The most I found myself hoping for was to finish high enough to stay in the game. And there's no joy in that. So I swore off competitive golf forever.

Forever lasted exactly two years.

It was my brother, Blue, who pointed me in the direction of law school and helped me figure out a way to pay for it. And upon graduation but prior to taking the bar exams, it was my brother, Blue, who saw how much I hated the idea of a career in law and helped me figure out a way to get back to doing what I was born to do: play golf. After suffering through the exquisite pain of law school, I suffered through the exquisite pain of Qualifying School and managed to regain my PGA Tour card. And that's when I made a promise to myself to take this gift seriously and play to win, not just to sur-vive. And I really, really meant it. But, you know, very few people truly un-derstand how impossibly difficult winning tournaments at the professional level really is. Tiger Woods has ruined it for everyone, because he makes it look so easy. And it's so not.

To win a PGA event, you must put together *four* exceptional rounds of golf in a row. Not two, not three, but four. On any given week during the sea-son, you'll see some player pull ahead on the leaderboard, shoot a sixty-five or sixty-six, create a stir, then the next day, slide inevitably down and down and down, to the anonymous land of nonwinners. That land of nonwinners, in fact, is where the vast majority of us live every week. Because we can manage to put a few solid rounds together, but rarely enough. Rarely four in a row. If tournament play was only eighteen holes, or even thirty-six, the world of professional golf would look very different.

So despite the promise to myself to become a winner, to achieve the goals I knew I was capable of reaching, I became, once again, a grinder. I posted just enough good finishes to keep my card, made a pretty good living after sub-tracting all the many expenses a pro golfer incurs, and even squirreled away a nice little nest egg of cash. Bottom line, I eventually came to accept my place in the world of professional golf. I was not the superstar I'd imagined back in my college days. Even though I'm still young, I had to realize I would probably never be a household name. If I was lucky, and worked hard, I would maybe be able to keep playing for a few more years. Then figure out something else.

Well, it dawned on me, as I was daydreaming behind the wheel, driving back to the hotel that night after the Pro-Am dinner, that that wasn't god-damn good enough anymore. The round earlier that day had given me a taste of what was again possible. My swing was humming, my putts were rolling true. I knew I had the skills. I knew I had the mental strength. I knew I had the luck.

I caught sight of my own eyes in the reflection. I saw something different in them; the look of a man who'd gone somewhere else for a few years, maybe lost his own definition of self, settled for who he was, not who he could be.

I was once again looking into the eyes of the former U.S. Amateur champion.

Back in the hotel room, the vodka stayed in the mini fridge. The television stayed turned off. And Sing Ten Wong's laptop stayed in the safe.

I had some golf to play.

CHAPTER TWENTY-SIX

The next morning, the alarm went off at five A.M. I was at the practice range by seven, warmed up and ready to go by my tee-off time of 9:37.

Each year for the Sony Open, Waialae Country Club changes its golf course from a par seventy-two to a par seventy. They do this by taking two of their par five holes and, with a flick of a magic wand, turn them into very long par fours. That makes Waialae one of the more difficult courses to score well on not only because of those lengthy fours, but players also lose two birdie-able par fives.

The number-one hole is one of the two transformed par fours. As such, it's the toughest hole on the course. I overheard one of the spectators nearby say most of the players that morning shot bogey there.

It's 480 yards to the center of the green. I knew from my earlier rounds this week that the fairway set up well for a fade. I have a natural draw, but I can hit a dependable fade if I don't get too handsy. I set my stance cheating down the left, targeting a bunker that lurked about three hundred out. I pictured the flight of the ball, and thought about a smooth takeback and exploding through the ball.

It zoomed high over the palm trees and folded over, dropping into the dead center of the fairway. Due to all the rain earlier in the month, the course was playing soft, so I didn't get a lot of roll. And that, too, added to the length. But that was a damn good start.

Zach Johnson teed it up next and laced an almost identical ball down the right center. Two younger guys I didn't know, one a rookie who looked all of twelve years old, finished out our group. They, too, had respectable drives, but both ended up in the rough.

Usually at tournaments, the guys are all chatty and loose on the first few holes, then get quieter and more serious as the round goes along. Caddies, too, are typically all-business on tournament days. Even Bobby seemed subdued. Until he sidled in close with a grin.

> You swing like that all day and we're going to be wearing big smiles come dinnertime.

The kids whacked their way out of the junk, both coming up short of the green with their second shots. Zach put his in a greenside bunker, but with the firmness of the sand there, he had a better-than-good chance of an up and down, what with the quality of his bunker play these days.

We'd gotten lucky with the draw of our morning tee-time. The winds hadn't really started up yet, and the greens weren't all tracked up. Bobby flopped some grass in the air and it blew away from him at a very slight angle.

Not much breeze. What's there is coming off the ocean from behind. You've got one-eighty-three to the pin. The greens are going to stick good until the sun heats 'em up.

I thought about hitting an easy six, but figured if I could get the ball a little higher in that helping wind it might give a nice soft landing and hold the green. So I changed clubs and busted a long seven iron. My Titelist got a good dig when it hit and trickled a few feet away from the pin. When I handed him back the seven, I gave Bobby a little wide-eyed look. He returned it with a cock of the head and mouthed the word *juju*.

I birdied the first. And the second. My twenty-footer painted the rim on the par four third, leaving me a tap-in for par. We approached the number four already two under.

The prevailing winds were just starting to pick up, and on this hole you're playing right into their teeth. It's a 197-yard par three with a ridiculously narrow, long green, and plenty of sand defenses that gobble up inaccurate shots. There are two ridges, one just short of the pin, one in the back. The ideal shot gets your ball past the first but not onto the second, or you're left with a very tricky downhill roll.

Zach had birdied the third so he had honors. He pulled a five iron from the bag and turned a nice little draw onto the front of the green. His ball almost crested the ridge, but the spin worked against him and it stopped just short, rolling back down toward the front of the green two dozen feet away from the cup.

I chose a six and staked it in the heart. My pill landed hard on the front swell, bounced just past the flagstick, ran up the back ridge, then caught and zipped back toward the hole. Bobby and I crouched over the six-foot putt and agreed there was no break to be seen. I stood, took a breath, rechecked the line, and died it in for our third birdie of the morning.

Waialae is the second-hardest course on tour to hit the fairways. But you wouldn't know it the way I was playing. My strategy of not hitting driver on every hole, mixing it up with a fairway metal or hybrid just to keep it in the short grass, was working perfectly. I found myself in the rough only once the entire round, and that was on the ninth, which has a fairway as narrow as Lisa Tan's waist. My second shot bounced off the side of the green but I still managed a par save there when my chip skipped once and pulled the string back to within a foot. Hole after hole I was Sugar Ray Leonard, finding my opponent's weaknesses with quick jabs and accurate hooks that were steadily wearing him down. When Bobby and I approached the tee box for the eighteenth, we looked up at the big leaderboard . . .

. . . and stopped dead in our tracks.

There, at the top, a full seven strokes ahead of the second-place player, were the words H. Doyle. I made some kind of involuntary sound, like a dog coughing up a chicken bone. Bobby took off his cap and let out a long whistle.

> Mother of God. I knew you was killing 'em out there. I didn't know nobody else was killing 'em too.

Zach Johnson ambled up beside us and put a hand on my shoulder.

> Feels pretty good, don't it?

> Man. That's quite a sight.

> Get used to it, Huck. You're in a groove.

I had to take a few extra practice swings at the tee just to get my heart rate back down. Judging from how far I bombed the drive, I didn't get it down far enough. The eighteenth is a severe dogleg left, and I unleashed a hard draw over the left side corner that disappeared from view behind the coconut trees. We found my Pro-V1 with the two red dots sitting quietly, about 240 from center green.

I caught my second a little thin, my first miss of the day, and I left it fifty yards short. But a soft pitch shot for my third hit the flagstick and dropped the ball next to the cup for an easy bird to finish the round.

We calmly shook hands all around, chatted briefly with the Golf Channel reporter, who thankfully didn't press when I gave some goofy explanations for my facial decorations, and headed into the scorer's tent to sign my card.

By the time all the players were finished, I'd kept my lead of eight strokes. I shot a sixty-two on the opening round of the Sony Open.

And for the first time ever, my name was at the top of a PGA Tour leaderboard.

CHAPTER TWENTY-SEVEN

Bobby and I grabbed a bite to eat in the clubhouse, then, like most pros do, we went right back to the practice range to hit some more balls. To keep the feel. To embrace the mojo. Golf is probably the only sport where players work on their game for hours immediately following competition.

After an hour of that, we said our goodbyes and I floated to my car and floated back to the Outrigger, not remembering a damn thing about the drive there. Back in my hotel suite, I thought about taking a short nap, but my brain was still buzzing from the day's incredible round. I kept switching on the Golf Channel to watch a rehash of the Open, just to see my name up there. H. Doyle. And in beautiful red numbers: 62. Because, well, truth is, I've never seen that before. Not at a professional tournament. I wanted to take a picture of the screen. I wanted to call everyone in my family, everyone in my life.

But that wasn't necessary. Because *they* were calling *me*. When I finally remembered to turn it back on, my cell phone had fifteen messages. They were almost all the same; congratulations, teasing about the reporter's quips during the interview, and concern that I was okay. I returned half of the calls until I got tired of talking about it over and over again, and turned the back phone off.

I went into the bedroom to shuck my golf clothes and take a shower, but my eyes fell on the cord leading from the closet safe to the wall socket. I resisted the urge to dig into Wong's computer files. I was leading for the first time in my professional life. I needed to concentrate on that, and that alone. The police would find out who killed Rick's dad.

That determination lasted the exact amount of time it took me to shower and dress. I looked at the safe again . . .

Oh, why the fuck not?

. . . and opened it, retrieving the laptop and carrying it over to the desk.

I mean, it's not like looking around in there was going to detract from my golf skills, right? I had the rest of the day to myself, so what could it hurt, right? In fact, a distraction would be a good thing, keep me from thinking too much about golf, right?

Right?

Those are the sorts of things I kept asking myself as I booted up the computer and clicked onto the web browser. When that program settled down and stopped throwing pop-ups onto the screen, I went onto Google and entered the name of a free disc-recovery program I knew about. Their website appeared at the top of the list and I clicked on downloads. That took me to their file transfer page. I selected the latest version of DiscHunter for the computer's operating system and requested a download.

Thanks to the hotel's high-speed Internet wireless network, all those ones and zeroes were safely beamed onto Wong's laptop within five minutes, and I fired up the program. It had a couple of options about types of deleted files I was looking for, so I selected all and clicked on start. The computer's hard drive started humming.

While it was working, I called my friend, the attractive, sometimes slightly aggravating, slightly confusing, slightly interesting assistant medical examiner for Los Angeles County, who'd left a congratulatory message on my voice mail but who didn't answer when I called the first time.

Hi, Doc.

Huck! You, I'm so, wow! Great round! I can't believe how well you're playing! That's so amazing!

Thanks. But it's just the first round.

I know, I know, but still. Wow. Top of the leaderboard! And you won the Pro-Am, too!

Yeah.

How's it feel?

Like it's just the first round, Doc. I'm not going to let myself get too excited. Let's see what happens tomorrow.

And Saturday . . . and Sunday . . .

Okay, okay, I get it. It was great seeing you on TV, though, but—and don't take this the wrong way—but Huck, you don't look so great.

Thanks. I told you I'd been mugged.

Yes you did, but, I, you didn't say you were that banged up. I'm so sorry I was so flippant about it when you called before! I was just trying to be, you know, playful.

It's fine. Looks worse than it is. Already feeling better.

For the most part.

Well, good. Good. So . . . wow. You're leading! I'm so excited for you!

Yeah. Thanks. Hey, did you manage to get a copy of that autopsy report yet?

Silence.

Maybe I should've chatted a little more before asking.

Doc?

Silence.

Yep. Shoulda chatted more.

Doc? You hear me?

Yes. I hear you. I'm curious. Is that the only reason you called?

Don't be silly! No! I wanted to share my great round with you. Did I mention I shot eight under?

Silence.

Judith, look. I told you, this is for my friend, Rick. His dad's the one who made it possible for me to even be playing in this tournament. I'm kind of obligated . . .

Well, *I'm* not.

No, you're not. Not at all. But I would very much appreciate your help. I have no one else to turn to. I promise I'll make it up to you.

I've heard that one before.

My turn to be silent.

Which did the trick.

She let out a big sigh.

I'm kidding, Huck. I'll get it for you. I've been, you know, a little busy.

Yeah, celebrating your ex-boyfriend's latest movie until all hours of the night. Instead of coming out here. . . .

I know it's a lot to ask. It would mean a lot to me, Doc.

I'll put in the request first thing. And really, congratulations, and I know you'll play as well tomorrow. Just . . . just, you know . . . stay out of trouble, Huck. It's all going so well for you right now. Now I'm worried about you.

I am. I am staying out of trouble. Don't worry. I'm just looking into this thing for Rick, that's all. It's not taking anything away from concentrating on the tournament.

Nor are those girls on the beach, I guess.

What girls?

The ones whose perky little asses and bouncy breasts are Xeroxed onto the inner walls of your skull. You know, *those* girls.

No girls here, Doc. I'm staying at an all-male geriatric facility. In fact, my shuffleboard lessons are coming up soon.

Uh huh. And the mugging, it didn't have anything to do with all this? What you're just *looking into*?

Shit. I hate lying to her.

Of course not. There's been a rash of tourist robberies here lately. I just got unlucky.

Which doesn't mean I'm not good at it.

Well, next time, just hand over whatever they want, promise?

Promise.

I mean, what's another secondhand Timex cost, anyway?

Har har.

I'll call you tomorrow when I have the report.

That's great, Doc. Thanks so much. Have a good night.

You too. G'night.

We hung up. I couldn't figure out why I was a little bummed as I stared at the phone in my hand. Then it occurred to me, we didn't really have the usual phone sex/flirtation thing going on this time. There's always a little lascivious undercurrent when we talk, even in those times when the discussion was about serious things. This conversation, in fact, felt a little clunky. Which, okay, was probably my fault.

Because, in case you haven't noticed, I kind of suck at relationships.

The laptop was still grinding away. I tossed the phone on the bed and went into the Internet browser's history file, which stores a complete list of all the websites the computer's user visited. That's another file that is easily deleted on a regular basis, and another one which most people don't bother to. Law-enforcement types love that fact, because your Internet history is a roadmap of every dark little corner of cyberspace you wandered into, when you did it, how long you stayed, and what you may have come away with in terms of downloaded material such as music, software or photographs.

The *DiscHunter* website was at the top of the list, followed by Google; the two sites I'd accessed earlier.

Next I saw a secure site, marked by the telltale *s* at the end of the http, for Bank of the Pacific Islands. That looked more like the general website used by customers to pay their bills online rather than a proprietary intranet location for employees. Sing Ten more than likely banked with his own bank.

There were some other financial institutions' websites, probably where Wong had investments. He'd evidently done some shopping recently with Saks, Brooks Brothers and Golfsmith, or at the very least, some browsing of their virtual stores. He favored *The Drudge Report* and *The Wall Street Journal*'s online edition, in addition to a whole host of blog sites and chat rooms. One in particular caught my eye; it had no title, just an ISP number. When I entered that address in the Internet browser bar, an innocuous dark blue welcome screen appeared, prompting for a password.

I went back to the list.

Wong obviously spent a lot of time surfing all the most popular free porn sites. And, a closer look revealed, a couple of the more specialized subscription sites. The decryption program was useless against website passwords, since most of those shut down access after a certain number of failed attempts. But I could at least see if Wong had taken home any souvenirs from those places. I minimized the browser's window and clicked open the "My photos" folder. There were two albums in the folder; one labeled "Family." One labeled "Work."

Nice try, Sing Ten, I thought to myself, *but I'm not that dumb.*

I clicked open the "Work" album. Thousands of tiny photographs appeared in rows of thumbnails.

I opened the first one. And then the next. And the next.

By the fourth picture, my stomach couldn't take any more.

CHAPTER TWENTY-EIGHT

I needed a drink. Make that plural. The laptop, which was still sorting through all the deleted files, went back into the safe. I thought about hitting the hotel bar. Decided to get a few questions answered instead.

Fifteen minutes later I parked under a streetlamp, mumbled a no-thanks to the pros hanging around there, and walked half a block to a strip club. The blue-and-pink neon sign said *BAN OK CLUB*. The G and K were burned out. Its real name was The Bangkok Club.

Oleo was seated on a stool just inside the front door, his tattooed bald dome reflecting the colored lights from the center stage. I gave him a nod.

Hey.

I had my hat pulled low and a pair of sunglasses on. He didn't immediately recognize me.

Twenty bucks. No touching.

I paid him.

I'm the guy who came by the other night with Detective Sagulio. Remember?

He looked closer.

Oh, yeah. Howya doin? I saw you on the news.

You saw me on the news? What was I doing?

Playing golf.

Shit. So much for being incognito.

Right. Yeah.

He jerked a thumb over his shoulder.

Some of your buddies were just here. Don't know their names.

Golf pros?

Yeah. Young guys. Like to party.

I had an idea about who that might be, but kept it to myself.

Your brother Lennie feeling better?

Yeah. For now. Can't seem to stay clean.

A few more customers came up and Oleo turned his attention to them. As my eyes adjusted to the dim light, I looked around the room.

There was a circular, low table in the middle of the room surrounded by chairs. Four or so guys were seated with drinks before them, watching a completely naked young woman stretch and crawl and flirt on the table. She rolled over onto her back and extended her legs into the air, crossing them at the knees, then opening them slowly, wider, and wider, and wider, back arched, head thrown back. The man with the best front-row seat leaned in as close as he could, almost knocking over his cocktail.

To the right of the main table was a small bar with a few shelves of liquor and a middle-aged lady bartender. At the other corners of the room were smaller performance tables. One was empty, the other two had girls giving similar shows to one man at a time. There looked to be a doorway in the back with a black curtain pulled across it.

I went over to the bar and ordered a vodka rocks. The bartender told me what I owed in a thick Russian accent. I wandered back over to stand next to Oleo.

How's business?

He shrugged.

Always horny dudes around. So why were you hanging with Paco?

Paco?

Sagulio. That's what we called him in high school.

You knew each other back then? Small world.

Small island.

Yeah. Well, I've kinda gotten pulled into a thing and he was trying to show me why I should stay out of it.

A thing.

A thing.

Paco says you should stay out of it, I'd listen.

Wish I could. I owe a guy a favor.

Three more men came up, looking very touristy and nervous to be there. Oleo repeated his twenty bucks, no touching mantra. They got some drinks and planted themselves at the main table. A lithe little woman of indiscernible heritage replaced the blonde and proceeded to show the world her innermost secrets.

Oleo kept his eyes moving to the street, to the customers, to the woman at the bar. She was watching us, too, with more than a little suspicion. I motioned in her direction with my drink.

I don't think she likes me.

She's the owner. Wants to make sure we're not doing a deal. All these years, she still don't trust me. Fuck her. So this *thing*: That what's got your face all messed up?

Yes, it is.

One of the girls at the corner table giggled, sat up, slid off, took her audience of one by the hand and led him across the room and through the black curtain. He must've said the right thing. My guess is, it involved numbers.

Oleo swiveled on his stool and turned to face me.

You come here to look at girls or not?

Not really. Wanted your opinion on a few things, that's all. Your street knowledge.

My street knowledge. Okay. Since you're tight with Paco. And so long as we ain't talking about nothing.

We're not talking about nothing.

He nodded for me to proceed.

Say, hypothetically speaking, somebody in this town needs somebody dead. And it's a very difficult job, not your usual run-of-the-mill hit. Is there a market for that kind of skill here?

Hypothetically speaking.

Not talking about nothing.

He thought for a beat, then shrugged.

Anything's possible. Are there dudes around who'd off someone for money? Shit yeah. Are there dudes who have extreme skills for that sort of thing? Depends.

How about dudes with military-type training?

Don't know about that. But I wouldn't think it'd be too hard to find someone. We got a lot of guys who do their time in the navy and don't want to leave paradise when the time comes. The problem would be getting the hardware.

Really? That's easy as shit where I come from.

Not here, man. Hawaii is crazy about gun control. Other than the cops, the only guy in the whole state who has a license to carry is the dude who runs the armory and repairs all the cops' guns. That's his deal.

What about black market?

We got that, for sure. You can get a ratchet, for a price. But the coast guard is pretty hard on smugglers. So any specialized equipment, bigger stuff, military grade, I don't know. Tough to do. Navy guys and Coasties have to turn in their weapons every time they leave the ship. Not allowed to go anywhere with them. And since nine-eleven those bases are ultrasecure. Nothing in or out that ain't approved.

How do you know that?

He laughed.

'Cause they come in here all the time, man. Matter of fact, there're some over there.

I looked over at the far side of the main table. Two young men with close-cropped hair, wearing polo shirts and jeans, were fully enjoying the view before them. I noted what they were drinking, thanked Oleo, got two more of the same from the bar, and sat down next to them. The guy closest to me raised an eyebrow when I slid their beers in front of them. I waved a hand.

No, no, man. It ain't that. My friend Oleo over there mentioned you're in the military, and this is just my way of saying thanks. Seriously. Thanks. I admire what you guys are doing.

They looked at each other, grinned, downed their brewskies, and reached for the fresh ones. The kid next to me looked all of twelve years old. Just.

Hey, mister. Thanks. That's mighty nice.

You guys deserve it.

I stuck out my hand.

Huck Doyle.

Seaman Lance Buckley. This is Dave. Seaman David Wilkerson.

Nice to meet you. What branch are you in?

The second kid, Dave, spoke up. He looked to be about four minutes older than Lance.

The United States Coast Guard, sir.

To which Lance added:

Semper Paratus!

My law school Latin failed me.

Always . . . ?

Ready. Always ready. That's us. For sure.

You based here?

Yessir. Flotilla Thirteen. Kaneohe Bay.

The girl on the table must've felt a little ignored by us. She propped herself up on all fours, facing away, and waggled her butt in our direction. That kept us all pretty much distracted for a few minutes.

Hey, Lance, let me ask you something. I saw a ship the other day with the number fifty-two on it. That wasn't you guys, was it?

Naw. That's a navy ship. Was it gray?

Yeah, come to think of it. It was.

Ours are always white and orange. What was the number again?

Fifty-two.

Dave piped up.

Yeah, I know that ship. Buddy of mine is a diver on that one. That's the *Salvor*. It's a salvage ship. They spend a lot of time pulling up or blowing up old munitions on the ocean floor. Stuff from World War Two. Fun shit.

There's still live munitions down there?

Oh, yeah. Tons of stuff that didn't go off. Every once in a while, a sport diver will bring one up, thinking it's a nifty souvenir. We had to confiscate some of those just last week. Guy had a live torpedo! Remember that, Lance?

Without ever taking his eyes off the girl's nether regions, Lance said yeah, he did. I noticed the boys were low on suds, so I went back to the bar and got a few more, including another vodka for me. The bartender was gradually warming to me. Maybe because I was tipping her five bucks a round.

So is that what you spend a lot of time doing, Lance? Stopping people from blowing themselves up?

Yeah. We actually do a little bit of everything. But drug and smuggling interdiction is probably what keeps us the busiest. Under DHS rules, we have the right to stop pretty much any boat we suspect may be carrying contraband.

Homeland Security.

Yeah. We're under them in peacetime, and under navy command in times of war. So right now, we function more as a coastal police force.

And you have a lot of encounters with smugglers?

Yeah. At least one a week. Mainly guys trying to get drugs into the Islands.

That must be pretty exciting.

Man, you have no idea. I love it.

I shut up for a bit and watched the show. I have to admit, I've never been that up close and personal with a stripper who wasn't Lindsey before. It was more than a little disconcerting. There were times when she would bring her crotch to within inches of our faces. I couldn't help but notice she kept her eyes tightly shut most of the time. Maybe going to her happy place. Maybe not wanting to see the raw lust on her audience's faces.

So, Lance, how do you Coasties do it? When you interdict someone you think is carrying something illegal?

We got mad fast ships, man, really fast. So we intercept them and holler at them over the loudspeaker that we're the coast guard and to prepare to be boarded for inspection.

Just like that? And do they let you?

Usually. We have a mark thirty-eight and two fifty-cals on the deck. Just the sight of those is usually enough to convince them.

And what if they're not?

Lance and Dave exchanged a grin.

Then we cook off a round to show them we mean business.

I see. So you literally fire a shot across the bow. Does that work?

Every time. Every time.

And when's the last time you had to do that?

They couldn't quite manage to pry their eyes off the girl this time. Mainly because she was attempting a tricky back-layover gymnastics move.

What was it, Dave, three months ago maybe? That old two-master?

His friend nodded.

Yeah, that was it. Turned out they had like a hundred pounds of drugs on board. Cocaine, mainly. Man, those women! They had these little thong bikinis and nothin' else on.

So you popped off a shot? Then what happened?

Then they got all kinds of scared. The girls screamed. The guys shit their little Speedos. And we had a good day.

The young Coasties laughed and gave each other a knuckle-bump.

Yeah. We had a good day.

So, wow, this is so interesting, guys. So one thing, how do you find the boats to interdict? How do you know who to go after?

This was obviously Lance's thing. His voice was full of enthusiasm.

Aw, man, that's the coolest thing. See, Homeland Security beefed up all our technology like crazy. We have equipment now that lets us see every boat and ship and, hell, skinny-dipper in the waters around the Islands. Top of the line radar. It's like the screens you see air-traffic controllers use. And not only that, we can plot where they came from with computers. So there are some places and kinds of boats, and just the way they try to avoid attention and if, like, for instance, they're making a run at night, that makes them more suspicious than your regular weekend sailors.

So, wait a minute, that's amazing. You're telling me you guys can know where every boat is at every single minute, day or night?

Yessir. Day or night. If they're in our waters, we know where they are.

Holy shit!

Holy shit!

Yessir. That's a big holy shit.

I stood, said *adios*, and gave them both another handshake. Lance thanked me again for the beers, then turned his attention back to the pretty young thing giving him a sight that would fuel his fantasies for months to come.

Halfway down the block, I remembered the other thing I wanted to ask Oleo about and doubled back. We talked for another ten minutes or so and then I headed back in the direction of the hotel.

CHAPTER TWENTY-NINE

I was a block away from the Outrigger when my cell phone buzzed. It was Rick.

Hey.

Hi, Huck. I didn't forget your request. Mother has agreed to talk to you. Tonight is good if it's good for you.

A glance at my watch told me it was not quite seven.

Oh? Okay. That's great. Any time in particular?

No, anytime is fine. She'll be here. Just so you know, though, the cops have already interviewed her at length. All of us, really.

I would've expected that. It go okay?

Yeah, I guess. They have a way of making you feel like you're a prime suspect, you know?

That's part of the technique, to see if there's any nervousness betrayed, that sort of thing.

Oh, right. So, Huck, just, you know, please be gentle with her. Okay?

I promise. See you in a few.

I'm actually at the bank, but I'll tell her you're on your way over.

Okay. Bye.

There were far fewer cars lining the street in front of the Wong's mansion this time. Walking to the house, I noticed the wake was still going on, although with only a handful of participants.

Mr. Doyle!

Li-Hua came down the entryway stairs to greet me, a surprisingly warm smile on her face.

Nice to see you again, Mr. Doyle.

Hello, Li-Hua. Call me Huck, please.

Motioning toward the gamblers, the gong, the white cloth flapping in the evening breeze:

I can't believe this is still going on.

Oh, yes. A man of Mr. Wong's position is mourned for many days. Many days. Ah, wake, yes? Wake will end with the burial this weekend, I think, but the mourning period will last for months. So you are here to see Mrs. Wong?

Yes.

This way, please. I will show you to her.

Thank you.

Li-Hua led me past the makeshift courtyard, where Sing Ten Wong's body still lay in state, and into a formal sitting room. Bao Wong rose from an armchair and extended an extraordinarily delicate hand. It felt like a small bird when I held it, but her squeeze was cool and firm.

Good evening, Mr. Doyle.

She had only the slightest accent; an attention to every syllable in *evening*, the dropped *r* in *mister*, of a Chinese person for whom English was a second language. I hadn't gotten a good look at her my first visit here. Her beauty, this close up, made my heart miss a beat. The family photo had done her little justice; it failed to capture the full effect of the fine curve of her nose, the feminine yet strong angle of her cheekbones, the graceful neck, the porcelain skin, the acres of obsidian hair swept up into a perfect bun, the eyes of limitless depth, at once full of pain and mirth, understanding and curiosity.

Bao Wong was simply exquisite.

And as I stumbled through my greeting and she motioned for me to sit, there was one thought searing my brain: *What man would ever need anyone other than her?* Then I remembered the images I'd found on Wong's laptop, and answered my own question.

She asked Li-Hua to fetch some tea and turned back to me with a smile.

Richard tells me you are a private investigator?

Well, yes. It's sort of an avocation of mine. At your son's request, I'm just trying to help the police figure out who killed your husband, and it's been my experience that sometimes people have an easier time talking to someone who's not a law-enforcement officer.

That's very kind of you. I understand you're a professional golfer, too. Playing in the tournament this week?

Yes, I am. Thanks to your husband.

He invited you?

He did.

And how are you playing?

Ah, very well, actually. Very well. So far.

I'm so glad.

Li-Hua appeared with the tea, poured it carefully, and retreated to another room. I took a sip, set the cup down, cleared my throat, and had no idea where to begin.

Mrs. Wong, first, let me say how very sorry I am for your loss.

She nodded.

I didn't know your husband well, but the short time I spent with him that, ah, that day, I enjoyed very much.

Again, a nod, betraying no feelings whatsoever. Her expression was relaxed, the corners of her mouth turned up ever so slightly in a polite, casual, smile. For some reason, I was nervous.

In, ah, in looking into something like this, it's natural, ah, normal procedure to talk to the people closest to the victim, and—

She leaned forward and put a hand on mine.

Mr. Doyle. Please do not be uncomfortable. You can ask me anything you wish.

Anything? Okay, then. Anything.

Thank you for that. Mrs. Wong, did you love your husband?

There was the tiniest flutter of her lashes, the slightest tensing of her lips. She took in a breath, and answered,

No. I did not.

Ever?

No. I never loved my husband.

She glanced at my left hand.

Mr. Doyle, have you ever been married?

No, I have not.

Then you will have a hard time understanding this, but sometimes a marriage changes from the kind we all idealize to something more realistic. A friendship. A partnership. But also, sometimes a marriage doesn't even begin with love and romance. Sometimes a marriage has a different purpose. To have children. To unite two families. To escape.

And yours? What was the purpose of your marriage?

I would have to say all of those things.

So if not love, how would you describe your feelings toward Mr. Wong?

She paused to add a squeeze of lemon to her tea and take a sip.

Fear, at first. Revulsion. Resentment, even. Hatred, at times. Eventually I suppose I came to appreciate some of his achievements, and how he provided for us. I know some people found him to be entertaining and funny. I never held that view of Sing Ten. In a marriage, one's true nature is laid bare. It's very difficult to hide your real self from someone who shares your bed, night after night, shares your holidays, shares your table. I saw his attempts at humor and philanthropy as nothing more than camouflage for who he really was.

I half expected to hear the sound from the next room of Sing Ten Wong turning over in his coffin. She continued,

My husband convinced my parents it was best for both families if they allowed him to marry me at a very, very young age. He was already a legend in our city. A man who escaped with nothing and returned very wealthy. On the surface, very generous. But his generosity always had a benefit to himself. I remember being terrified when he came to get me. It was not what I wanted. It was never what I wanted. But when I look at my children, at the life apart from Sing Ten I've been fortunate enough to lead, I realize how lucky I am. But that doesn't make me love him.

Mrs. Wong, did you tell this to the police?

They never asked.

What *did* they ask you?

Where was I when he was murdered.

And where were you?

Here.

And there are friends or staff members who can corroborate that?

Yes.

How and when did you hear your husband had been murdered?

Mr. Ching, a vice president of the bank, called me from the hospital shortly after Sing Ten was pronounced dead.

That must've been one of the calls he made on my phone, I thought. Then it occurred to me it might be interesting to see who else he called. I made a mental note to check my phone records from that day.

Bao Wong was watching me coolly, that slightest of smiles still gracing the corners of her lovely mouth. She seemed strong, in charge of her emotions, so I went for broke.

Mrs. Wong, do you have reason to believe your husband cheated on you?

This time, no fluttering of eyelashes, no tensing of her lips. Just a hint of a nod.

Yes. Constantly. But Mr. Wong would not see it that way. As cheating. In fact, many in my culture have forever viewed men having affairs with other women as the natural state of a marriage. They believe men are not capable of monogamy. Especially not powerful men. And should not be held to that.

But women should?

This time, the smile increased ever so slightly. Especially in her eyes. I found myself envying whoever the lover was who visited her thoughts just then.

Mr. Doyle, may I ask you a question?

That took me a bit by surprise, but I shrugged.

Sure.

Do you think I killed my husband?

I paused to think about it, given what we'd just talked about. I must've been deep in thought for a bit too long, cranking through the possibilities, because she spoke up again.

The policeman who interviewed me said next of kin, especially the spouse, are always at the top of the list of suspects.

Well, it's true that spouses are usually the first suspects, only because in a large percentage of murders, it's a spouse who committed the crime. Do I think you actually did it? No. From what I know about the murder, and I was there at the time, I'd say there's no way on earth you pulled the trigger. Do I think you might have hired someone to kill your husband?

I watched her response for a moment before answering.

I honestly don't know yet.

CHAPTER THIRTY

Bao Wong thanked me for my frankness and invited me back if I needed any more information. At the front door she lowered her voice.

I have only one request in return. Richard does not need to know any of what we discussed. As a friend of his, surely you can understand why.

I nodded in agreement, shook her strong, tiny hand. On the way back to the hotel, I checked my phone's call list. Unfortunately, I'd placed enough calls to push whatever numbers Sam Ching had dialed out of the phone's short-term memory. So I called my cell phone provider's twenty-four-hour service line and asked that the most recent bill be faxed to me care of the Outrigger. That would have an itemized list of every call placed or received by my phone.

Wong's computer was silent when I pulled it from the safe. The deleted file recovery program was finished with its work. There were literally thousands of emails awaiting my perusal. After opening a random number of them, the contents of which were inconsequential, it became clear there were simply too many to pore over in any reasonable amount of time. I'd have to figure out a way of culling the herd, so to speak. Which meant looking for patterns, irregularities, red flags.

I clicked over to my keepers folder and pulled up the email written in Chinese. In another window, I fired up the Internet browser and navigated to a popular foreign language translation website. I then copied the Chinese characters from the message into the translation box and clicked enter. What appeared was almost unintelligible:

> *Your request without a doubt. We will not hold the post in the deal little position. You will discover that a way convinces their you the proposition in bank' In the future will grow s biggest interest. If you in this, are unable you to know the consequence. G.W.*

Computers can't always translate the written word perfectly, especially when imperfect grammar and colloquial idioms are used. Still, this paragraph did give me a few clues: It hinted at a threat, at some tension. And it was written by the mysterious G.W.

The undeleted messages contained a total of seven emails in Chinese written by the same individual. The translations were equally as garbled, but here and there, the author's intentions were clear. Coupled with the responses Wong sent which I'd pulled up from the deleted sent files, they gradually painted a distinct picture of the origin and details of the merger, and why BOPI's chief executive officer was so determined to bring it about in the face of considerable opposition from the bank's board of directors.

There was a knock at my door. Through the peephole, I recognized one of the hotel security men who regularly sweep my room for bad guys.

Yes?

Fax, Mr. Doyle.

I fumbled around in my pocket for a tip, opened the door, thanked the guy with a five-spot. The list of calls over the past week showed the seven Sam Ching placed on Saturday. One was the Wong's home number, which seemed to confirm Bao Wong's alibi. A long distance call began with the numbers 01186. Two others began with 011852. According to the helpful international operator I got on the hotel phone, 86 is the country code for China; 852 for calling Hong Kong.

The digital clock next to the bed said 9:41. Even though my tee time wasn't until 12:07, I wanted a good morning workout. But there was one last email from G.W. that I hadn't yet looked at. When I clicked it open it contained no text, just a small icon that indicated an attached file. A double-click of that launched a video player program inside a separate window.

I had discerned from the email exchanges that Sing Ten Wong was being blackmailed.

The video I was now watching told me how.

CHAPTER THIRTY-ONE

What I went back to ask Oleo earlier was if he knew a man named Anders. He raised an eyebrow and didn't answer.

Look, I saw his Maserati parked here when I came with Officer Sagulio.

So? He owns some buildings around here. Pays me to keep an eye on his ride when he's in the area on business.

I glanced around the neighborhood. Rundown brick buildings. Shuttered stores. A dodgy looking Thai restaurant directly across the street.

He owns buildings around here? How does that make sense as an investment?

Got no idea. I made my millions in the stock market. Why do you want to know about Mr. Anders?

I heard some things. Rumors. About young girls. Really young girls.

That's when his eyes turned hard and his head slowly returned to scanning the street, the dancers, the patrons, like the turret of a tank looking for a target.

You have a good night, now. Y'hear?

We're still under the rubric of not talking about nothing.

Wrong. We're not talkin'. Now don't make me lose my temper.

I fished around my pocket for a business card and held it out for him.

If you change your mind, my cell number's on this.

He patently ignored my outstretched hand and instead tilted his head just enough to give me a *go fuck yourself* sneer. I left it at that. A guy the size of Oleo, with a temperament to match, you can only push so far.

But back in the hotel room, watching the little, grainy video of a naked Sing Ten Wong having his way with a very small, very young girl, I was reminded of my chat with the tattooed Samoan bouncer. Because on the video, barely visible through the apartment window behind the bed, were the blue-and-pink neon letters N OK CL.

Traffic was light. I was there by shortly after ten, standing in front of a decaying brick apartment building on South Kukui Street with a Thai restaurant on the first floor.

The Bangkok Club, with the missing G and K in its garish sign, was behind me as, presumably, was Oleo, still manning his post inside the door, scanning the oglers, the oglees, the passersby. I didn't think he could see me from this angle. I didn't much care if he did. I was in a really bad mood.

Looking up, I tried to picture which window would have the angle that revealed the strip club's sign, and I decided it had to be the one on the third floor, to the left of the fire escape. A dim light glowed from somewhere inside.

There was a door to the side of the Thai restaurant with one of those buzzer intercoms. I started to push some random buttons to see if some careless soul would shut me up by buzzing me in, but I noticed the severed wires hanging out of the bent frame and instead reached for the knob and pulled the unlocked door open.

The stairwell smelled of old urine, Thai spices, and dead rats. There was one working light bulb on the second-storey landing. The third-floor landing was illuminated only by the streetlamp and neon sign outside the window.

I tried the door of the room I was guessing was the right one. No go. A large, expensive deadbolt was mounted a foot above the doorknob. No sound from inside.

I looked closer at the lock. It was a Medeco. Like the key that I'd found in Sing Ten Wong's briefcase. I fumbled around in my pocket for the key, hoping I hadn't left it on the hotel room dresser when I scooped up my change that morning.

Nope. My fingers found its distinctive shape and I pulled it out.

Slipped it into the slot.

The lock clicked open almost silently.

It was a small living room, definitely not the room from the video. A door on the far wall most likely led to the bedroom I'd seen. I looked around in the pale light. A couch, two chairs, a table with some magazines. No TV. A desk sat in the corner with an outdated computer and cathode ray monitor on it. I eased through the door and into the room to get a closer look. As I closed the door, I noticed the lock was the kind that required a key to open from both sides.

And there was no key in it.

A software box and some manuals were stacked next to the computer. The writing was in Chinese script but the box's yellow design and logo were of a popular series of language courses.

A short hallway led to a small kitchen, fastidiously neat. A bag of bread sat on the counter, alongside a bowl of fresh apples and bananas. That's when I heard the laughter.

Girlish laughter. Coming from the room to the right of the kitchen.

Putting an ear to the door, I listened hard for any indication a man was inside. I heard nothing but young voices, giggling and talking in Chinese.

I backed out of the apartment, careful not to trip over any furniture, closed and locked the door. Walked down the stairs. Out of the building. To a vacant corner where I was sure no one could hear me.

Found her number on the card in my pocket and called.

Fifteen minutes later, a cab pulled over down the street from the Bangkok Club and she stepped out.

Li-Hua! Over here.

She spotted me, waved, paid the driver and walked briskly across the street, hugging her sweater close to her chest and looking around nervously.

Mr. Doyle. Good evening. I have never been here before. It is very scary at night, yes?

Yes, but you'll be all right. I promise. I just need you to do some translating for me, just for a bit.

And, frankly, I couldn't think of anyone else to call until I knew what's going on.

She nodded.

I understand. I will do what I can to help.

Very good. This way.

We went back into the building and up the stairs, pausing outside the door. I leaned in close to her ear to whisper.

> There are some young girls in this apartment. I think they've been held here against their will, but I don't want to scare them. So when we go inside, I need you to call out to them, tell them not to worry, that we're here to help, and for them to come out into the living room. Tell them we are not the police and they are not in trouble in any way. We're simply here to help them.

She looked confused but nodded.

Yes, okay.

I again unlocked the big deadbolt and opened the door. We took half a step inside and, at my signal, Li-Hua spoke up in a moderately loud but calm voice.

There was a momentary outcry of surprise from the room, then silence. But after she repeated the same phrase a few times, the bedroom door opened and two faces peered around the corner.

Li-Hua gestured to herself and to me as she spoke in soothing tones. The girls looked at each other, then came all the way out into the living room. They appeared to introduce themselves with a slight bow. Li-Hua motioned for them to sit on the couch.

We came into the room and I shut the door behind me.

Ask them if there's anyone in the other bedroom.

She did, and they both shook their heads no.

Do they expect anyone to come back here tonight?

A short conference, then Li-Hua turned to me.

No. They say the *house mother*, yes? The house mother lives upstairs, but she's already gone to bed for the night. She, ah, she checks on them sometimes during the day to make sure they're okay, bring them food, and to see their language lessons. Also to . . . I am sorry, I'm not sure I understood that last part.

She turned back to the girls and asked something. They responded. Li-Hua looked at me with something approximating shock on her face, turned back to them, asked them something else, then put her hand to her mouth.

Mr. Doyle! They said, she brings men, to teach them . . .

I started to put my arm around her shoulders to steady her, thought better of it under the circumstances, and simply patted her on the back.

I know. I know. I'm sorry you had to hear that. But that's why I called you. I suspected this was going on here. And now, we have to figure out what they know and how to make it stop.

Their names were Jiao and Luli. Both girls were fifteen years old. For an hour, through Li-Hua, I quizzed them about their lives and the operation going on in the building. Her empathy, calming nature and closeness in age to the two girls helped them open up, despite the dire repercussions they'd been warned about from the moment they set foot in Hawaii.

They told us there were other girls holed up in other apartments, about eight at any given time, they guessed, although they weren't exactly sure how many were there just now. Girls came and went; once they reached a certain level with their English skills, and other skills, I assumed, they were sent elsewhere.

Jiao and Luli came from different cities in central China not quite three months ago. They both thought their parents were sending them to the U.S. to go to school, but when they got here, they learned exactly what kind of schooling was their destiny. Once they arrived inside the apartment, the nice man who accompanied them from the front stoop of their homes, onto the plane, and, posing as their father, through U.S. customs, turned suddenly cold. He introduced them to the woman who would oversee their lives and education from that point on, the house mother, then promptly disappeared.

Then they told us about the man they called Xiong Mao. Li-Hua turned to me to explain *xiong mao* literally translates to *bear cat*. The Chinese name for panda bears.

The Panda Bear they described was a short, funny, somewhat pudgy man, who visited them on an almost daily basis until about a week ago, to show them all the many ways a man likes to be pleasured. I was pretty sure the Panda Bear was the man I'd seen in the video. The man whose killer I was trying to track down.

Please ask them if they are forced to be with other men.

With tears welling up in her eyes, Li-Hua repeated my question. They looked at each other, then nodded in unison. Li-Hua reached out for both of their hands before telling me what they said.

Yes. With many other men, they say. To practice what Xiong Mao taught them and to practice their English.

I'd heard enough. I flipped open my phone. Started to call the police.

But that would lead to questions of how I found the place. How I got the key.

Which would inevitably reveal Sing Ten Wong's involvement.

Which made me think of Rick, and what this revelation would do to him. I wanted to mull all that over before exposing his family, so instead of calling Five-0, I called my brother. He answered on the third ring, his voice phlegmy and disoriented.

Yeah? Vida Blue Doyle. Who is this?

It's me.

Huck? What the hell? Everything okay? Shouldn't you be asleep?

Who's the special agent in Hawaii who handles crimes against children?

CHAPTER THIRTY-TWO

Before Special Agent Vida Blue Doyle took a bullet to the neck, his areas of focus within the Bureau were cybercrimes and crimes against children. One often involves the other. He promised to call back with the name of an FBI agent on Oahu, even though I refused to tell him why I needed it.

You don't want to know. Trust me.

Huck . . .

Trust me. I'll fill you in later.

I was absolutely not going to leave without Jiao and Luli. But that presented a whole host of problems, not the least of which was the minute the house mother arrived in the morning, she'd know the jig was up. She and the rest of the girls would instantly disappear, and the men of the pedophile club would almost certainly be alerted. I wanted those bastards caught.

As Li-Hua helped the girls pack up their few belongings, I took a quick check around the apartment. A close inspection showed the camera that recorded Sing Ten Wong committing any number of felonies had to have been hidden inside an air conditioning vent in the front bedroom. It was no longer there, but the paint around the vent was missing some large flakes where the metal cover had been removed.

Blue called back. Gave me the name, number and email address of the special agent in charge of the Violent Crimes and Major Offenders squad, or VCMOP, based in Honolulu, who just happened to be a woman.

The computer in the apartment was not connected to the Internet and there was no phone in the whole place. I didn't want to use my cell phone because, again, I didn't want to have to answer a whole lot of uncomfortable questions. Not yet. Not until I knew how I wanted to play this hand. When the girls were packed and ready, I checked the hallway, then we quietly exited the apartment. Down the stairs, out the front and quickly back to my car, where the hookers hanging around the streetlight made some snarky comments about how young girls can't possibly be as much fun as they are, and hey, if I wanted a foursome, why didn't I just say so?

Two blocks away, I spotted a payphone booth next to a convenience store. Special Agent Christine McLeavy was dubious at first, insisting I give her my name and explain more fully how it was I knew about this place. But I laid on enough legal jargon to show I had something between the ears other than a vivid imagination, and she guardedly agreed to take a look at the building on South Kukui Street. I pushed harder.

It has to be tonight. Otherwise they're gone.

We'll be there within the hour.

Good. And Agent McLeavy, keep checking your email. If I can dig up anything else that's how I'll contact you.

I'll keep an eye on my BlackBerry. But if you don't want to tell me your name, at least give me some way to refer to you. Something other than *anonymous tipster.*

For some reason, the symbol that had been carved into my various courtesy cars and hotel room came to mind.

Call me Xi.

Chee?

Yes. Xi.

I hung up. Got back into the car. Drove toward Waikiki on deserted streets.

Their faces in the rearview mirror told me Luli and Jiao were scared. And I couldn't blame them. They had no idea if they'd just jumped from the frying pan into the fire. But they must have been hoping that, at the very least, maybe they wouldn't have to service those disgusting older men anymore.

It was too late to take the girls anywhere but my hotel. I dropped them all a block away with instructions to come up to my room in ten minutes, then I drove to valet parking and went up to the penthouse suite alone. When they knocked on the door and I showed them in, Jiao and Luli's jaws dropped at the display of wealth around them. The difference between their little apartment, and certainly their homes back in China, and the place they now found themselves in was enormous. They told Li-Hua they hadn't been allowed out of the apartment once since arriving there.

The two young women walked slowly around the suite, touching fabrics, pushing light switches, giggling about the opulence and gadgets. I showed them the bedroom and had Li-Hua explain that that was where they'd be spending the night until I figured out a safe place for them to go.

Jiao asked a question. Li-Hua looked at me, and the first little smile I'd seen on her pretty face all that evening peeked out. She shook her head with a laugh and said something to the girls, who both giggled with apparent relief.

I retrieved the laptop from the safe, as well as a few articles of clothing. We said our goodnights and I closed the French doors that separated the bedroom from the rest of the hotel suite.

> Li-Hua, thank you. Really. I know this wasn't easy, but I couldn't have done it without you. I have one last request. Is it possible for you to be back here in the morning? I've got to do some research, but I want to get them to a safehouse, and there might be a language problem.
>
> Yes, certainly. I will be back in the morning. At what time would you like me to be here?
>
> Let's say eight?
>
> Yes, eight. Thank you.
>
> And, listen, you can tell no one about this. Absolutely no one. Not right now. It would put those other girls back at that building in danger.

And maybe you, I didn't add.

> Yes. I understand.

She opened the door. I stopped her to give her cab money, then had to ask;

Her question, just then. It made you laugh. What did she say?

A blush came to her cheeks and she put her hand to her mouth to cover the smile.

She asked, are they safe with you in the same apartment? Will you be expecting, ah, to visit them in bed?

I was mortified. Of course they'd be wondering that, after all they'd been through, all the depravity they'd been exposed to. I felt like an idiot.

And what did you tell them?

I told them no. You are a man of honor. They are safe with you.

I closed and locked the door when Li-Hua left, then moved over to the dining area table and booted up Wong's laptop. I had a hunch about that nameless ISP address, the one that was password protected. I was hoping Wong was like ninety percent of the rest of humanity: lazy. When the website prompted, I typed in five letters and hit return. I was right.

Money gained me access. Doesn't it always?

A Chinese title appeared at the top of the page. I highlighted that script, opened a new Internet browser window, and pulled up a translation website. When I pasted those characters into the window and hit enter, the English translation appeared.

It said, *The Relaxation Club.*

Pedophiles with a sense of humor. That only pissed me off more. I went back to the original site. The cursor turned into a finger when it rolled over the Chinese characters, so I clicked on it to enter. The next level appeared to be some sort of chat room. The layout was barebones, consisting only of a series of questions and comments, in English, I was relieved to see, from anonymous persons, identified only by five-digit numbers. There was absolutely no overt indication of what the discussion was about. Scanning back over months of these terse messages, it became apparent this was nothing more than a digital message board, where members of this murky club could stay in touch without revealing their identities, rate the qualities of their latest conquests and, it appeared, schedule their next appointment with a girl.

There were no names in any of the messages. When I tried to dig into the website's properties to find out who established and maintained it, I was prompted for an administration password. This setup was the ultimate in anonymity. The most recent posting was from yesterday. *When does the new produce arrive?* asked 48771. There had been no response. But reading over the requests and replies, I picked up on the terminology. That gave me an idea.

I opened another window in the browser and went to Gmail. In five minutes I had a new email account, signed up under a bogus name. The hotel's Internet system would be the ISP of record, which couldn't possibly implicate me. Next, I composed a message to Special Agent McLeavy and included the chat room's Internet address and password:

> This appears to be the website these men are using to arrange their dates with underage girls. You'll notice they don't use real names, but by scanning through the months of queries, you can see the code words used. It seems to me it shouldn't be too difficult for you to set a trap. If I can find any other useful information, I'll forward it along. You can contact me via this email address, but if I find out you're trying to track me down, I'll disappear.
>
> Happy hunting,
>
> Xi

I hit "send," then clicked over to Google and found the name of the Honolulu battered women's shelter. Jotted that on a notepad, shut down the computer and, since I couldn't go back into the bedroom to return the laptop to the safe, I stuck it inside the gas fireplace, out of sight behind the chain-link side curtains.

I was asleep on the couch within minutes.

CHAPTER THIRTY-THREE

The buzzing of my cell phone woke me. Momentarily confused as to where I was, I fumbled around for it and knocked it off the side table. By the time I retrieved it from under the couch, it gave its missed call bleep. I pushed "send," saw who it was, and pushed it again to return the call.

Hi Doc.

Well, good morning little Mary Sunshine. You sound sleepy.

I scanned the room for a clock and found one on the kitchen wall. Ten after six. I'd forgotten to set the alarm.

I was up late. How're you?

I'm good. I hope I didn't wake you.

No, no. I needed to get up to answer the phone, anyway.

She giggled that raspy way I like so much. That started a glow below the Mason-Dixon line. It had been a long time since I'd heard that sound. In person. Very much in person. Usually when I do that certain little thing.

So, I almost thought you'd be out on the range getting ready for the round.

Yeah, well, I'm headed there. After breakfast.

And after taking some young girls to the women's shelter. No way was I doing to tell Judith about last night's little adventure. She'd give me another earful about why I should be focusing on golf and not trying to solve other people's problems.

Not that she'd be wrong.

You getting on a plane soon, Doc? I'm ready for my house call.

That's part of why I'm calling. I had to move my flight to the morning. A city councilman woke up dead yesterday and it looks like somebody gave him a little painkiller cocktail. It's going to be a late night but I promise I won't miss the flight. It doesn't leave until eight-thirty. I'll be there in plenty of time to watch you tee off tomorrow. Although I'll be a tiny bit sleepy, I'm sure.

A pang. The part of me that is used to rarely playing on Saturdays immediately became suspicious. If her flight doesn't leave until tomorrow, that means she'd know if I made the cut or not in plenty of time to cancel the trip. Which is actually not a stupid thing to do. No sense coming all the way out here if I wasn't going to play. Then I remembered what I shot yesterday.

But for some reason, it still bugged me.

You know, if you're that busy, why don't we just ditch this plan and I'll see you when I get back?

No! No, no, no. I want to come out, honest! We'll have a blast and I'm *so* in need of some R&R. Plus, I can't wait to tag along with the rest of your groupies and watch your little butt tense up when you putt.

My butt doesn't tense up when I putt.

Oh no? I'll take video next time.

Seriously, though, it's a long way to come. . . .

Huck. If you don't want me out there, just say so. Otherwise, I'm coming if I have to use those big wings I ordered from Victoria's Secret. Along with that new lingerie, of course.

Another warm tickle, this one all the way to my toes.

Okay, just making sure. Can't wait to see you.

Well, you better do more than just look, mister. Now, the other reason I called, I have some information on the case you shouldn't be looking into because you're playing so damn well you might actually win this tournament.

Oh? Great! Whatcha got?

Sing Ten Wong's autopsy shows he definitely died of myocardial infarction caused by blunt force trauma to the right ventricle. No sign of drugs in his system. Moderate-to-severe arterial plaque buildup indicates he was at near risk of coronary heart disease. Other than that, he was relatively healthy for an overweight, middle-aged man.

Wait a minute. Blunt force trauma? He was shot in the heart!

Technically, no. He was shot, true, by a fifty-caliber weapon. You don't see that size bullet everyday.

That sounded like military. Some sniper rifles use .50 cal. Judith was still talking.

I've worked on dozens of drive-by shootings, domestic killings, drug hits, you name it, and I've never come across a slug that large. Anyway, the projectile pierced his back, entering between the ninth and tenth ribs, fracturing both, before impacting the right ventricle. But it did not actually enter the heart. The force of impact evidently was enough to cause the heart to stop. That also explains why there was very little blood.

Jesus Christ! So the bullet had just enough momentum to poke through his ribs and smack his heart but not enough to pierce it?

That's right. And guess what else?

She was enjoying this way too much.

I don't know. He has a third nipple?

No. The bullet went in backwards.

I wasn't sure I heard her right.

You want to say that again?

Happy to! The round entered the body backwards. The nose of the bullet was literally pointing in the direction from which it came. Very strange.

Don't bullets sometimes bounce around inside a body? You know, rico-chet off bones and things? Couldn't it have just gotten turned around?

Yes, they often do. That's how gunshots cause so much terrible damage to the human body. But as I said, this one was pretty much out of gas when it hit Mr. Wong, and it hit him facing the exact opposite way a bullet normally flies.

The wiring in my attic was smoking pretty good by now. Not only were my thoughts still fairly scattered from being up late and waking up early, but I just couldn't latch on to the nonsense she was telling me. Then, in the en-thusiastic voice Judith reserved only for the most bizarre cases that come across her surgical table, she threw the high-voltage switch all the way open and fried what remained of my brain:

And Huck, get this! Chemical analysis of the bullet and chest cavity found traces of sodium, chloride, magnesium, potassium, sulfate and calcium.

Okay . . .

Know what that is?

Cotton candy?

Seawater!

Judith rattled on a bit about how cool this whole thing was, seeing as how a medical examiner always loves a good mystery involving dead people with things that aren't the way they should be, so long as they eventually solve them, of course, and then we said our *adioses* and I stumbled into the suite's kitchen to make a cup of that really thin complimentary coffee with that really minuscule complimentary coffee maker.

The bedroom door cracked open and two young faces peeked out. They giggled and shut the door. I heard laughing. Then the shower. I picked up the hotel phone and ordered an assortment of breakfast food.

Blue called right as I was signing the check and the waiter was setting the spread on the dining room table.

Hey, little brother. Guess you were busy last night.

How would you know that?

Well, a priority notice went out on the Bureau's flash line about four o'clock this morning giving the heads-up about a raid on an apartment building in Honolulu. Two people arrested, a man and woman. Three potential juvenile victims of statutory rape, kidnapping and white slavery were rescued unharmed and are currently in protective custody. A sting operation is currently up and running to apprehend suspects. The operation is under a tight lid, but they expect to make contact with their first suspect later today.

Thank God she kept her word. . . .

Wow. They work fast, don't they?

Yeah. Wonder how that happened.

Little bird must've told them.

That has to be it. Hey, Huck . . .

Yeah?

Hit 'em long and straight today.

Will do. Thanks for your help.

Anytime. Thanks for not listening to me.

About what?

About not getting involved.

Anytime.

The women's shelter was more than happy to admit the two girls. I had to be vague about their circumstances, and mine, but it seemed to me the nice lady on the other end of the phone was used to a certain amount of obfuscation.

Their ultimate concern was creating a safe haven for abuse victims. Little else mattered.

Jiao, Luli and I were fed and dressed, the laptop was returned to its warm and cozy safe and the girls were practicing their very limited English on me when Li-Hua arrived. As we were leaving, I pulled her aside.

I don't want you to ask them to lie, but if they could forget me, forget my name, forget they came to this hotel, it would be a great help to me. I have more work to do, and if the police found out I was the one who broke up this operation, well, I'm afraid I won't be able to finish it.

Yes, of course.

She had a little conversation with them in the doorway, and they nodded emphatically, turned toward me, nodded again. Jiao said something. Li-Hua translated.

She wants to know what happens now?

Good question.

Now . . . they live their lives. I think if they want to return home to their families in China, that will be arranged. But if I remember correctly the U.S. government has a policy of not deporting victims of this sort of crime. So if they choose to stay, I think they'll be allowed to. The nice people at the women's shelter will have all the answers for them.

We got out of the car a block away from the shelter so I wouldn't be seen by anyone there. I gave Li-Hua cab fare to get her back home after making sure the girls were settled and a translator was available to help them. Luli and Jiao gave me awkwardly tearful hugs, with a lot of hand grasping and head bowing. I was fully embarrassed.

Then Li-Hua leaned up and gave me a kiss on the cheek and I felt my face grow hot.

Enough of this mushy stuff. I'm a highly trained professional athlete, after all. We said goodbye for, oh, about the two hundredth time that morning and I pulled away from the curb.

Looking back in the rearview mirror at the three young women walking down the street, hand in hand, I sincerely hoped their worst days were now behind them.

CHAPTER THIRTY-FOUR

There is no other game as fickle, as elusive, as humbling as golf. Not a player in the world can predict what he or she will shoot that day, how the putts will roll, how the gods will bless or damn. No amount of training or confidence can ensure a great round. In fact, the *only* sure thing about professional golf is within about half an hour after the last player's ball rolls into the cup on any given Sunday evening, that week's money list is produced by the PGA Tour's computer in Ponte Vedra Beach, Florida.

Even though the Sony Open is the season's first full-field event, the only players not thinking about that money list, not thinking about being in the top 125 on that list by the end of the season, are the guys who'd won exemptions. Make it in the top 125 money winners, and you keep your card another year.

Win any tournament, win a two-year exemption from qualifying for the right to play in a given tournament. Win the U.S. Open, the British Open, the World Series of Golf, the Tour Championship or the Player's Championship; win a ten-year exemption.

Win The Masters or the PGA, and you're exempt for life. You never again have to Monday qualify. You never again have to worry about Q-School. You are a PGA Tour professional for as long as you can swing a club. That is what every one of us dreams about.

I had to deflect a few questions about my appearance from the assembled media as I made my way to the practice range and warmed up, but everyone was pretty friendly and supportive, and it was obvious they enjoyed having an unknown at the top of the leaderboard, for however long that lasted.

Huck, do you think part of the reason why you're so far ahead is because Tiger's sitting this one out?

Like a lot of the really big names, Tiger Woods often skips the first few events of the season so as to go into the big opening events fully rested. Some of the guys play the lucrative made-for-TV events in the off-season, so if they're going to be at their best, something has to give. The PGA Tour doesn't like it, but that's the reality.

You know, I'm really just playing against this course. If Tiger was here, I'd have to make the same shots. Sink the same putts. Yes, I'd be looking behind me maybe a little more. But I hope it wouldn't shake me.

Bobby shooed the guys away, and we moved over to the side a bit to kick some balls into the rough and work on distance control out of the long stuff. We finished up with a few dozen putts and headed over to the first tee, the one that started my birdie-fest yesterday.

This round didn't start off quite as spectacularly. I posted pars until the fifth, where I smashed a huge drive to the right side of the fairway and slam-dunked a nine-iron into the bottom of the cup for an eagle two. That started a run of birdies for the next three holes.

The number thirteen at Waialae is the second most difficult hole on the course for this tournament. Even though I was striking the ball well, I was having a little trouble hitting a dependable fade, which didn't bode well for this hole considering the fairway cut hard right almost 90 degrees. I'd have to get a little creative.

The line of tall trees on the right would limit how far I could start my ball that way, but I decided to take the risk, aiming just left of the nearest one and crushing a solid drive that sailed over the far kiawe trees, and drew back left just beyond the fairway bunkers that mark the dogleg's turn. The landing zone was only twenty-four yards wide at that point, and my sweet little Titleist found it just fine.

My second shot was a little over two hundred yards, with just a hint of a helping breeze at my back. Bobby and I conferred.

You don't want to be short on this. You got four traps on either side of the green. This one gets baked pretty good by the sun so it'll be firm. Anything coming in hot will run to the back.

I'm thinking a five.

That's good. That's a good club. They tucked the pin in the front left, behind that leading bunker. It's a sucker's placement. You reach the sand there, you can't put your third near enough to the cup.

Maybe a cut shot? Start it left of those three tall trees to the back and bring it to the center?

I like that.

He waited for me to slide the five-iron out of the bag and then heaved it onto his shoulder and moved a few paces away. I set up aiming down the left side, and swung with my wrists more firmly in position than normal, cutting through the ball, with a high finish on the follow-through that kept my hands from rolling over on impact. This imparts a side spin on the ball that gives it a sharp but controllable left-to-right track.

The dimpled white projectile started off as straight as the side of a pyramid, then dove hard into the same kidney-shaped bunker my caddie had advised me to avoid.

When we got up to the ball, though, it wasn't nearly as bad as it could've been. Instead of burying itself, which is what I feared when it hit the sand so hard, the ball had run up the face of the bunker, then trickled back down, leaving me a slightly uphill lie. I was able to get the wedge under it softly enough to throw the ball close to the cup. I saved par with a two-foot putt. Walking off the green, I spotted Mr. Shades hanging back in the crowd, that fucking wiseass grin plastered on his face.

We finished six under for the day. When Bobby and I walked off the eighteenth green, not only had I made the cut, my name was still at the top of the leaderboard, and I still led the tournament by eight strokes.

Vijay Singh's name was just under mine, tied with three others for second place. He plopped down next to me at the scorer's table and gave me a thump on the shoulder.

I told you it was your week, Huck.

Well, the week's not over. Two more rounds to go.

Good luck with that, kid. You're playing really well.

Thanks, Veeg. You too.

The press conference took a little longer this time. There were more reporters. More cameras. More questions about how my face got messed up.

But one thing was different. I was no longer the one-day wonder.

I was the real deal.

CHAPTER THIRTY-FIVE

By the time I made it out of the broadcast booth and checked my cell phone, I had thirty-five missed calls. Most were numbers I didn't recognize. The ones I did recognize, from friends and fellow Tour pros, were most likely congratulatory in nature. I was reluctant to return those . . . well . . . because I didn't want to tempt fate by celebrating too early. I had two more days to go. Two more days to play at the same level. And I wasn't going to do anything to screw that up.

But the one number on my caller ID I did return was from a certain homicide detective.

Sagulio.

Hi, Detective. It's Huck Doyle.

Mr. Doyle. Thanks for calling back. I wanted you to know I spoke with Mrs. Wong and she gave permission to show you the autopsy report of her husband. I understand you've already interviewed her?

Yes, I did.

And what was your take on her?

Gorgeous. Stunning. Ethereal.

I don't think she had anything to do with the murder.

You're aware their marriage was less than perfect?

Yes, but frankly I think she's incapable of killing anyone, or having anyone killed. Just my hunch. I'm still convinced Sing Ten's murder is connected with this financial deal somehow, although I don't know how.

I wasn't ready to give Sagulio what I knew about the blackmailing. Point of fact, I might never be ready . . .

Well, Mr. Doyle, I have to agree. I don't think she's the type. We haven't ruled anything out yet, though.

. . . but I could help him out a little, considering he'd asked Mrs. Wong about sharing the autopsy.

Detective, did you know the coast guard has some sort of technology that allows them to know exactly what boats and ship are where in Hawaiian waters? They literally track them with radar like air-traffic controllers.

Is that true? Hadn't heard about that. We don't exactly have close relations with the military. Their boys get a little rowdy on shore leave.

Well, I was thinking it would be interesting to see what boats were offshore Waialae at the time of the shooting. The shot had to be fired from the water, right?

Correct. Had to be.

So the shooter had to come from a boat, maybe even slipped up close wearing diving gear, since the bullet left traces of seawater, right?

He was silent for a beat.

You've seen the autopsy?

Oops.

No, not yet, but I did hear about a few details.

Well, you're right. Seawater was found in the entry wound. That tells me the bullet was, at some point, submerged.

Makes sense. But how do you explain the bullet being backwards? How does that happen?

Big sigh on the other end of the line.

Beats the hell outta me.

Sagulio said he'd get back to me after he checked with the Coasties, and caught himself just before hanging up.

Hey, Doyle, one last thing. Those guys who roughed you up and trashed your car, any idea yet what they were after?

The mental images that flashed through my mind: The laptop in my hotel safe. The emails on the laptop. The financial documents on the laptop. And, probably of foremost concern to the fellows trying to recover Wong's computer: The video clip blackmailing Sing Ten, sent to him by the still-mysterious G.W.

Uh, no. No idea.

Uh huh. Seen any of them lately?

Just at the tournament every fucking single day.

Nope. Must've given up.

Yeah. Right. That must be it. Well, be careful, Mr. Doyle. Something tells me you and they have unfinished business.

We clicked off. I found my loaner car in the parking lot, started it up and headed back toward Waikiki. My phone buzzed just as I pulled into valet parking. I couldn't help but smile when I saw the name.

Hey there, Blue!

Huck! *Man!* What a great round! We had everybody on the whole floor crammed into my room, watching it. You probably heard us yelling all the way across the Pacific.

My brother has had little to celebrate since catching that bullet. It occurred to me that giving him a moment of happiness felt even better than being at the top of the leaderboard.

Yeah, going pretty well, huh?

Better than pretty well. You've got it together. You look so calm and under control. That putt you made on the twelfth. Unbelievable.

Bobby, my caddie, gave me great reads all day. Really. The guy knows every inch of this course as if he built it himself.

As I made my way through the hotel lobby and up to my room, Blue and I talked through every hole I played that day. His memory of the lies, the club selections, the shots I used every time, was incredible. It was as if he'd been there, and in a way, thanks to the entire round being broadcast on the Golf Channel, he was.

He put Lindsey on, who was so excited I could barely understand her. But her ebullience was contagious, and I found myself getting caught up in it all. Which I couldn't afford.

Hey, hey, Lindsey, hey! Wait a minute! I haven't won anything yet! Hold on!

You were so great, though! I've never really watched a whole round of golf before and it was so exciting!

Well, I have at least thirty-six more holes to play before we can really celebrate, so please, let's just calm it all down a bit, okay?

She agreed. Calmed it down a bit. Put the phone back to Blue's ear after wishing me good luck. Then started yelling and laughing again in the background.

Jesus, Blue, please tell her we've got a long way to go still.

Don't mind her. She's just never seen—

—me do so well?

No, I was going to say, a really exciting round of golf before. Never been interested. Now I think she's hooked. So, Faldo and those guys gave you major grief about your face, didn't they?

Yeah. They don't see too many golfers who look like they just went five rounds with George Foreman.

About that, I found out a little more about the people trying to buy into BOPI. Specifically, the CEO of the investment group, Wei Wu.

I flashed back on the country codes of the numbers the bank's senior VP, Sam Ching, had called from my phone.

The guy in Hong Kong.

Right. He lives in Hong Kong now, but he's from mainland China. He's a retired four-star general of the People's Liberation Army. Formed Zhonghua Holdings Limited two years ago with millions of his own money and a small group of international investors.

They must pay their officers better than we do.

They most certainly don't. The CIA believes he made a considerable fortune through redirecting portions of arms shipments to North Korea, Iran and terrorist groups. He may also have benefited directly from the narcotics trade among Chinese army troops. There's a vibrant drug industry, especially in the farflung provinces. Soldiering in bleak outposts can be pretty boring, and there's no way for the drugs to reach these places except as part of resupply convoys. Which means higher-ups have to be in the loop.

If the CIA knows about this, doesn't it stand to reason the Chinese leadership does too?

Oh, they must. But the Asia analysts think General Wu probably has some hefty leverage, in the form of embarrassing or incriminating information or materials, which would severely damage the power structure in Beijing. Early in his career, he was brought up on charges of extortion. So he's definitely got it in him. He also maintains considerable loyalty among many of his troops and junior officers, and put dozens of them on his own private payroll, at a tidy raise, when he left the army. Wu is very protected in many ways. The Chinese government seems resigned to allow him to conduct his business as he sees fit, so long as he doesn't damage the People's Republic.

What happened with the extortion charges?

Dropped. When the key witnesses recanted their testimony.

Of course.

Of course. And one other thing you'll find interesting. I checked with the airlines. A person named Wei Wu left Honolulu on the eight-forty A.M. flight to Hong Kong the morning Wong was murdered.

Fuck me.

Well put.

The conversation gradually shifted to his locomotor therapy sessions and the various happenings at the Rancho Los Amigos rehabilitation center my brother calls home. Before we said goodbye, Blue made me promise to put all this aside until after I hoisted up the Sony Open trophy on Sunday. I said I would.

And I almost meant it.

Except for the fact that there, then, in the information Blue got from the CIA, was the G.W. of the emails. *General Wu.* A greedy former military man who wanted to buy into a Western bank, and found a way to get a weak, vulnerable pedophile in an influential position to make it happen.

The man Wong undoubtedly met with the morning he was killed.

What I couldn't understand was, by all accounts, prior to Wong dropping dead of a gunshot, the merger was on track to happen. John Ng said as much. The billion-dollar deal was, forgive me, in the bank.

So why in the world would Wu have his precious goose murdered just when it was about to lay the fourteen-carat egg?

CHAPTER THIRTY-SIX

When I got back to the hotel, I had very limited options. I could hit the bar, which I promised myself I wouldn't do until the Open was over. I could go surfing, but there's always an off chance of sustaining some sort of injury in that endeavor, so I nixed that as well. I'm not much of one for languishing on the beach. Without alcohol, that is. So that, too, was a nonstarter.

Leaving me the following possible activities:

1. Watch a movie.

2. Wander around Waikiki.

3. Nap.

4. Read a book. Which would quickly lead to number 3 above.

5. Shop. Which would immediately drive me to drink.

6. Exercise. But I was already a bit weary from the round and all the adrenaline shooting through my veins.

So I chose number seven.

Crack open Wong's laptop and see what else I could see. As I retrieved the computer from the safe I could hear Blue's voice in my head. I could hear Judith's voice in my head. Hell, I could hear Kenny's voice in my head. All telling me to focus the fuck on golf and leave this thing until later.

But, see, I have a theory about that. I think if I zero in on my game too much, I'll break something. I'll overanalyze a missed putt, fixate on my swing plane and fine-tune my way out of this comfy groove I was in. So I figure a distraction would be a good thing.

I booted up the computer and wandered back into the Relaxation Club's chat room. The FBI had been busy. There was a whole new series of messages announcing the availability of *new fruit*, and a flurry of responses requesting a date to *go shopping*. By my count, six pedophiles were either already in custody or headed there within the next few days. I wondered if Anders was one of them, and if I'd be seeing him at the golf course tomorrow.

For the next hour, I pored over Wong's tax returns and financials. His family was definitely not hurting; between cash, investments and real estate, good old Sing Ten had socked away almost $22 million. Then I noticed something funny. Up until two years ago, Wong had maintained savings, checking and money market accounts with BOPI. And only BOPI. He had investment accounts with other institutions, but he'd done his banking only with his own bank.

But then he opened up an account with a Swiss bank based on the Island of St. Vincent in the Caribbean. And, according to the documents, the account was under the name of a limited partnership: Xiu Xian Ltd.

I clicked open the Internet browser, pulled up the translation website, and entered the name of the partnership. It took less than a millisecond for the English words to appear in the little box.

I stared at them in disbelief.

Xiu Xian. *Leisure. To be idle. To relax.*

Wong was evidently the Relaxation Club's banker.

A quick Googling provided me with the offshore bank's website. Man, was it slick, and because it wasn't limited by U.S. banking regulations, it advertised very high rates of returns for all its financial instruments. As such, of course, those deposits weren't insured by the FDIC, but hey, what's a little risk when the rewards are eight points above prime?

There was a button on the upper-righthand side of the site for account holders to log in. Thanks to Wong's financial records I had the name of the account holder, which in this case was a twelve-digit number. But I didn't have the password.

I gave it a shot. Typed in *money*. The screen changed to an angry red:

INCORRECT PASSWORD.

I started to try the combination of his birth date and the word PearlR Wong had used to disable his computer's security, but then noticed a button at the bottom of the page to assist the account holder in the event, alas, he lost his password. Clicking on that took me to a very pleasant and welcoming screen that asked me three personal questions presumably only Sing Ten Wong would know: his mother's maiden name, his social security number and his place of birth.

The tax documents gave me his social. The newspaper bio gave me the other two answers. I entered that information and the screen happily announced they were sending the password to my email account of record.

Five minutes later, the message appeared in Wong's Outlook inbox.

Two minutes after that, I was looking at an online balance sheet showing the Relaxation Club had just over one and a half million dollars in an interest-bearing account.

I noticed irregular deposits every few weeks of exactly the same amount: $20,000.

That seemed a bit random, but when I navigated back over to the Relaxation Club's message board, the timing became obvious. The deposits corresponded exactly with the dates the pedophiles went *shopping* for *new fruit*. In other words, once they were notified a virgin was available, they made an electronic $20,000 deposit to the numbered account to lock in the date. And then they had their fun.

Twenty grand's worth.

The price of innocence.

As satisfying as it was to shut down that operation and sic the FBI on those assholes, it didn't lead me any closer to find out who killed Wong. I knew who was blackmailing him. I knew how. I knew why. But I had no evidence yet that General Wei Wu was the guy who wanted the portly banker murdered.

I closed out of the Xiu Xian sites and went wandering back through Wong's once-deleted emails again, hoping to get some sense of whether Sing Ten had, perhaps, threatened to expose the scheme. Or was backing out of the deal. Anything. Any fucking thing.

After an hour of futile searching, my eyes were droopy and my back hurt. I shut down the laptop, placed it back in the safe and hopped in the shower for a quick refresh before heading out for dinner. I was toweling off when my cell phone buzzed. I didn't recognize the number.

Hello?

Huck?

It was a woman's voice. Slightly familiar.

Oh, I'm so glad you're there. It's Lisa. Lisa Tan.

I pictured her face. Her hair. Her bikini. The flat stomach with the belly-button piercing.

Yeah, hi! How are you? Haven't talked in a while.

Since some guys chased us through a pineapple maze and you got pissy at me, I didn't say.

I know, I know. I was rude to you when all you're trying to do is help Rick, and I'm sorry. Are you . . . can I . . . I need to talk. Can I come up?

Come up? You're here at the hotel?

Yes. It's a long story. Is now a bad time?

No, of course not. I was just going out for a bite. We can go somewhere together. Have you eaten yet?

She hesitated a moment before speaking.

Well, actually, it's, I'm, it's just that, it's private. What I need to talk to you about.

I see. Sure. Okay. Why don't I order room service then?

That would be perfect. Thank you.

Great. I'll track down a menu.

I gave her my room number, hung up and hastily straightened up the room, setting some plates, glasses and utensils on the table. I fumbled around for some clean clothes and had just managed to pull on some jeans and a t-shirt when there was a quiet knock on the door. Even distorted by the fisheye lens of the peephole, she was gorgeous. I did notice she looked very upset, or nervous. When I opened the door, she stepped up to me without a word and threw her arms around my neck. Her face was wet with tears.

Hey! Hey, are you okay? Lisa?

She spoke into my chest.

I'm so sorry. This is so embarrassing. I'm, it's been . . . such a terrible day.

She looked up at me.

It's so horrible. Luke and I, we broke up. I found out he was cheating. I still can't believe it.

Oh, Jesus, I'm really sorr—

But the truth is, Huck, I'm glad. I'm glad. Because . . . well . . .

Yeah, okay, so, I don't know how it happened exactly, but then we were kissing. And then we were on the couch and my t-shirt was off, and then hers was off. And that was really, really great. But then she kind of pushed away to catch her breath, which I didn't mind so much because it gave me a great view, until she stood up that is and said *Wait we can't do this it's too soon.*

I started to say *Hey I understand completely.* But then she was back on top of me again and we took up where we left off. Before I knew it, her shorts were on the coffee table. My jeans were on the floor.

Then she stood again. Which was really great. Even better view. Hello, black thong. Hello, belly-button piercing. Hello, little tiger tattoo. And said she needed to use the bathroom for a second and she'll be right back and don't go anywhere and by the way do I have a thing against wearing under-wear?

I'd just gotten out of the shower when you called. Dressed in a hurry.

She leaned back over to give me another kiss.

Oh, don't misunderstand me. It was a nice surprise. I like surprises.

Then she turned, another really great view, and walked into the bedroom. A second later, I heard the shower start and she peeked around the corner.

You reminded me, I could use a quick rinse, too. Do you mind? I'll just be a minute. Why don't you order room service? I'll take any kind of grilled fish they have. And wine. Lots of wine!

Then she was gone again. I looked around the room for the room-service menu, couldn't find the damn thing anywhere, then eventually I realized I'd left it next to the phone in the bedroom and went in there to retrieve it.

Which startled Lisa, who was standing next to the closet.

Oh! You scared me!

Yeah, I saw that. That's not the shower. . . .

I know, silly. I was looking for one of your shirts to wear when I come out. Men like that, right? It's sexy?

That's a good look, yes. I prefer what I'm seeing right now, though.

She giggled, winked and disappeared into the bathroom. Not before giving me another peek of perfection.

I found the menu and ordered. As I was putting the phone back down on the receiver, I remembered someone I meant to call that evening.

Judith.

I looked up and saw my reflection in a decorative mirror on the wall. I was suddenly deeply embarrassed. And disappointed. In myself.

You fucking dog.

I was dressed by the time the shower stopped. Lisa emerged from the bedroom a few moments later wearing one of my Polo shirts and, I assume, nothing else. She stopped in her tracks, noticing I was no longer *au naturale*.

Is something wrong?

Yeah, yeah. There is. I'm sorry, Lisa. I, see, I'm sorta seeing someone.

Oh.

And as much as I'm attracted to you and all, well, I just can't.

She moved over closer to me. I could smell her clean skin, her wet hair.

Are you sure? It doesn't have to mean anything. Just, just, you know, a nice moment.

It would mean something to me, though. I'm sorry.

Something howled deep inside me, a pain-torn wail of objection. Which I somehow managed to ignore.

Lisa sat on the edge of the couch and gave a wan smile.

I'm not really that way, I hope you know. Not wild like that. It's just been a horrible day.

I know. I know that's what it was. Don't worry, it's totally understandable.

She stood, wrapped her arms around my neck, and gave me a light kiss on the lips. I could feel all of her through the thin cotton of my shirt.

You're such a gentleman. She's a lucky girl.

Well, I feel terrible about you and Luke . . . but may I say he's a fucking idiot to cheat on you.

Lisa Tan shrugged and set about recovering her various articles of clothing. I found something to occupy my attention as she dressed. When she straightened up after pulling on her flip-flops her deep brown eyes looked miserable.

Now I'm embarrassed. I think I should go.

No, no, no. Look, I think all that . . . whatever that was that just happened . . . I think that just shows we've got some mutual attraction going on. We can handle that. Right? We're adults. Stay. Dinner will be here soon.

But she shook her head, moved toward the door. Opened it.

I can't, Huck. I'm sorry. I'm just too uncomfortable now. I'll call you.

Then she was gone.

I stood looking at the door long after it closed, wondering what the hell had just happened. Finally, I flopped down onto the couch, felt around in the cushions for the television remote I knew was there and clicked it on. I thought about calling Judith, but frankly, I was afraid she'd sense something was up and I'd end up spilling the beans. Don't get me wrong; I'm not stupid enough to believe you should never lie to your woman—no relationship can survive complete honesty—but I needed to assess how to play it if her female ESP kicked in and she busted me.

Just then there was a faint knock at the door. The peephole once again revealed a slightly distorted vision of Lisa Tan loveliness. I opened the door.

Hey. You leave somethi—

Mr. Shades stepped into view from the side of the hallway and launched his foot just past my right ear. I thought I'd slipped the kick and started to step forward with a straight punch to his solar plexus when he yanked his heel hard into the back of my head.

I saw a spurt of blood fly from my nose. Then the hallway carpet came up and smacked me in the face.

CHAPTER THIRTY-SEVEN

I heard the voices first. Garbled. Indecipherable. Then realization gradually dawned that the voices were speaking in a foreign language, and the following things became apparent: I couldn't move my arms. My neck hurt. My face hurt. I was sitting down.

I opened my eyes and lifted my head to look around me.

Lisa sat in a chair across from me. She was awake and looked frightened but calm. It appeared her arms were tied down much as I now noticed mine were, with plastic zip ties holding them firmly to the chair arms. Three men stood a few feet away, watching me closely. One was Mr. Shades. The other two could've been his twin brothers, since they all wore sunglasses and dark suits. Mr. Shades smiled and spoke. It was the first time I'd ever heard his voice. I didn't much like it. He had the faintest of accents.

Hello, Huck, my old friend. Did you have a nice rest?

Blow me.

I was in a very bad mood. He didn't seem to take offense.

This can be easy or difficult. That depends on you. There is a laptop computer in the room safe over there. We are going to take it with us, and if you cooperate, you and your lady friend here will be unharmed. What is the combination?

When I was sixteen, one of my best friends, Mikey Donnelly, went missing for three days. Mikey was a full head shorter than any of us, but he was solid and fearless. Got a black belt in Tae Kwon Do by the age of fourteen. Took down guys twice his size if they gave any of us shit.

I don't know at exactly what point Mikey got mixed up in dealing drugs. He never offered any to me. But when the cops found Mikey in an abandoned house in the San Fernando Valley, tied up like this, and very much dead, they told the newspapers it had been a drug deal gone bad. No amount of training or fierceness or attitude saved Mikey that day. Because he simply fucked up. His belief in his own abilities betrayed him.

So I found myself thinking about Mikey just then, because here I was, in a very similar situation, with guys who probably had no reason to let me live and every reason to eliminate an eyewitness. Or two. I glanced over to Lisa, who was urging me on in silence, because there was a cloth napkin shoved in her pretty mouth.

These men had already committed assault. What was taking place in that hotel suite now was tantamount to kidnapping. Obviously, committing serious felonies was no big deal. I figured these guys had something to do with Wong's murder. I was sure they wanted the computer because it contained evidence of General Wu's blackmailing of Sing Ten Wong. The only thing that could save our lives right then, I realized, was time. Call me a pessimist, but once they had the computer, chances were very good Ms. Lisa Tan from BOPI and Mr. Huckleberry Doyle from the PGA Tour would be dead. I had to drag this out as long as possible. Which wasn't going to be pleasant.

Huck? You still with us? Don't make us hurt you. What is the combination?

I looked up and gave Mr. Shades a big ol' smile.

B, left. L, right. O, left. W,—

His foot caught me just under the left eye, shaking up my snow-globe pretty good. When my brains once again unscrambled, I felt something warm and sticky drip down my cheek and land on my lap.

We don't have much time, Mr. Doyle.

I became aware he had my left index finger in his hand.

Listen closely. I'm going to break one finger at a time until you tell us. And if you're still a tough guy after that, I'll start on your knees. Then your legs. Then Ms. Tan over there gets to become a cripple. You will tell us eventually. They always do. Do you get the picture yet?

I nodded slowly.

Good. What is the combination?

I shrugged. Sighed deeply. Cleared my throat. Spat a thick wad of bloody gunk on his shiny black shoe.

B . . . left. L . . . right. O,—

Lisa screamed through the gag. The sound of my finger snapping was similar to a leaf-covered twig being stepped on; sharp but muffled. There was nothing muffled about the pain; it was more intense than anything I'd felt in a very long time. I fought back against the glittering stars and beckoning twilight that began closing in on my peripheral vision and somehow managed not to make a sound other than a quick intake of breath.

Opening my eyes, I looked at each of the three men closely, memorizing their faces, their height, their build. Just in case.

Just in case I was wrong. And did make it out of this alive.

Mr. Shades let go of my now-crooked index finger, wiped his shoe on a pillow he retrieved from the couch and got a firm grip on the middle finger of the same hand.

Chance number two. What is the combination?

No, no, wait! Don't! You know what will happen if you break that finger?

He raised his eyebrows. At least I think he did, behind those Foster Grants, because his forehead furrowed as he sneered.

Your career as a golfer is over?

No! It means . . .

I raised the middle-finger of the other hand.

. . . I'll have a harder time telling you to go fuck yourself.

The sneer faltered a bit. I clinched my stomach in preparation for another searing jolt of pain, determined not even to make a peep of sound this time, but just then there was a loud knock on the door followed by a very familiar voice:

Room service! I got yer fuckin' shitty-lookin' grilled fish and veggies!

The three Stooges looked at each other, looked at Lisa, looked at me, completely baffled.

I managed a laugh through pain-clenched teeth.

Hey, that's just the room-service waiter. Don't mind him. I've been here a week. He and I kid around like that. He's harmless.

Mr. Shades leaned over and whispered into my ear.

Get rid of him. Or he joins you.

Got it.

I raised my voice.

Hello, asshole! I'm not feeling too well all of a sudden. You mind coming back at ten-twenty-four?

Silence. His voice came back somewhat less jovially.

Ten-twenty-four? You shittin' me?

I winked at my three hosts.

Not shittin' you. You heard me. Ten fucking twenty-four!

Suit yerself.

Mr. Shades looked quizzically at his partners, then back at me.

Why exactly ten-twenty-four?

It's an inside joke. You wouldn't get it.

He shrugged . . .

Ah, well. See if you get this. This is our little inside joke.

. . . reached for my finger and braced himself for the best leverage when the hotel door exploded inward and 260 pounds of meat and mean was suddenly in the room. For a split-second I caught sight of the actual room-service waiter's shocked face in the doorway, before he turned and ran.

Two of the men in suits leapt at my dad, throwing lightning-fast punches and kicks, which seemed to have about as much effect on Pete as rocks would on a tank. He didn't even flinch, just took the blows on his arms and head and belly and thighs, waited for the opportunity and grabbed one of the guys by the leg, swinging him around like an Olympic hammer-thrower before slamming him into his buddy. Both men went down.

Pete was on them instantly, those massive arms chugging like oil derricks, smashing his big fists into both men's bodies and faces. The designer sunglasses were in pieces. And suddenly, neither man looked so good.

Mr. Shades, momentarily frozen to his spot, shook himself out of his shock and moved over toward Pete, angling to get behind him.

Pete! Six o'clock!

Pete whirled on him, took a few kicks to the forearms and landed a solid right to Mr. Shade's chest, sending him staggering backwards, gasping for breath.

Unfortunately, he'd staggered backwards against the dining-room table. On which lay the silverware I'd put out in expectation of a nice dinner-for-two earlier that evening.

Mr. Shades picked up a steak knife. Held it like someone who knows how to knife-fight. And started toward my dad.

Drop it!

That from the doorway. Where two policemen now stood, guns drawn, with the room-service waiter and a hotel security guard watching close behind.

Mr. Shades was no dummy. The knife bounced on the hotel room carpet.

CHAPTER THIRTY-EIGHT

The earnest emergency medical technician, as luck would have it, was the same one who'd informed me my broken nose was probably broken a few days earlier. As she splinted my finger, cleaned up my face, and applied a butterfly bandage to the half inch-long gash under my left eye, her eyes showed a million questions.

Finally, she could keep quiet no longer.

Who did *you* piss off?

Who the fuck *doesn't* he piss off?

That from Pete, who stood over to the side, wrapping up his interview with Five-0.

Ten minutes earlier, the three Stooges were hauled off to jail in handcuffs, two of them looking quite a bit the worse for wear. Mr. Shades was the only one who wasn't bloodied and limping. He shot me a smile as he left the room.

Detective Sagulio showed up and was talking with Lisa and Pete when I emerged from the bedroom in a fresh set of clothes. I didn't want the Honolulu PD to get their hands on the computer, so while changing I quickly pulled it from the safe and stuck it inside my suitcase. All three turned to me with varying looks of pity, concern and exasperation on their faces. Sagulio spoke first.

What did I tell you? These guys play rough.

Yep.

Any idea what they were after this time?

Nope.

Lisa's eyes widened. Pete snorted.

Sagulio blinked.

Ms. Tan here said they asked about something in the safe.

Yeah. I know. But the safe's empty. No reason to use it. So I don't have any idea what they thought was there.

Mind if we have a look?

I shrugged.

It's open. Help yourself.

The detective motioned over one of the other officers and asked him to check out the safe. He turned back to me.

You're lucky your father happened in when he did.

No shit.

That took him by surprise. But I was in no mood for a lecture. The meds the EMT gave me hadn't yet kicked in. My everything hurt. Especially my finger. Lisa reached out a hand to take a closer look at the splint, which was nothing more than a thin aluminum tray and elastic wrapping.

That doesn't look very substantial. Are you going to get a cast?

No. They generally don't put casts on fingers, just a splint. It'll be fine.

I'm so sorry about the tournament. You were doing so well.

I looked at her in surprise.

What do you mean? I'm still playing.

Her turn for surprise.

But you have a broken finger! How can you hold a club?

I held up my hands as if I was gripping a golf club and waggled the pinky and ring fingers of both.

You use these two fingers to hold on to the club. The index fingers don't factor in much at all.

I'd been lucky. Mr. Shades obviously didn't know shit about golf, or he'd broken one of the other fingers instead. The EMT advised me to go to the hospital to get stitches, an x ray and a bigger splint for my hand. I told her I would. But I wouldn't. A bigger splint could be a problem for my golf grip.

Pete wanted to know if I thought I'd be able to play as well.

I'm leading a tournament for the first time ever. I'm damn well going to try.

Detective Sagulio tried to talk me out of it, saying I was an even bigger target now, but I waved him off.

Fuck them. They're in jail. And probably headed to a long stay in prison.

Pete and the detective exchanged looks, then looked away.

What? What did I miss? They're going to jail, right?

Sagulio:

Yes, they are. But not for long. We can't hold them.

Pete:

They're fuckin' exempt from prosecution. Nobody can touch them.

Me:

What do you mean, nobody can touch them? Try charging them with assault and battery. Kidnapping. Attempted murder. Hell, vandalism of a rental car!

Sagulio shook his head.

They are all official employees of the Chinese Consulate. They have diplomatic immunity. The most we can do is file an official complaint with the State Department and hope they kick the bastards out.

All I could muster to say was a heartfelt,

Fuck me.

The room phone rang. It was the hotel manager, informing me the door wouldn't be fixed until Monday and he was terribly sorry but there were no other vacancies available but they'd found a room at another hotel and they'd be happy to arrange to move my belongings for me. Not that I could blame him; I'd become a very big pain in the ass. But I was way past being considerate.

I'm sorry, Mr . . . ?

Collins.

Mr. Collins. My room has been ransacked. I have been assaulted, twice now, in your fine establishment. And you're throwing me out? How do you think that's going to look to the jury when my attorney is asking your boss, on the stand, about the lack of security measures you took to ensure the safety of your guests?

He sputtered on the other end of the phone.

Well . . . I'm sure I . . . just a moment please.

The Bee Gees entertained me while I was on hold. I cut a glance to Pete. He looked amused. The manager came back on the line.

Mr. Doyle, I've just been informed we have a cancellation. And I'm happy to tell you, it's an even nicer suite than what you're in. Our honeymoon deluxe.

That's great news, Mr. Collins. Thank you.

And we will also be boosting our security. There will be a guard on your floor at all times. We will not have a repeat of your earlier troubles, I assure you.

Excellent. Thanks again.

We hung up. Lisa turned to Pete.

Mr. Doyle? I'm sorry, do you mind? One question. How exactly did you know to burst in like that?

Simple. He gave the radio code for *trouble at the station*. Ten-twenty-four.

It wasn't that much of a stretch. Every cop teaches their kids the ten-codes. Sagulio chuckled in amazement. Lisa's mouth was agape.

And . . . that was enough to go on? What if you'd misunderstood him, or he was just joking around?

Look at his fuckin' mug, for chrissakes! I seen that face looking worse and worse on TV all week long. Call his brother, who tells me Huckle-berry here's into something deep but can't tell me what. Fuck that, I says. So I figure on taking a little hop out here to make sure everything's up and up. Plane landed early. Found the hotel. Get to the door, and he gives that signal? What the fuck else would I think?

Lisa and Sagulio both make that little head bob of comprehension. Pete chuckles.

Besides. It's just a door, ya know? If I was wrong, that is. Just a door. But this guy . . .

He chucks me in the shoulder. Which also hurt. Not that I minded.

. . . this guy. I know Huckleberry.

I thought he was getting all mushy, until he added:

He's always fuckin' up.

CHAPTER THIRTY-NINE

The cops finished up their crime scene investigation, packed up and left. Sagulio took off a few minutes later, after tossing a couple more words of caution in my general direction. And asking, one more time, if I was sure I didn't know what those goons were looking for. It was obvious he didn't believe me, and I honestly felt bad about lying to him.

Hey detective, just so you know, I think I'm close to figure some things out. And when I do, I'll pass it all along.

Fair enough. And just so *you* know. We checked with the coast guard and got a list of boats in the area at the time of the shooting. We're making our way down through them now. That was a good lead. Thanks.

Any time.

Lisa disappeared into the bathroom to freshen up, came back into the room, leaned over to give me a kiss on the cheek and said goodbye.

Please be careful, Huck. I'd hate to see you hurt. More than you have been.

Pete and I both watched her go. I couldn't help but think about her condition of undress less than two hours earlier. A lingering, torturous, surreal memory.

She's something.

Pete gave a snort, which I took to be loyalty to Lindsey, my ex-girlfriend. He could never understand why I let her get away.

Yeah. She's something. Hey, that reminds me, I gotta go check something out. I'll be back later.

Okay, I'll leave your name at the desk. They'll give you a key to the new room.

See ya.

I was asleep when I heard the key card in the lock. I woke up just enough to make sure the hulking form feeling his way to the suite's second bedroom was, in fact, my father, and returned to my codeine dreams.

The calls started at six A.M. First it was the wire services, then the newspapers, then the TV stations. All wanting to interview the PGA pro who'd been assaulted. After a dozen times of saying *no comment*, I asked the hotel operator to stop sending them my way.

Pete and I took our breakfast on the balcony, overlooking the beautiful white beaches of Waikiki. Even he couldn't hide his appreciation of the view.

My body felt like it'd been thrown into an industrial-grade washing machine and put through a dozen spin cycles. The painkillers helped ease the throbbing in my finger and face, but I wasn't going to let myself take enough to kill it altogether for fear it would also dull my golf game. Tee-time was 2:05 that afternoon. I had to work out the kinks before then, so I planned on heading to Waialae early to have one of the trainers at the gym trailer there put me through some good stretches, followed by a long workout on the practice range to see if I had to adjust my swing to compensate for my new injury.

Judith was on the United flight scheduled to land at 12:30, and she was planning on getting a cab over to the golf course, spending the day following me around, then having a lively evening of good food and fun. She was unaware that my dad was now our roommate. It was going to be interesting to gauge her reaction to that bit of good news.

Pete belched and set down his coffee cup. He was wearing an astoundingly ugly Hawaiian shirt, khaki shorts and black socks with sandals. The getup screamed *tourist*.

So, Sport, got something to show you. You ain't gonna like it.

He reached into his pocket and pulled out a cell phone . . .

I got a hunch yesterday about a certain friend of yours.

. . . flipped it open, pushed a button on its side and held it out for me to see the tiny screen.

On which a video was playing.

Of Lisa Tan. Talking. With Mr. Shades.

It was a short clip. Pete flipped the phone shut and set it on the table.

Don't know what they was sayin'. They were speaking Chinese.

Lisa's Korean. She doesn't know Chinese.

Yeah? Well, that wasn't Korean, that's for sure.

How do you know?

I had a Korean partner for five years. Heard him talk to his nagging wife eight hours a day. I know what Korean sounds like, believe me. Ain't that.

I motioned toward the phone.

What tipped you off?

Something funny about her, last night. Too cool a customer. She shoulda been more freaked out by all that happened, you know? More upset. She didn't even strike me as being particularly afraid when all the shit was going down. Made me think she knew she wasn't in danger. And knew more than she was saying. So I leave here and follow her. She drives about ten minutes, talking on the phone the whole time, then pulls over at a park across the street from, you guessed it, the Official Consulate of the People's Republic of China. Half hour later, *he* shows up. They get in her car, drive to another park next to the beach, sit on a cement wall not twenty feet away from where I pulled over.

So, how'd you shoot that video without them noticing you?

Pete picks up the phone, opens it, slouches down into his seat, puts the cell phone to his ear like he's talking on it, holds it that way for a few seconds, then shows me the video he just shot of me staring incredulously at his little demonstration.

Nice trick.

I thought back on Lisa earlier, excusing herself to go to the bathroom, standing next to the closet, coming up with the quick explanation about wearing one of my shirts. Then I remembered how she allowed the bikers to force us off the road. After they vandalized my loaner car while we were surfing. Which no one other than Lisa knew we were doing.

Damn. She's good.

Yeah. Guess she is. So maybe it's time you let me in on things.

He was right. So I did. I left nothing out. Showed him the video of Sing Ten and the little girl. Showed him the Relaxation Club's website. Showed him the translations of the blackmail messages.

So, the General has this guy Wong over a barrel. It's all going in his favor, right?

I nodded.

And you didn't find anything says Wong was backing out of the deal?

I shook my head.

Then it don't make sense he'd kill him. Wu's not your guy. He's a crook. But he's not your guy.

I agreed. Then described the forensic evidence about the bullet.

Jesus H. Christ. Never heard about nothin' like that before.

Me neither. But I have a theory. Something I saw in a newspaper article, years ago.

I told him a little idea I was chewing on, and he offered to talk to a few people who might know.

Hey, Pete, I didn't have a chance to thank you. For saving my ass. And my fingers.

It was fun. Those little fucks hit like pussies.

The pain I was feeling in my face, my neck and my head took exception to that statement, but I let it slip.

By the way, I have a friend arriving later today. Judith Filipiano? The Assistant M.E. for Los Angeles County.

He gave me a long look.

Yeah?

And . . . she's staying here. With me.

Well, I didn't think she was shacking up with *me*! So, whatcha saying? You want to arrange a signal? If this van's a-rockin, don't come a knockin' sorta thing? Hang a DO NOT DISTURB sign on the door knob?

I was thinking we'd find you another room, actually.

I got a room . . .

He motioned to where he spent the night, in the second bedroom.

. . . and I got a boy of mine somebody's trying to do a number on. So I'm staying right here. You get all erectile dysfunctiony with your old man in the next room, well, that's just tough.

Pete went into his bedroom and emerged a few moments later in a garish yellow Hawaiian shirt, black shorts and knobby black leather motorcycle boots. He grinned at the expression on my face as he plopped a ridiculous floppy hat on his head.

Think I'll pass as a tourist?

When Pete left, I put the laptop into the room safe and took a long, steaming-hot shower.

My cell was beeping when I got out. It was Pete. I called him back without listening to the message.

Hey. What's up?

Our guy? The one with the sunglasses and shiny shoes?

Yeah?

I'm watching him eat breakfast.

How'd you find him?

My new buddy, Sagulio, mentioned they'd keep him in the slammer overnight. I made sure I was there when they let him out.

Where are you?

Pete told me and promised to keep an eye on Mr. Shades until I got there. I dressed quickly and called the front desk.

Hi. Huck Doyle. Is there by any chance a bunch of media types hanging around the front of the hotel?

Why, yes sir. There are. Lots of cameras and reporters. A few have tried to find out which room you're staying in, but we've posted extra security and are checking that everyone passing through the lobby has a room key.

Good. Thanks. Could you please have valet parking take my car out of the garage and park it up the street, then bring me the keys? And I'm in a bit of a hurry.

Certainly.

When the valet guy handed me my keys, I tipped him the last twenty in my pocket, then slipped out the ocean side of the hotel and walked up the beach half a block to where he'd told me my Toyota courtesy car was parked.

Traffic was heavy, this being a Saturday in paradise, but I found a spot a few car lengths away from where Pete was parked and joined him in his rental car. He pointed out the diner where, through the big plate-glass window, I could see Mr. Shades sitting at a table by himself. The restaurant was right next to a bank, which gave me an idea. I opened the car door.

I'll be right back. Call me if he comes out before I return.

Where you goin'?

To make a withdrawal. Can I borrow your hat?

Pete took off his floppy Gilligan cloth hat and tossed it at me.

Your fuckin' fault if I get sunburned, now.

I was in the bank for less than five minutes. As I approached Pete's car he pointed behind me. I turned and saw Mr. Shades exit the diner and head down the street, then turn right to take a shortcut through a park. No one else was around. On Saturdays in Waikiki, everyone is at the beach.

Catching up to Mr. Shades was easy, since by the pace of his walk he wasn't in any hurry. He stopped to light a cigarette just as I reached him.

Hey.

He turned. Didn't recognize me at first with the silly hat. Then slowly lowered the lighter and blew out a long stream of smoke from his nose. Suddenly, as if the thought occurred to him this might be a setup, his head rapidly scanned left and right.

Don't worry. No cops around. Just the two of us.

He visibly relaxed. The smartass smile returned.

You're not looking so good, Doyle. How's the golf game?

Thanks for your concern. I'm fine. I hear you're leaving town.

No comment from the consulate employee. Just a shrug. A draw on the cigarette. A pop of the mouth as he let some smoke out, then pulled it back in and sucked it down deep.

So, I have a few questions for you. Considering our last little meeting, I think you owe me some answers.

He laughed. Kind of a silent laugh. More like a hiss.

I owe you shit. You stuck your nose in the wrong place. You got hurt. Big deal.

How many fucking times have I heard that? And usually from assholes.

Yeah. Maybe I did. But, look, you've got diplomatic immunity. Nobody can touch you. So what'll it hurt?

Another shrug. Another draw. It was obvious to me he was curious. Otherwise he'd just turn and walk away.

You didn't kill Wong, did you?

I already knew the answer. I just wanted to hear it from him.

No.

He was too valuable, right? To your boss?

My boss?

Yeah. General Wu.

I couldn't see his expression through the sunglasses, but the tilt of his head revealed his surprise.

Very good, Doyle. Very good.

So if you guys didn't kill him, who did?

He flicked the cigarette and looked at the burning cherry as he spoke.

Don't know. We've been trying to find out, too. Whoever did cost us all a lot of money.

You're leaving. If you really want to find out, tell me what you know. Any lead will help.

We don't have any leads.

What about the Chinese government? Easy enough way to quash the deal.

He let out a real laugh this time.

Doyle, the government of China is scared to death of my boss. They know if he found out they killed it, by killing Wong, the General could bring the whole lot of them down. So, no. It wasn't China. I have no idea who murdered that guy. And at this point, I don't care.

Because without Wong, the merger can't happen.

He shrugged.

There'll be others.

Not if I can help it, I thought.

Yeah. Well. One last question. I know about Lisa Tan. She's on your team. So who else? Who else at the bank is a spy for Wu? Sam Ching, right?

Doyle, this conversation is now over.

He turned to leave.

Okay. Fair enough. Had to try, right? Hey, you asked how my golf game was.

Mr. Shades stopped and looked back with that shit-eating grin plastered all across his face.

I did. Yes.

I tossed him a golf ball . . .

Pretty good, actually.

. . . which distracted him just long enough . . .

Swinging well today.

. . . to connect just below his right eye with a solid overhead right. I felt something crunch under my knuckles. Other than his designer sunglasses, that is. Probably his cheekbone.

He went down hard. Lights out. That's when I saw the little tattoo on the side of his neck that looked like an L with a line through it.

The Chinese number seven.

On the way back to Pete's rental, I played catch with the roll of nickels I'd gotten from the bank, feeling better than I'd felt in days.

Here's your hat. Thanks. See ya later.

I tossed him the nickels.

Keep the change.

Pete just grunted. But he couldn't hide the barest rumor of a smile.

The twenty-minute drive to the country club was uneventful.

Thank God.

CHAPTER FORTY

Bobby Carter was waiting for me at the training trailer. The caddie raised his eyebrows at my bandaged face and hand.

Tough night?

Yeah. The finger's broken but I'm hoping it won't screw up my swing. I need to stretch, but first off I want to see if I can hold a fucking club with this thing.

Broken? *Sonofabitch!* How'd you do that?

Sheer stupidity.

Well, you're so far ahead I think all you have to do to win this thing is hang on. So let's see what you can do.

He hefted the bag on his shoulder and we walked over to the practice range. There were some other players warming up there. I felt a few odd looks and some sotto voce comments between them, but no one said anything to me directly.

From the crowd outside the media tent, it looked like one of the big names was giving interviews. I knew they wouldn't leave me alone forever, but I hoped to dodge the spotlight as long as possible.

I pulled a wedge and tried out my grip. Took a few swings. Hit a few balls. It wasn't bad, just a twinge of pain on impact, but I did notice the temporary splint pushed the ring finger of my left hand a little out of position, which might have some effect on my long irons and driver.

Bobby, is there any way to trim this thing down a bit? Maybe even give it a little bend so it wraps around the shaft more?

You think that's okay for the finger?

It's just for two days. How much damage can it do?

He shrugged.

Whatever you say. There's a machine shop over there, just behind the maintenance shed. We can probably make a few adjustments there.

We found a work table with a vice and a hacksaw. Bobby carefully unwrapped my finger and took off the aluminum splint. He then shortened it by about half an inch and also bent it slightly. He also cut the corresponding finger off of my golf glove so it would fit over the injured digit.

It hurt like hell when I put it back on since I had to now bend my index finger to match the curved metal, but the pain subsided once we had it wrapped up again. I gripped the pitching wedge again, and it definitely felt less awkward. I gave Bobby a pat on the shoulder.

That'll have to do. I'll meet you back at the range in half an hour.

To his credit, the guy in the fitness trailer only asked two questions: *You okay?* And, assured I was, *What do you want to do?*

Work out some kinks in my back and get my hammies warmed up.

He nodded and we got down to business. Thirty minutes later I was ready to hit some balls.

A pack of media types surrounded Bobby and my bag at the range. For just a second, I thought about slipping into my car and going to one of the other driving ranges in the area to practice, but I realized I'd have to face the music eventually. No pun intended.

Ten feet away, one of the cameramen spotted me. They crowded around, questions coming in a flurry. I just smiled, held up my hands and waited for them to subside before speaking.

> Fellas, I know you're curious about what happened to me and how I got so damn beautiful over the past few days. Because of an ongoing police investigation into the events surrounding my injuries, all I can tell you is there are some really bad guys who, for some reason unknown to me, came to believe I had something that belonged to them. And they've tried everything from threats to violence to get me to tell them where it is. Problem is, though, I have no idea. It's all a big case of mistaken identity. Let me repeat that: I have no idea where the item they're looking for is. But thankfully, the very competent officers of the Honolulu Police Department arrived just in the nick of time and have the suspects in custody.

Don't I lie purdy?

My statement did nothing to abate the questions.

> Huck, you're saying this doesn't have anything to do with gambling debts you owe?

No. I have no gambling debts. I'm not a gambler. Except when I'm going for the green in two on a long par-five.

> Could this be retribution for helping expose the Giordano crime family's activities in Los Angeles?

Who? Just kidding. No. I'm telling you the truth. These guys, who are definitely not Italian, wanted something they thought I had. End of story.

What about rumors that this was a smackdown by a jealous boyfriend of a woman you've been sleeping with?

I couldn't help but laugh.

You know, I really do wish that one was true. I really do. Because it would mean I was actually getting some. No jealous boyfriends, nope.

But you're known as something of a ladies' man on Tour.

Right. Well, tell the ladies that. Please. I don't think they're aware.

Is it true your finger's actually broken?

Yes.

I held it up as evidence.

Are you going to withdraw, then?

Not a chance. Sorry, boys. You'll have this mug to look at a few more days.

That elicited a murmuring of surprise. A couple guys asked the same question at once:

You're not withdrawing? How can you play with a broken finger?

Simple. I'll use it to putt.

Chuckles all around. I took a few more questions, then begged off to practice. They all stayed to watch, no doubt to see how a guy with a broken finger can actually hit a golf ball.

Turns out, not too well. At least, not at first. The problem wasn't anything technical, per se. The changes we'd made on the aluminum splint worked well enough. Like with most injuries, though, be it a sore knee or back ache, psychologically I just couldn't push the damn thing far enough out of my mind to not baby it during the swing. Which starts an exponential breakdown of the complicated mechanics that allow one to hit a golf ball in a controlled fashion.

But knowing it was a mental problem, and, by the way, nine-tenths of all swing issues *are* mental, meant I had a chance of working it out. So for the next two hours, in front of Bobby and the gathered nattering nabobs of negativism, aka the sporting press, I hit ball after ball after ball. Slowly, the throbbing pain caused by the centrifugal force of the blood rushing to my mangled finger at the apex of each swing began to recede in my awareness. Slowly, things began to feel natural, grooved, smooth.

By the end of the session I was confident I could play. I might not be able to drive the ball quite as far as usual, but I could play.

Oddly enough, the bandaged finger seemed to actually help my putting. My usual bugaboo with the flat stick is breaking my wrists too much on the takeback. With the splint forcing my finger off the putter's shaft, I was more keenly aware of maintaining the desired triangle of my arms, and rotating my waist and shoulders back and through the putting stroke as opposed to just using my arms and wrists.

When I finished practicing, I bid the reporters and cameramen adieu and retreated back to the fitness trailer for a good rubdown before lunch.

I was in the clubhouse, nursing the one beer I was going to allow myself before the round, when Judith walked in, looking slightly jetlagged from her overnight flight from LA, but otherwise beautiful as usual. She was in a pale-blue sleeveless top and white shorts, which showed off her long, tanned legs. I smiled all the way south. Thinking, *That is mine tonight.*

She spotted me.

And stopped in her tracks.

What the hell happened to you!?

That from twenty feet away and at full voice. Every pair of eyes in the place looked at me. I tried to shush her as I stood. She didn't move.

Don't shush me! What happened to your face? Oh my God! Huck! *What happened to your hand?*

I reached her in two steps, put my arm around her, put my mouth next to her ear and said, ever so gently and with ever so much affection:

Will. You. *Please.* Keep. Your. Voice. Down?

She allowed me to lead her to our table, but stared at my battered face every step of the way.

Jesus, Huck, you look like you've been beaten with a shovel.

Yes, I'm aware of that. Nice to see you, too.

And your finger!

Doc, listen. I'll tell you everything. I promise. It's not as bad as it looks—

That's what you said on the phone. I shouldn't have believed you.

Seriously. I'm okay. Now, let's try again. Hi, Doc! So happy you could come!

I leaned over and gave her a hug. She returned it, arching her back, putting her lips against my neck. She felt absolutely wonderful. But the warmth of her body was missing from her voice when she spoke.

I'm just, I'm sorry, Huck. But seeing you like this is a shock.

I know. . . .

And you're winning a tournament for the first time ever. . . .

I know, I know. . . .

It just seems like, I don't know . . .

Like what, Judith?

Nothing.

What?

No, nothing. This isn't the time. I'm sorry. I'm sleep deprived and cranky. Don't mind me.

She made a valiant attempt to shake it off.

Really, here, take two: Girl enters restaurant. Sees boyfriend. Walks sexily over to his table in her fabulous new Tory Burch sweater.

Then it was her turn to lean over and wrap her arms around me. She gave my ear a kiss, which sent vibrations all the way down to Florida.

I'm really, really glad to see you.

That was better. The waiter came over and we ordered a light lunch, with wine for her, and in very quiet tones so as not to be heard by the other diners, I filled her in on exactly how it was I came to look like I'd been beaten with a shovel. The only detail I left out was specifically what Sing Ten was doing in the video that put him in the position to be blackmailed.

Judith and I parted ways after the meal with another kiss and a promise from her that she'd be at the first tee by 2:05, which was by then only about thirty minutes away. She wanted to freshen up a bit since she'd come to the club straight from the airport. And I wanted to stretch one more time before starting the round.

Waialae, like most country clubs, has a strict no-cell-phone policy, so I turned mine back on in the fitness tent to check messages.

One from Rick, asking did I know anything yet and are my facial injuries related to my investigation into his father's murder. I decided not to call him back until after the round.

One from Blue, wishing me luck. Lindsey hollered something in the background I couldn't quite make out.

One from my accountant, Lenny, saying there was an offer on the Aston Martin and was I sure I really wanted to go through with this.

One from Detective Sagulio, informing me that the three gentlemen who roughed me up now had official State Department protests lodged against them and were expected to be recalled to China within days. As soon as one of them got out of the hospital.

The last one was from Pete, who'd been at the coast guard station all morning and had some very interesting information. I called him back. He was right. It was very interesting information, which put Sing Ten Wong's death in a whole different light.

I sat absorbing that for a good five minutes, until the helpful personal trainer came over and asked if I felt okay.

Yeah. Fine. Just . . . yeah. Fine.

The stretches felt really good. My finger was throbbing, signaling the codeine Tylenol I took that morning was wearing off, so I popped another. The suggested dosage was for two at a time, but all I needed was just enough to keep the really sharp pain at bay.

I changed into the uniform of the day, and headed out to the first tee to do battle.

CHAPTER FORTY-ONE

Vijay Singh was my playing partner in the final pairing of the day. He took in my bandaged finger and face with alarm.

Huck, what the hell have you been doing, man?

Got in a little scrape, but it's okay. I'm fine.

Yah, well, I hope so.

As every golfer knows, the swing you have on the driving range isn't always the swing that shows up on the course. And even though I felt confident that morning, the moment I stood over the ball on the number one tee, I knew something was different.

My first drive was a little toe-hook that nestled behind a tree, which blocked any possible second shot to the green. I chipped back onto the fairway, knocked my third shot twenty-five feet from the pin, and two-putted for a bogey.

My par putt on the second eased up to the cup, then caught the rim and sling-shotted two feet away, a power lip-out you don't often see on Bermuda grass.

I managed to cobble together a string of four pars before my next bogey, but I was dropping strokes like I had a hole in my pocket. I was finding myself too often in the rough, and chopping it out of that evil weed sent an electric jolt of agony from my broken finger all the way up my arm. Even Judith, who was following along in our gallery, was finding little to cheer about. By the time we reached the tenth I'd given back five to the field. With the wind and the way the course was playing, thankfully no one was really making a hard run at me yet, but even so, my lead had dwindled to three.

Vijay stepped closer on the tee box and spoke quietly.

How's the finger?

Hurts. But no excuses. I was hitting well on the range. Gotta find it again.

You will. Mind if I make an observation?

Golf is the only sport where players call penalties on themselves, as Davis Love III famously did during The Masters a few years ago. That cost him the championship but gained him a legion of admirers. For Davis, it was more important to win fairly than simply to win. In that way, the world's greatest game is, too, the world's most honorable game.

Golf also happens to be the only professional sport I know where contestants routinely ask and offer advice of each other, even during a match. It harkens back to the reality of who the opposition really is. It's not the other golfers.

It's the golf course. And the conditions. And yourself.

No, Veeg, please do. Really.

I think you're compensating for the bandage by cupping your wrist at the top, maybe subconsciously trying to keep from dropping the club head since you don't have that finger supporting the shaft anymore. It's pulling you off-plane.

That makes sense. I'll keep that in mind. Thanks for that.

Don't mention it.

The tenth is the shortest par four on the course, only 351 yards. Yesterday, I nearly drove the green. This day, I had to play it more conservatively. I pulled my hybrid, thought about what Vijay had said, focused on keeping my wrist flat at the top as I shifted my weight to my back foot and laced a straight shot down the center of the airstrip, about 225 yards. Next shot, my pitching wedge threw the ball to about ten feet, but couldn't drop the birdie putt.

Still, it felt like maybe I could stop the bleeding, and I wrestled the next seven holes to a draw. As I walked down the number-eighteen fairway, a familiar voice boomed out of the crowd.

Hey Huck! Hang in there, man!

It was Buddy Mano, the radio personality from my Pro-Am group.

Hi, Buddy. How're things?

Good, man. Been watching you all week. You're doing great. Don't give up, you're still in this thing.

Barely. . . .

Yeah, thanks. Doing my best.

Well, I've got an idea. When you win this thing tomorrow, stick around a few days. A friend of mine has a place up at Sunset Beach near the Pipeline. Luke Pendergast. Pro surfer. Really great guy, you'd like him. Knows every break in the islands.

That name was familiar.

Luke? He used to date a girl named Lisa Tan?

Not used to. My girlfriend and I had dinner with them last night. How do you know Lisa?

She fucked me over. She's a corporate spy. She's a liar.

Lisa works with a friend of mine.

And I despise her. Even though she's still the hottest thing around.

Wow! No shit! Well then, you gotta come out, okay?

Yeah, we'll see. Thanks, man.

Not a fucking chance. I was hoping she'd soon be in jail. Or at least unemployed.

My drive had left me 269 to the green. Normally, that's a three-wood for me. But I just wasn't feeling it. So I hit a hybrid to within fifty yards, flopped a pitch shot over the edge of the bunker, and watched as my ball caught the fringe of the green, banked left and rolled to within a foot and a half of the pin.

I knocked it in for my only birdie of the day.

I walked off the green still four under for the tournament. But it was no longer my name at the top of the leaderboard.

It was Vijay Singh's. He'd torn up the back nine, birdieing five of the last holes.

CHAPTER FORTY-TWO

The mood was at dinner, shall we say, dark. Judith ordered fish, I felt like having a steak. The waiter recommended Kobe beef imported that day directly from Japan. *Sure,* I said. Whatever. Before he left I downed my second Kettle One and asked for another. Judith took note but said nothing. I made a valiant effort to break the heavy silence.

So maybe you should take some beach time tomorrow. It's bound to be more enjoyable than walking the course with me again.

Huck, I came here to watch you play. And to be with you. You're going to do better tomorrow. This is still winnable for you, isn't it?

Not a frickin' chance. . . .

Yeah. But it's going to be tough.

Well, you're tough.

Yeah.

We lapsed into silence again. The heat we felt at lunch was oddly missing. After my drink came, she finally asked the question that had been burning a hole in her pocket.

So, really, what I don't understand is, why would you get yourself involved in this mess? Why even allow the distraction?

I told you. Rick's father is the one who invited me to play. I felt like I owed him.

But the minute it turned violent, or even once you found out about the blackmail, and the pedophile club, couldn't you have just turned that over to the police? It's just like with those mobsters back in LA. Why is it you can't leave these things to the proper authorities? I mean, really, you could've been killed.

I had no answer for her. I just stared at my glass, watching a rivulet of condensation meander down its side. Judith wouldn't let it go.

Do you want to hear my theory?

It took every fiber of willpower I could muster to not say *no*. Still, all I could manage was a lukewarm response.

Sure. Let's hear it.

She leaned forward and put her hand on my arm.

I think you have a compulsion to save people, bordering on obsession. Which is admirable and wonderful and I love that about you. I really do. But it's not your job, and it could very well eventually cost you your career, if not your life. Huck, you get into these dangerous situations and you're lucky to get out of them. It's only a matter of time before you don't.

I eased my arm out from under her hand to take a drink. I could've used the other hand, of course. But I didn't.

She wasn't finished. She began counting on her fingers.

Don't you see the pattern? These young girls you rescued from the pedophile club. That was so heroic. But you didn't have to do that personally. And that little girl who was abducted a few years ago you found. Tracking down the men who killed those two women. You had the information that could've put them away. Instead, you go after them yourself.

Not entirely accurate, but I didn't feel like arguing.

And then there's this. Every other relationship you've had, with the exception of this one, involves a woman who is damaged or messed up or in serious need of rescue. Especially Lindsey. You have such a weakness for damsels in distress.

Judith didn't know it, but she was now swimming in shark-infested waters. She took a big breath.

And I honestly think it all comes back to your mother.

I blinked.

What?

Your mother. The simple fact that for some reason you blame yourse—

Wait. Wait a goddamn minute. What do you know about my mother? We've never talked about her.

Don't get upset, Huck. I'm just trying to under—

What do you know about my mother?

She physically recoiled, sitting back in her chair. Probably, at that moment, deeply wishing she hadn't started this conversation. But she had. It was too damn late to put it back in the bottle. So I repeated my question.

What do you know about my mother?

Well, *because* you never talk about her, I was curious. I wanted to know more about your family. That's understandable, right? So I found the medical records and the newspaper accounts of her suicide.

I couldn't look her in the eye. She leaned forward again, and her hand found mine. Until I moved it.

Huck, she had a terrible, horrific, painful disease which, back then, and even now to a large extent, has a very poor prognosis. No one could blame her for wanting to spare herself, and all of you, from that nightmare.

I don't blame her.

No, of course not, you shouldn't. But I think the reason you risk yourself to help these other people, people you don't even know in many cases, is because . . . really . . . because you couldn't save *her*. You were just a little boy!

I took a long swallow of vodka. My eyes met hers, but I gave her nothing with them.

Go on.

You couldn't save your mother from cancer. From killing herself. You couldn't save your brother from the bullet that paralyzed him. You couldn't save your father from himself. Doesn't it strike you odd that you're the only member of your family who hasn't been terribly damaged? Who has somehow escaped extreme tragedy? Isn't it possible that the guilt you feel for being spared has compelled you to risk yourself time and again to somehow make up for your good fortune? Or even, God forbid, ensure that eventually something truly bad *will* happen to you? That you *will* then be a full-fledged member of your wounded family?

My stomach had tightened to the size of a raisin. I realized I was clenching my jaw so hard that my teeth were beginning to hurt. So I calmly lifted the glass to my lips again and finished the last of that wonderful, icy, clear elixir. Craving six or seven more.

Judith stood and came around the table, squatted down next to my chair, put an arm around my shoulders, and spoke very, very softly.

Huck, I really think that's why you've almost sabotaged your golf career again and again. You have all the markings of a self-destructive bent. You drink too much. You drive fast. I think you really can't bear being successful. You can't imagine being truly happy and fulfilled. Because you don't think you deserve it. Not with the suffering all the people you love have gone through . . .

That was enough. Instead of ordering another drink, I set my glass down and motioned to the waiter with the universal signal for *check, please.*

. . . and I truly believe that if you really want to reach your potential. If you really want to be the champion golfer you can be. That I *know* you can be. Then you have to concentrate on that, Huck. You have to focus on yourself for a change. It's time. You have to focus on yourself. It really *has* to be about *you* now. At this level you simply *must* be, I hate to say it, but . . . *selfish.*

When the waiter brought the check, I signed it, stood up, stepped away from the chair and forced myself to look at Judith. She, too, straightened up, her eyes searching mine for some reaction.

Don Dahler

I handed her the key card to the room. Let out a long sigh. Gave a nod toward the beach.

I need to take a walk. I know you're jet-lagged. Don't feel like you have to wait up.

And I left her there, crumpled. Afraid. Regretful.

I started to stroll down the beach, spotted a liquor store across the street, made a quick detour, then, with a fresh bottle of Grey Goose in hand, I returned to the still-warm sands of Waikiki. There was a concrete breakwater about two hundred feet away, near an oceanside park, where musicians, artists and purse-snatchers plied their wares. I stopped next to the wall, leaned against a palm tree and let myself slide down until my butt plopped into the sand. Sounds carried from here and there on the breeze. Music. Laughter. Birds. Distant honks of cars. The rumble and hum of the city.

The cobalt sky before me melted into the Pacific with little distinction between the two, except that the swells tended to elongate, then collapse, the reflections of the stars, making them appear to reach out to me, only to change their minds.

I sat there. And I watched. And listened. And thought.

About nothing. And everything. My phone buzzed in my pocket. A text message from Judith, saying goodbye. Saying good luck. Saying how sorry she was for bringing up my mother but she hoped we'd get past this and she couldn't wait to celebrate the win back in LA. Saying she loved me.

I flipped the phone shut, wishing she wasn't on that plane. But also glad she was.

A kid walked by with his parents, a boy of eleven or twelve. Little League age. Which made me think of baseball and, in the random way the brain sometimes works, Mickey Mantle.

I caught the millionth rerun of the movie about Mantle and Maris's run for Ruth's single-year home-run record on cable a few weeks ago. It's one of those films I can't possibly turn off if I start watching it.

Mantle's pure talent and innate knowledge of the game are what made him great. His lack of discipline, his penchant for fun, his unquenchable, Achillian thirst for alcohol, all the other records he could've broken had he just taken his gifts a little more seriously, all that is what made him human. And yes, I can see my own self in his reflection. Not the greatness; the weakness.

Mickey Mantle learned how to play golf late in life, but he managed to turn his home-run hitting power swing into a fairway-eating golf swing. He was known to bomb drives over 350 yards, and this many decades before technology and conditioning created three-hundred-plus hitters on the Tour. He played with a persimmon-headed driver which had a club head the size of a baseball.

It was said that he was happiest on a golf course, where his demons were at bay and his natural athleticism allowed to take flight, away from the heavy burden of expectations, of being America's hero, of knowing he was imperfect even as a nation worshiped the ground he walked on. Mantle's friend and golf instructor, Marshall Smith, said in a *Golf Magazine* article after the ballplayer had died, had it not been for golf, we would've lost Mantle to those demons years before he finally succumbed to liver cancer.

I'm not sure how long I sat in the sand, thinking about the Mick. Thinking about my life. My past. My whatever is next. But the beach strollers were far fewer by the time I stood, stretched and started back toward the Outrigger.

Bottle of vodka in hand.

Its seal still unbroken.

Pete was sitting on a chair he'd pulled over next to the balcony, smoking a cigar, feet propped up, looking out at the moon. I set the bottle of Goose in the freezer and walked into the bedroom. No Judith. No Judith suitcase. I came back out into the living area just as Pete popped a perfect smoke ring.

The girl is on the red-eye back to LA. Said to tell you she hopes she didn't hurt your feelings. Said call when you get back to town. If you want.

Okay.

She's a real looker.

Yeah.

Smart.

Yeah.

I pulled another chair over next to Pete's and sat back, looking at the moon, enjoying the cooling air coming in off the ocean.

You do know they don't allow smoking in these rooms.

Not in the room, Sport. My feet are outside.

Nice. A self-serving technicality.

The blue, aromatic wraith he sent crawling toward the stars disintegrated in the breeze.

And just what the fuck ain't?

CHAPTER FORTY-THREE

Sunday morning I called John Ng and told him everything.

I'll get you the laptop later today. It has the evidence of the blackmailing on it. I'll email you the video of Ms. Tan talking to General Wu's guy. The phone number Sam Ching called from my phone is a direct line to Wu's investment company in Hong Kong. I realize that's not a lot to go on, but it's a place to start your investigation. I'd have the Justice Department take a peek at his and Ms. Tan's financials, just in case they happened upon a sudden large amount of cash. And I'm sure the U.S. State Department would like to know about General Wu's actions. They can shut down any future dealings he might have with other American banks by classifying him persona non grata.

Yes, certainly. I'll contact the all the appropriate government agencies myself. I just can't believe this is possible. Sam Ching has been with the bank longer than I have! And Lisa Tan, as Mr. Wong's personal assistant, she has the highest level of access to all the bank's records. If they are both truly compromised it could be devastating for the bank's security.

It seems to me access and trust are the two most valuable weapons for spies.

Indeed. I'm just shocked that they could do this.

That's always what the neighbors say of the mass murderer next door. The flimflam artist. The tax cheat.

The pedophile.

There were a few things no longer on the laptop. His collection of child pornography. And the email message containing the video clip of Sing Ten Wong violating a young spirit. If that ever got out, it would devastate Rick and his family. Not to mention the little girl herself. I couldn't let that happen.

Because I know what it is to endure the sins of the father.

Whether he was forever slumbering in the dark soup of nothingness, or reaping the anguish of ultimate divine justice, or floating incorporeal through and around us living things, Sing Ten Wong was beyond the reach of human punishment. So it served no purpose to bring that shame to the people who would suffer solely because of their relation to a weak, venal, sick little man.

When I hung up with the bank executive, I called Detective Sagulio. He was incredulous at first, but finally had to admit it all made perfect sense. The ballistic and forensic evidence, the timing, the angles; there simply was no other answer.

Nice work, Doyle. Nice work. We were stumped.

Thank you, Detective. Now, on to the next for you, right?

Unfortunately, yes. A nasty domestic dispute turned deadly.

You sound like a local news anchor.

God, I hope not. So, Doyle. I'll be watching you today. Go out and win this.

I thought you didn't like golf.

I don't. Not yet, anyway. Kinda silly game. But I like you.

I'll do my best, thanks.

It's been my observation this past week that your best is pretty damn good.

We clicked off. I placed one last call.

Hello?

Rick, it's Huck.

Hey there! I saw you on the news. You've gotten the shit beaten out of you! This is all because of your investigation into Pop's murder, isn't it?

I'll explain everything tomorrow. Where can we meet?

I have to be at the cemetery at sundown.

That was as appropriate a place as I could imagine.

Perfect. I'll see you there.

Okay. Hey . . .

Yeah?

Good luck today.

Thanks, Rick. See you later.

I met Bobby at his favorite diner for breakfast. I'd asked him to bring his course book, the one full of the notes he'd been making all week about how I hit certain shots and what the distances were for each hole. He ordered eggs over-well and ham; I ordered an omelet. The waiter poured us each a big mug of coffee and moved over to the next table. I blew on my coffee and took a sip before speaking.

So here's the thing. We can't win this if we don't make a few adjustments.

He nodded solemnly.

I think you're absolutely right, Mr. Doyle.

Bobby, you gotta start calling me Huck.

After you take the championship, I'll call you Huck. Until then, you're Mr. Doyle.

Okay, fine. So anyway, this is what I think we need to do. I can't depend on my driver with this finger the way it is. It's causing us too much trouble, having to hack out of that fucking forest they call a rough.

Yes.

So we leave the driver in the bag on everything but the two par fives, and we play hybrid and longs. Hybrid and longs.

Yes, okay. Yes.

But what that means is, we have to be dialed-in on the distances. I'm going to be hitting greens in regulation *at best* this way, so that approach has to be with the perfect club. If we're to have any chance of going low, there's no room for error.

I understand. You're right.

So let's figure it out now.

For the next two hours, Bobby and I went over his notes, hole by hole, plotting which clubs put us in the most advantageous positions and how best to attack those greens.

Then we went to the Waialae practice range and pretended we were playing the round that way, hitting my drive, checking the distance, hitting the second, checking the d, making adjustments to the plan as my actual swing and ball flight dictated.

There were plenty of questions from the media about whether my injury had cost me the championship, but I wouldn't take part in their pessimistic game. Instead, I talked about how great this golf course was, how fortunate I am to be playing the greatest game here, and how, like a gigantic puzzle, there are eighteen beautiful holes to figure out out there waiting for me.

It's a game, boys. It's meant to be fun.

But, Huck, you came so close to running away with this thing. You were playing some of the best golf of your life.

I shrugged and gave them a smile as I stood up from the interview table.

The day is young.

I had decided, sitting on the sand last night, that I might not win today. But like someone once said of Winston Churchill:

There would be no defeat in my heart.

CHAPTER FORTY-FOUR

By the time Vijay and I stepped onto the number-one tee box, the wind was screaming off the Pacific a steady fifteen to twenty knots, with gusts of up to thirty. We'd been spared this facet of Waialae's geographic location most of the week, but on this course, the wind was usually part of the natural defenses arrayed against we interlopers. Players had been posting big numbers all morning, with some of the world's best shooting close to eighty. I saw a lot of drawn faces and downcast eyes in the courtesy tents. No one was threatening the lead.

When the starter announced our names, the audience gave an enthusiastic greeting, hoping, I'm sure, for someone, anyone, to mount some kind of an attack on a golf course that had beaten all comers this day.

We shook hands and Vijay gave me a wink.

Let's have a good round.

Yeah. Let's do that.

Veeg proceeded to smash a monster drive down the left side that caught a tree limb on the way down and ended up five feet into the long grass. The gallery groaned. They'd seen that happen all day long.

When I approached the tee with a hybrid in hand, there was a hum of surprise from the onlookers. It was 480 yards to the hole. No one else that day had hit anything but driver here. They must've thought I was crazy. But I fired a low-flier that cut through the wind and landed 220 yards out. And as was our plan, I laid up my second with a pitching wedge to one hundred.

Vijay powered his second from the rough, but it fell out of the sky and ended up short-sided in the righthand bunker.

Bobby and I stood over my pill and had to reconsider what we'd laid out for that hole that morning.

The problem was the wind. Ordinarily I'd hit a gap wedge with this distance, but that sends the ball very high and there's no telling what the winds would do with it up there. So instead, I pulled a nine-iron from the bag and hit a firm chip. My Titleist scooted up onto the putting surface and came to a stop three paces from the cup; not perfect, but not horrible either.

The big Fijian thumped a gorgeous bunker shot to within two feet.

I drained my nine-footer. He, too, saved par.

Humans: 1. Golf course: 0.

Game on.

Vijay's drive left him apparently stymied behind the palm trees on the next fairway, but somehow he carved it out of the thick grass and was able to turn it around and through a thatch of palms, ending up just off the front of the green.

I painted the flagstick on my third and popped it in for another par. Vijay matched it.

Humans: 2. Golf course: 0.

But on the third, Waialae had its revenge. Vijay's drive found the water hazard on the left.

My ball had a tight lie on a part of the fairway that had been trampled down by the crowds crossing to the other side. I called a rules official over and he agreed I could take relief, so I dropped it onto the healthier turf a yard away.

The pin placement was front left, protected by a greenside bunker. Bobby set the bag down next to me, took off his cap and rubbed his head.

Wind's cross, gonna push you away from the flag when it gets close. You got two-oh-one to center, minus three since they plugged it in so far up.

Thinking about a cut five-iron, but with a cross-wind that might turn it too much.

Yeah, I think you're right.

So how about if I lay it down the left side, maybe shoot at that fountain there in the lake and let it ride the wind back right?

I like that.

My ball hit the green just right of the pin, but released and rolled fifteen feet away.

Vijay was sitting three in the drop zone. His fourth found the right edge of the green, but he rolled in a magnificent thirty-footer to save bogey.

I crouched over my ball, looking carefully at the line. Bobby stood behind me, scrutinizing the same thing. His voice came from just past my right ear.

This one's tricky. There's not a lot to it, but there's a change in the grain about ten feet from the cup. See it there? Where the color of the grass changes?

Yeah, got it. That'll nudge it right just a bit.

Yep.

Okay.

My putter swept back and forward in a smooth pendulum, starting the ball slightly left of the hole. Then it curved back and dropped in the side door.

The match was tied.

For the next three hours, I shot nothing but par. It took a few creative saves and a lot of scrambling to make up for my lack of distance, but we were fighting the course and the wind to a draw, which was the absolute best we could expect.

Vijay dropped two more shots on the ninth and the twelfth, but battled back with birdies on the difficult number thirteen and the short sixteenth. Walking up that fairway, I couldn't help but notice there were no bikini-clad twenty-year-olds and their portly sugar daddies hanging out at Anders's pink stucco house.

The gallery was huge at the number seventeen, and as we squeezed our way through the crowd that surrounded the tee box, I realized that this was where it all started a little over a week ago. This was where Sing Ten Wong fell over dead, unleashing a cyclone of events that changed so many lives.

I hadn't thought about him for a long time. He was no longer my concern.

The people he damaged and deceived were.

I took a moment to look around. The big green Sony Open billboard was to the back of the tee box, barely managing to stay upright in the howling winds that were charging off the Pacific. The waves were huge and angry, their tops whipped off as soon as they formed. There were no pleasure boats out there this day. No navy vessels. Only the most foolish of seagulls struggled to crawl their way across the gray sky.

Bobby was watching me, a bemused look on his face.

How ya doin', Mr. Doyle?

I'm good, Bobby. I'm good. So what do you think?

Well, you're looking at one-ninety-one to the pin. With that wind coming hard from left to right, it's going to be tricky getting it in close. I think anything on the plate is good. The grain here grows toward the setting sun this time of day.

Okay.

I set up aiming down the ocean side and smacked a hard six-iron. It cleared the front bunker, but put a pair of roller skates on and ended up about eighteen feet past the pin. Bobby took the iron from my hand.

Sometimes that's as good as a man can do on this hole.

No complaints. Let's bring this thing home.

Vijay's pill landed in the sand trap I'd barely missed. His bunker shot came out quicker than he probably expected, meaning he must've caught it thin, and the ball shot past the cup to just inside mine. He marked his ball and as I moved past him to get a read, he chucked me on the arm with a sly grin.

Show me the line, hey?

My putt tracked nicely, rolled up to the cup, perched itself on the edge and took a nap right there.

The folks in the gallery cheered. They were getting their money's worth this day.

I tapped in for my par. Vijay followed my line almost exactly and rolled his in, too. The crowd roared again. We were all square going to the eighteenth, and every person on that golf course had an ear to ear grin.

Including Vijay and me.

The reason Waialae switches their out and back for this tournament becomes obvious in times like this. The eighteenth is simply a marvelous finishing hole. It has an exciting ratio of risk to reward, favoring the long-hitters. This 550-yard par five saw four eagles this week.

Not today. Today the girl was a bitch.

As I stood to the side of the tee box, watching Vijay set up to hit his driver, I suddenly missed Kenny for the hundredth time that week; my friend, my partner, my usual caddie. He'd been on my bag through all the hard times. It was a shame he wasn't here for this. But I had to admit, the man who was with me this week, Bobby Carter, was a big part of the reason I was in this thing at all. His course knowledge and pointed advice had gently guided me through this treelined minefield. I turned to him and extended a hand.

No matter what, Bobby. No matter what. It's been a pleasure.

He took it and squeezed hard, his eyes filled with emotion.

No, the pleasure's mine, Huck. This has been the best week of my life.

I started to reach for my club when it dawned on me.

Hey! You called me Huck!

That's right, I guess I did.

And for only the second time that day, I pulled my big driver, Excalibur, out of the bag.

Time to cut one loose.

I set up aiming at the bunkers way down on the left, and laid into a big, no-nonsense boomer that rose like an F-18 on takeoff straight over the coconut trees, straight over the sand traps, cutting the corner of the dogleg. My ball hit the firm turf and caromed across the fairway.

When we got up to it, Vijay's little white orb sat safe and sound on the short grass, 260 yards from the flag stick.

Mine, when we finally spotted it, was deeply buried in the long grass. I'd taken a 340-yard bite out of that fairway, leaving me only 212 to the hole. But I was looking at about the worst lie I could imagine. Especially for a golfer with a broken finger.

Bobby's voice was nonchalant, but I knew he was concerned.

Whatcha thinking? Lay up to a hundred out, then knock it close?

I shook my head.

Veeg is looking at a three-wood to the green, maybe even just a long iron with the wind behind us like it is.

He'd be shooting for a birdie at least, with an eagle not out of the question, and the outright win. To have any hope of reaching the green, I'd have to muscle it out of that nasty crap and get the ball up into the jet stream.

I reached for my hybrid club.

There's no laying up now, Bobby. Time to go for it all.

The ball was barely visible. To pull off this shot, I'd have to do more than just make good contact. I was going to have to slam down on the back of that unfortunate little Pro-V1 with every bit of strength I could muster. And no matter what the outcome, one thing was for sure:

This was going to hurt.

CHAPTER FORTY-FIVE

A man named Lum Ching hiked up the Manoa Valley a hundred and fifty years ago, to the top of Akaka Peak, and gazing back down toward the mighty Pacific raging in the distance, decided the view was the most extraordinary he'd ever seen.

After some calculations with a compass and a mirror, Ching declared it to be an extraordinary spot. The pulse of the watchful dragon of the valley, he called it. He predicted people would come from across the seas and gather at that place to pay homage.

The Chinese immigrant declared the valley to be sacred ground, and as such, the perfect location for a haven for the living and the dead, because in his faith, the two remain forever intertwined. He gathered a group of his countrymen, and they eventually purchased thirty-four acres of the valley to create a final resting place for all their people who travel to and settle in these islands. They named their organization Lin Yee Chung: *We are buried together here with pride.*

Rick and I stood on a hillside above the still-lush valley, surrounded by tombstones, carved stone figures of curly-haired lions, and burial sites described by low, concrete borders. The resort hotels and office buildings of Honolulu reached toward the sun in the distance. A mound of dark earth at our feet marked Sing Ten Wong's grave. My friend finished saying his prayers to his father and lifted his eyes to wander over the thousands of relatives of thousands of other sons and daughters.

We're like sea turtles. *Hai gui.* We carry our homes, our Chinese identity, with us, wherever we go. And we make the new place like the old.

But you adapt, too. To the new. You become something different. I mean, you said you buried your father earlier than is the custom back in China.

Yes. But the mourning period will continue for another hundred days. Traditions should be respected as much as possible. I think we change our surroundings more than our surroundings change us.

Maybe not. Maybe it's just that one you see, and the other you don't.

He considered that for a moment.

Yes. You might be right.

It's never easy letting go of a belief. Rick was absolutely certain his father had been murdered by someone involved in the merger deal. The fact that he was being blackmailed, even though I withheld the tawdry details of how that was accomplished, only bolstered that belief. Because his father was such an important man, not only within the bank but within Hawaiian society at large, there was, in his mind, no possible explanation other than murder. The shady characters involved in the negotiations, the bullet to his heart, everything pointed to a corporate assassination. When I explained to him what actually happened, he even questioned if I was part of the coverup, that perhaps the perpetrators had gotten to me and convinced me to concoct an outrageous explanation for Sing Ten Wong's death. But in the end, logic held sway. Rick came to grips with the tragic reality of what fate dealt his family.

The ship's log shows that at 9:53 A.M. the Saturday morning Rick's father fell dead, the Coast Guard Cutter *Integrity* intercepted an Indonesian-registered yacht approximately five miles off Waikiki. From intelligence forwarded to them by Homeland Security, the Coasties had reason to believe the boat contained a substantial shipment of heroin and other drugs bound for the Honolulu market. The pleasure craft was hailed, and ordered to stop engines and submit to inspection. Instead, perhaps thinking the much-smaller boat could outrun the large ship, the Indonesian crew turned about and pushed hard for international waters.

Bad move. The cutter quickly maneuvered in front of the yacht, again demanded its captain heave-to and fired a single round from a deck-mounted .50-caliber machine gun across its bow to put an exclamation point on that order.

The Indonesians stopped.

The bullet did not.

Because the Indonesian craft sat lower in the water than the cutter, the Coast Guard action report states Seaman Charles Folling fired the deck gun almost parallel to the sea, which still cleared the deck of the yacht by eight feet.

The maximum range of a .50-caliber round is four and a half miles. Figuring the bullet left the barrel at a speed of 2,910 feet per second, it took approximately eight seconds for the projectile to lose trajectory. Its angle of descent was extremely shallow, and when it made contact with the uncharacteristically calm ocean that day, it skimmed the water and became airborne again and again, like a stone skipping across a pond. The round continued on for another second or so until it either made more direct contact with an ocean swell or the reef located three hundred yards from the shore, and began tumbling end-over-end, ultimately punching into Sing Ten Wong's back, expending the last of its momentum by breaking two of his ribs and slamming into the banker's heart which, already stressed by arterial plaque, high cholesterol and hypertension, shut down from the shock of the impact.

Death was instantaneous.

After Pete's meeting with coast guard officials, subsequent ballistics tests confirmed the bullet found in Wong's chest had, in fact, been fired by the .50 Browning machine gun on the deck of the *Integrity*. A coast guard board of inquiry determined no breach of procedure on the part of Seaman Folling nor his commander, but suggested a servicewide procedural review for future such interdictions within twenty nautical miles of land.

It wasn't only difficult for Rick to accept that his father had not been murdered, but also, that a man as important, as accomplished, as Sing Ten Wong would meet his end in such a random fashion.

Pop's death was just some absurd accident? A bullet can really do that? Go further than its normal distance?

Yes. There was a case years ago of a little girl on a playground taking a .22-caliber bullet to the head. Turns out it was fired from miles away and skipped all the way across a lake before killing her.

I can't remember when I'd seen that in an article, but it stuck with me, perhaps because of its tragically bizarre nature, or perhaps because it involved a piece of metal similar to ones that crippled and killed two people

I love. What rang a bell was the fact that the bullet entered Wong's body backwards with traces of seawater on it. That's what made me think it was something other than a deliberate act. Exactly *what* it was, divine retribution, capricious fate, instant karma, I have no idea. Nor do I really care. I'm sorry my friend lost his father. I'm very grateful for what his death accomplished. Neither Wong nor the other members of the Relaxation Club being caught up in the FBI dragnet would be raping little girls ever again.

Rick and I turned from his father's grave and began the hike back to the parking lot. We reached his first, and we shook hands goodbye. He motioned to my other hand.

That going to be okay?

Earlier that afternoon, the doctor at Queens Hospital had reset the bone, put the finger in a larger splint, and strapped it securely to the finger next to it. It now looked like I was wearing half a boxing glove.

Yeah, it'll be fine. Won't be picking up a golf club for a few weeks, though.

Well, I know I said it before, but I'm really sorry you went through all that. If I'd known it was going to be dangerous—

Rick, it's okay. I'm fine. But, listen, promise me something. The things these people were using to blackmail your dad, well, there's always a chance they could someday become public. You need to be aware of that possibility. And if that does happen, you have to protect yourself... *from* yourself. You are not to blame. Okay? You are not to blame. You're going to have to separate the man who did these things from the man you loved as your father, the great man, as you once described him to me, who did so many things for so many people.

He nodded. I could see a million questions in his eyes. I could tell he wanted to know exactly what his father did, but in the end Rick decided to keep the vow he'd given Sing Ten Wong all those years ago. To never peek into the other side of his life. He got in and rolled down his window.

People all have their secrets, don't they?

I just shrugged. *Some darker than others*, I didn't say.

I watched him drive off, then checked my watch. Too late to call her, so instead I sent Judith a text message to her cell, which began with the three most difficult words in the English language.

You were right. Home tomorrow. Let's talk.

Don Dahler

EPILOGUE

One of the only bonuses to traveling as much as professional golfers do is all the frequent-flier miles we rack up. And because of those miles, most of us are members of every major airline lounge. My flight home was delayed by some bad weather over Southern California, so I sat in the United Red Carpet Club, killing time. I know; killing time indoors in Hawaii is a crime. But I was already checked in, my courtesy car returned, and frankly, I was buzzing pretty good from a combination of painkillers and one itty-bitty little beer. So sue me; I wanted to sleep on the long flight.

What I didn't want to do was to keep thinking about Rick and his dad and how a bizarre accident led to the unraveling of one man's grand illusion. To this day I can't fathom how someone can seem so jolly and generous and harmless to one part of the world, and so vile and selfish and destructive to another. That .50 round the Coasties fired that day did more good than they will ever know. It ended a nightmare for an untold number of girls.

For the twentieth time that day, I pulled out my cell phone and played the little video message I'd received that morning. It was of Blue, in a harness, suspended over a treadmill, with four guys helping him move his legs as if he were walking, grinning like mad into the camera. Laughing. Sweat streaming down his face. I could hear Lindsey's voice behind the camera urging him on. Laughing. Cheering. In two days, I'll be there with them, laughing and cheering, as my brother continues to fight his way back from that terrible injury.

I flipped the phone shut. Wiped my eyes on my sleeve. Spotted a bank of computers over to the side, and remembered the bogus email account.

Better tie up that little bit of business, I thought, intending to disable the account.

There was only one message waiting for me. From FBI Special Agent Christine McLeavy:

> Dear Mr. Xi: I wanted to bring you up to date on the results of the information you supplied us about the pedophile club. We rescued a total of five young women; three in the initial raid and two more who sought sanctuary at the Honolulu Women's Shelter with the help of a man they refuse to name.
>
> The offshore account you pointed us to has proved helpful in linking various deposits with the travel schedules of some of the men, and in two cases, the suspects were careless enough to use their own personal accounts to make deposits, which we were able to trace.
>
> I tell you this in the sincere hope that you are not one of these men who abused these young girls who eventually had a change of heart and turned in your friends. Instead, I choose to believe you are a man who somehow saw what was happening and figured out a way to stop it. A man who could have looked the other way, not gotten involved, left it for others to sort out, but who didn't.
>
> For that you have my, and the Bureau's, deepest thanks.
>
> There was one thing that puzzled all of us, I must admit. When we gained access to the offshore account with the number and password you supplied us, we noticed the account was almost completely drained of funds. Six large transfers of a quarter-million dollars each had been executed just hours before we got your last message with the financial information. Would you know anything about that? No, I suppose you wouldn't. Neither did the women's shelter, which received a sizeable donation, and the five girls who now have college funds established in their names.
>
> I looked up your pseudonym, by the way. *Xi* is the Chinese word for the number seven. My researcher said it's actually considered bad luck, even death in some uses. But then she went back and dug a little deeper. And she found out that the number seven has another mean-

ing to the Chinese people. It means *togetherness*. That's why I think you chose that name. Because we are in this together. To help those who can't help themselves.

My best wishes to you for your future, whatever that may be.

Christine.

I deleted the message and cancelled the email account, just as the club room attendant called my name over the PA system. She held out two boarding passes when I got up to the desk and said when she explained my situation, the United Airlines manager agreed to comp the companion seat.

Thirty minutes later, I ducked through the doorway of the 777, found our seats, and strapped in my beautiful new friend who would be traveling back to LA. with me.

The golden, soaring, flame-shaped trophy . . .

. . . of the Sony Open.